A COBBLER'S TALE

——— *A Novel* ———

NEIL PERRY GORDON

Cover and interior design by Tabitha Lahr

Published 2018
Printed in the United States of America
Print ISBN: 978-1-7326677-0-9
Digital ISBN: 978-1-7326677-1-6
Library of Congress Control Number: 2018910645

For Alla, my love and muse.
Your tears touch my soul.

CHAPTER 1

VIOLENT SEAS, JULY 1910

The *SS Amerika* sailed up through the Elbe River and an hour later entered the mighty North Sea. Pincus tried to make himself comfortable on his bunk of steel pipes with stained and tattered fabric stretched over its framework.

The gentle motion of the seas and the humming of the steamship's engines encouraged the weary Pincus to doze off. His desire for a restful night's sleep was dashed as he awoke to a violent tremor and devastating explosions of waves crashing against the ship's hull.

Trying to assess the assault on his senses, he looked around and saw others gawking at the horrors as they clung to the railings of their bunks.

"What is this?" Pincus cried, as a few men with poor grips fell off their beds like rag dolls. Pincus could see the faces of men screaming, but their voices were inaudible over the sea's fury upon the steamship *Amerika*.

Beads of warm sweat started as a slow trickle down his forehead and slender nose. *Am I getting seasick?* Pincus wondered. Nausea washed over him, along with a devastating hopelessness.

His eyes stung as the sweat gushed out of him. He wanted to rub it away, but he did not want to loosen his iron grip.

The ship's jerking motion was too much for Pincus to keep down his dinner. He launched the simmering contents of his stomach as a projectile that spewed from deep inside his throat and landed on the floor below his upper bunk. He wasn't alone either. His fellow neophytes joined in the action. Regurgitated stews of meat and potatoes coated the floor.

Men were praying to Hashem—to God—for relief from their suffering. Lanterns swayed back and forth, creating eerie patterns of darkness and light. Just as he thought that nothing but death itself could be worse, a warm, malodorous cloud rose from the boiling bile from the floor below, and with every laboring breath, he felt the smell of sickness enter his lungs. He moved in and out of consciousness as his misery deepened.

Then he felt coolness seep into his brain. As he struggled to open his eyes, a man's face was inches away, his hand applying a wet rag to Pincus's forehead.

"I need to get you up on deck," said the stranger.

"I can't move," moaned Pincus, as he tried to raise his shoulders.

"Don't try. I'll carry you," said the man, as he lifted him off the sweat-soaked bed.

Cradled in the arms of the giant man, Pincus asked, "Where are you taking me?"

"Up on deck. You need to hang onto me."

Pincus wrapped his arms around the man's sturdy neck and muscular chest. The man lifted Pincus up and walked through the metal hatch door. Traversing the maze of narrow doorways and metal staircases, they made their way topside. Moments later, with Pincus draped over the stranger's back like a sack of dirty laundry, they burst out onto the main deck.

Still hanging on to the stranger's back, he saw dozens of other seasick passengers from steerage. Those immune to seasickness were providing comfort to the suffering. Although the ship still heaved from the churning black sea, it was a relief to inhale the sweet smell of the salt water.

The man found a spot to prop up Pincus along a wooden storage box that blocked the sharp winds.

"Here, you need to eat something," the man said, as he handed him a piece of bread from his coat pocket. Pincus, unused to such kindness from a stranger, thanked him as he took small bites from the stale, crusty loaf.

As the nausea settled and some color returned to his pale complexion, Pincus worried whether he could manage a ten-day voyage. What he feared most was that he would become ill, fail the medical inspection at Ellis Island, and then be shipped back to Hamburg in steerage again.

Pincus looked up at the large man who had easily carried him up from the bowels of the ship. He figured that this fellow had to be at least 200 pounds, much more than his slight, 135-pound frame.

"Who are you, and why are you helping me?" asked Pincus.

"My name is Jakob Adler, and you're sick. I'm well and able to help," explained Jakob, with a comforting smile.

Pincus held out his hand. "It's nice to meet you, Jakob. My name is Pincus. Thank you."

Jakob reached out to shake the smaller man's hand. "You're welcome, Pincus."

Pincus removed his glasses and pulled a cloth from his coat pocket. He cleaned off bits of bile still clinging to their frame before repositioning them on his slender nose. They gave him a better view of Jakob Adler's imposing figure. With his short curly brown hair, large catlike emerald eyes, and small nose, Pincus doubted he was a Jew. His imposing stature was impressive, but he seemed approachable, almost gentle.

"I don't think I have ever felt so sick!"

"That was rough. You should rest here. I wouldn't go back to steerage until it's cleaned up," said Jakob. "Where are you from?"

"I'm from Krzywcza," said Pincus. "It's in Galicia."

"I'm from Warsaw."

"I've never been there." He sat up and looked out into the dark sky. "Actually, this is the first time I have left Krzywcza," Pincus added.

"We are both leaving our homeland for a new life in America," said Jakob.

"Krzywcza is not my homeland anymore," whispered Pincus, afraid of who might be listening. He leaned over so Jakob could hear him and continued in an audible whisper. "Jews are being forced to emigrate. They want us to leave the country."

"Yes, I know. I'm Jewish too, and I'm going to America to escape religious persecution and economic hardship so I can be safe and earn a living."

"You're a Jew?"

"I am, Pincus, and I hope to settle and establish a business in New York. What about you?"

"I'm a cobbler. I want to open a business."

"Maybe we can look out for each other, help out. It's good to have friends," Jakob said, smiling.

"It sure is," Pincus said, trying to manage a smile in return.

CHAPTER 2

THE DECISION

P incus quickly folded a letter and placed it under the counter as the door to his shop opened. It was Mendel Beck, who needed to push his way through by leaning against the heavy door with his shoulder. In his hands he carried several pairs of black leather shoes.

Mendel was a friend whom Pincus had known since they were children growing up together in the shtetl. They had many fond boyhood memories of running and playing together in the forest surrounding the town. Their paths in life had diverged when the boys turned thirteen. Pincus had begun his apprenticeship under his father, learning how to repair shoes, while Mendel had continued his Torah studies as a scholar in the study hall known as the *beit midrash*.

"Pincus, when will you fix this door before it kills someone?" pleaded Mendel, dropping the shoes on the countertop.

"What for?" Pincus said, more as a statement than as a question.

Mendel tilted his head and smirked at his good friend as if he understood. "Any news from Hersch?"

"Good timing," he said, as he reached for the letter he had just hidden and held it up for Mendel to see. "Just arrived today." Pincus smiled and handed the letter to Mendel. "He says I should come."

Mendel squinted at the words on the weathered page. "Can I bring it to the light? It's so dark in here."

Pincus's slight hand gesture indicated that was fine.

Hersch was Pincus's cousin, the son of his uncle Benjamin, a carpenter who had emigrated to America seven years earlier, which now seemed like a lifetime ago. Right before he left, Hersch had pleaded with Pincus to go with him.

"Clara isn't ready to emigrate," Pincus had said sadly, as he removed his glasses to polish the lenses with a soft cloth that was tucked inside his cobbler's apron pocket.

"Pincus, you need to convince her. Things will only get worse here—you'll see. In America you can proudly be a Jew and make money. I hear that the streets are paved with gold," Mendel had said, with a great smile that seemed to occupy his entire round face.

"Yes, I know. That's what everyone says," Pincus had replied. "I want to leave here. I do."

Every year since Hersch's departure, Pincus had received a letter from him, and every year Pincus had read it, folded it, and placed it under the worn wooden counter. After each letter, he would torment himself with the same questions. Was he putting off the inevitable? Would life in America be easier? What would the future hold for his family if he didn't go?

But Pincus knew that ignoring the facts would prove to be foolish. He had been reading and hearing reports that the government, feeling the pressure of the poor economic conditions, was blaming the Jews again for the plight of its citizens. Rumors had spread that the Jews were destroying the very fabric of life in the region. They were the cause of the troubles, and if they left the country, the other citizens' problems would cease.

Mendel returned to the counter and handed the letter back to Pincus. "He says you should come."

Pincus placed a hand on his cheek, looked at Mendel's bearded face, and said, "Maybe it's time. But Clara is pregnant, and it would be a bad time for her to take such a long sea voyage."

"You know, Pincus, many men go alone first to establish themselves. Find work and a place to live and then come back for their family once they're settled," Mendel advised.

Pincus nodded as he thought about what his friend had said.

Mendel continued, "The ticket agent for the shipping line will be in town again soon. You should purchase your ticket to America. I wish I could go with you. Sara is very ill and I can't leave her. But you should go."

As Mendel left the shop, Pincus decided he would tell Clara soon. This would not be easy. He had tried many times to bring up the possibility of emigration, but Clara was frightened of uprooting her family and moving to a country whose calling card was that the streets were paved with gold.

"Only a fool would believe that," she would say.

As he locked up his little shop, he took a moment to scan the place where he had spent nearly ten hours a day, six days a week, for the past twenty-three years, taking time off only for Shabbat. The gas lamplight flickered on the wooden shelves that lined the walls, filled with the backlog of shoe repairs for his loyal customers. The trade was good to him and his family. He would benefit from these skills in the New World, because people always needed their shoes repaired.

As Pincus walked home that night through the town he had known his entire life, he believed that he was ready to leave Krzywcza. One reason was that he was not well liked by the other Jewish men in the shtetl. He had tried for years to get elected to the *kahal*, an exclusive Jewish community council that oversaw civil and religious affairs. But as a tradesman and not a scholar, he was not accepted into that elite segment of Jewish society. He would complain to Clara, "They mock me by bringing me their dirty, worn-out shoes."

I have been dishonored enough. I am going to America. Clara must understand, Pincus insisted to himself. But he knew that this argument would not convince Clara. He would need to explain the logical reasons for going. He practiced the words out loud.

"Clara," he began, using his arms to orchestrate his intentions, "it is time we emigrated to America. Life here is bad and will only get worse. But I must go alone and establish a business and a residence for us. Then, in one year, I will come back for you and the children."

It was a ten-minute walk to the Potasznik family home, the deed to which Pincus had inherited when his mother, Sussti, had passed away a year earlier. Four years before that, his father had died of a heart attack right in his cobbler's shop while polishing the shoes of the rabbi, of all people.

Pincus liked the house. It was considered large for the neighborhood and could comfortably accommodate his pregnant wife, Clara; his eldest daughter, Jennie, age eleven; Moshe, the middle child, a fun-loving nine-year-old; and the baby, Hymie, who was just two.

Also living at home was his mother-in-law, Sadie. A snarl twisted his lips when he thought of her. She feasted on challenging Pincus at every opportunity. This news would certainly send her into a frenzy he would prefer to avoid.

Just like the other men in the shtetl, Sadie did not show the respect he believed he deserved. Not only that, she poisoned Clara's mind whenever she could. Just a few evenings earlier, Pincus had arrived home late, forcing the family to wait for him before they sat down for dinner.

As he walked in the front door, Sadie started in on him. "Well, look who's decided to show up."

"Sorry I'm late. I met Mendel on the way home, and we got talking about America," Pincus said.

"America again, Pincus? When will you get it through your head that this idea is nothing but a fantasy?" Sadie insisted.

"It's no fantasy, Sadie. My cousin Hersch sends me letters and tells me how wonderful life is there."

"You're a fool, Pincus. Now, sit down so we can finally eat. Your children are hungry," Sadie concluded, dismissing his words with a flick of her wrist.

CHAPTER 3

THE RABBI'S SUPPORT

Two weeks later, Mendel returned with news: "The ticket agent for the Hamburg-Amerika Line will be making rounds through Krzywcza in a few days."

"Good, I've been waiting," Pincus said, holding up the bank notes he needed to secure his passage.

"When are you telling Clara?" Mendel asked.

"Tonight, for sure."

"You told me that a few weeks ago!" Mendel said with a smirk.

"I know, I know," he said nervously. "But I really must tell her tonight. My mother-in-law will be out with the *Schechter's* parents. They're going to hear a lecture from some Yiddish writer at the firemen's hall. I don't want her around when I tell Clara."

"Good luck, Pincus. You're going to need it!"

....

Pincus glanced up at the cloudless evening sky and was relieved the rains had finally stopped. For the first time in days, he could walk home without getting soaked. But, on the bright side, the heavy rains had been good for business.

As his father used to say, "When the streets are muddy, we rejoice."

The last few days had been very busy, as many of his regular customers had dropped off their mud-caked shoes for repairs or polishing or both.

His father, Scheindl, had begun Pincus's education in the cobbler trade when he turned thirteen. Even before his apprenticeship had begun, he had often watched his dad replace a heel or a sole. By the time he picked up a razor, a knife, and a file or tried his hand on the sewing machine, he already knew the basic skills of shoe repair.

During their days working side by side, his father amused Pincus with interesting stories about their customers.

"You can learn many things about a person by their shoes, Pincus," instructed his father. "You see that young man who just left here? He has ambition. He wants to be an important man one day."

"How do you know that, Papa?"

Pointing for effect with a sharp razor used for shaping leather soles, his father explained, "That was Josef the tailor, a young man just starting out in business. He has only one good pair of shoes. He brings them in every Thursday and waits patiently for me to polish them. Did you notice they really don't need it every week? That means he always wants to look his best. That's a sign of an ambitious man."

His father's favorite expression was "The best way to understand the soul of a man is by examining his sole," which always got a smile from Pincus.

He continued, "Repairing shoes is an honorable profession and will always put food in our family's bellies and a roof over their heads. Never take this trade for granted."

"Why are some tombstones the shape of shoes?" Pincus asked.

"When the Messiah comes, Hashem will command the resurrection of the dead, and they will need shoes for their journey back to Zion," his father replied.

Pincus also learned that, according to the code of Jewish law, when a Jew puts on his shoes, the right shoe always goes on first.

"When you're tying your shoes, the left one is always first," his father said. "When you take them off, the left shoe is also first. This is because the right foot is more important than the left. So, the right foot should not remain uncovered while the left is covered."

He father concluded, "You must remember not to insult your customers by ignoring these customs."

Being respectful of his shoes and of his father, Pincus carefully avoided a few deep mud puddles and several shallow ones during his ten-minute walk home. After dozens of mini-detours around the muck, Pincus found himself standing at the front door of the shul. He had told no one except Mendel about his plan to emigrate to America. *Maybe I should talk to the rabbi before I talk to Clara*, he mused.

The synagogue was the spiritual center of the town, and its leader was Rabbi Shapira. Pincus, like all Jewish boys in the shtetl, had started his Torah studies at the age of three. Although Pincus had shown promise by being able to memorize passages from the Torah, the rabbi knew—because of who his father was—that he was destined for the cobbler's shop. This exemption from advanced studies had made Pincus unpopular with the other boys. His friend Mendel, a promising scholar, sometimes needed to defend him from occasional bullying.

Pincus had never sought out the rabbi's advice before, but now, he thought, it couldn't hurt to ask, as he walked through the large double wooden doors and into the dark and empty synagogue. The rabbi was busy on the bimah, preparing for the evening services. He looked up in surprise and said, "Pincus, I am pleased to see you, but services don't start for another hour."

"Oh, I know that, Rabbi. I was hoping to speak with you privately for a few minutes," Pincus began feebly.

"Sure, of course. Let's sit in my office," the rabbi said. What's troubling you?"

"Well, it's not troubles, really. I need your advice on something."

The rabbi leaned in and stroked his beard. Pincus had always liked the way the rabbi ran his fingers down his long gray beard. He had seen him do it in the same way for as long as he could remember.

"I have decided to emigrate to America!" he blurted out. "I'm leaving Clara and the children behind while I go ahead to get established. I'll come back for them in a year and bring them to join me in the New World." He looked at the older man whose dark-brown eyes were widely spaced on his long, thin, and gentle face.

The rabbi looked at Pincus carefully and said nothing for a few moments as he let the announcement sink in. Impatiently Pincus said, "So, what do you think?"

With the biggest smile he could muster, the rabbi said, "I think that's wonderful news."

"You do?" said the startled Pincus.

"This is a good decision, and I approve. Things are not good for Jews in this part of the world and will only be getting much worse. The sooner you can get established and return for your family, the better and safer you all will be."

"I had no idea you would be so supportive, Rabbi," Pincus said. "I still need to tell Clara and the children, but I'm planning on doing that tonight."

"Don't worry. You can assure Clara that we'll support her while you are away." "Really? This is helpful," Pincus replied with relief in his voice.

The rabbi stood up from his desk and walked over to the large window that looked down the street to the market square. "You will be on a sacred journey. Not just for the benefit of your family, but for the other Jewish families from Krzywcza who want to emigrate to America. What I would like you to do when you arrive in America is to get yourself established. You know, with a place to live and with your cobbler business. Then I want you to start a Landsman Society."

"A Landsman Society, what's that?"

"Its purpose will be to establish a support system for those emigrating to America from Krzywcza. This is very important for our people who want to move from a place where their families have lived for generations to the New World where they know nothing and nobody. There are many Landsman Societies already established. They help families get jobs, find places to live, raise funds in an emergency, locate relatives, and organize committees to call on and help the sick and to properly bury the dead," the rabbi said.

"I have many things I must do first before I can start such a society," Pincus reminded the rabbi.

"Of course. I know that. Take your time, get settled, and then start the Landsman Society of Krzywcza. The people of Krzywcza will be eternally grateful, and you will become a very important and respected man."

"Thank you, Rabbi, please let me think about it. First I must talk to Clara and the children," said Pincus with renewed enthusiasm.

CHAPTER 4

THE NEWS

The sun had set by the time Pincus found himself standing in front of the dilapidated wooden home where he had lived and slept every day of his thirty-five years. The lanterns were lit, casting uneven light across the entry vestibule.

As he entered he heard a cheerful "Papa," and saw his eldest son, Moshe, emerging from the shadows at a run.

"Moshe, my boy," Pincus said, as he lifted up the happy-go-lucky nine-year-old and kissed him on the cheek. Pincus saw that his unusual show of affection startled Moshe. But Moshe loved it and returned it with a smile and a hug around his neck that touched his father's heart.

Moshe returned to playing with the family cat, Manu, after his father lowered him back down to the uneven wooden floor.

"Jennie, Hymie, come to Papa," Pincus called out.

Jennie, the eldest girl, eleven years old and years beyond that in maturity, was clearly suspicious of her father's uncharacteristic behavior. She squinted at him as she approached, but Pincus ignored her expression and smothered her with kisses. Hymie was simply caught up in the celebration and smiled, as any naïve two-year-old would.

Clara was not a suspicious woman by nature, but her husband's overly demonstrative display of affection clearly puzzled her. She stood there observing him with her hands on her hips. A baby bump rounded out her flour-dusted cotton apron.

"Pincus, what's going on?" she said, trying hard to hold back a smile. But her big brown eyes couldn't fool anyone. Pincus knew she was happy to see him like this.

"Children, go to your room. Your mother and I need to talk," said Pincus.

The children's complaints rose in a crescendo that blended in with the smells and textures of Clara's baking, a familiar sensory experience that Pincus noticed and thought he would never forget.

Once Jennie, Moshe, and Hymie were tucked away in their bedrooms, Pincus pulled a chair out for Clara and sat down across from her, their knees just a few inches apart. He leaned over, clasped her flour-coated hands, and looked into her eyes.

"What is it, Pincus?" Clara asked nervously.

"Clara, I have just come from the shul where I had a very good conversation with the rabbi. He wants me to go to America and start a Landsman Society, so we and other families can settle there."

"He wants you to go to America and start *what?*" she asked.

"A Landsman Society. It's an organization that assists Jews settling in America. It offers help in finding a place to live and work as well as money for medical treatments and burials. It's a support group, and the rabbi wants me to be its founder," he said as he squeezed Clara's hands.

In one swift motion she stood up, yanked her hands from his grip, and knocked her chair over.

"What are you saying, Pincus?" she asked, shaking her head as if something needed to be dislodged from her ears.

"Sit back down, Clara, and listen," he calmly implored, righting her chair. "I am buying a ticket, and I am going to America."

"Without us?" Clara asked, stunned, as she slowly sank back down onto her chair.

Pincus studied her face and leaned over again, trying to be convincing. "Clara, you can't travel now in your condition," he said, placing his hand over her belly. "You and the children will stay here while I get established. The rabbi said that the shul would take care of you and the children."

"Is that so, Pincus?" Clara said with such thick sarcasm that she surprised him. "You really think the men in that synagogue—who, as you say, show you no honor—will take care of us while you're gone? For how long, Pincus, how long will you be gone before we see you again?" Her questions came fast now.

"Probably no more than a year at the most," Pincus said, trying to avert a crisis. "The rabbi said this was a good idea. He warned that it wouldn't be safe for Jews here very soon. It's for the future of our family."

"And when do you plan on leaving?"

"As soon as I can. The ticket agent will be making his rounds again. Then I will buy my ticket and set sail for America."

"So I will have this baby without you?" she said, placing her palms on the underside of her belly as if to emphasize that the event was only a few months away.

He nodded and quickly said, "Your mother will help with the baby, Clara."

She offered Pincus a grimace of disgust, rose quickly to go, and slammed the bedroom door behind her, leaving him alone in the kitchen to ponder what he had just done.

....

The ticket agent leaned over the counter in Pincus's cobbler shop as he transcribed the travel details. "Okay, let's see what we have so far," he said, reading from a ledger on the counter between the two men.

Pincus had run into the ticket agent a few days after sharing the difficult news with Clara, and they had made arrangements to meet at his shop early in the morning before he opened for business.

The ticket agent was well dressed. His black hair looked as if it were pasted to his skull with some substance that gave it an unnatural shimmer. Pincus also noticed and approved of the man's pristine, black leather shoes.

"Now, Mr. Potasznik, let's discuss your accommodations. First class provides the ultimate luxury with a beautiful stateroom for twelve hundred fifty krones. But if that's not in your price range, you may consider second class for two hundred fifty krones. You would have nice quarters that you share with another single man. Then there is third class for a special price of only one hundred twenty-five krones, but for the most basic accommodations."

Pincus had put aside a thousand krones for his journey, but third class didn't sound so bad, and he could save the money. "I'll buy a third-class ticket," he said with a smirk of self-gratification.

"One last thing," the agent added as he finished recording the details in his ledger and handed Pincus the boarding ticket and receipt. "When you get to immigration at Ellis Island, you will need to answer some questions. Some are easy, like what is your name or what country are you from? But some you need to learn, things such as what is celebrated on the Fourth of July or what is the name of the American president who freed the slaves? You should study. Take this pamphlet. It has answers to most of the questions you may be asked."

Pincus took the pamphlet, receipt, and boarding ticket, and realized he was really going to America. Next would come the hard part: saying goodbye to Clara and his children.

That night, as Clara waited for him in bed, he busied himself preparing his valise for the journey. He packed and unpacked, intentionally avoiding conversation with Clara. Once she fell asleep, he lay down gently, being careful not to wake her.

When morning came, Pincus was awake and ready before Clara, Sadie, or the children arose. Moshe woke up first and approached his father, pointing to the valise.

"Are you going somewhere, Papa?" he asked.

"Yes, Moshe, I'm going to America," Pincus said.

"Can I go too?"

"Not yet," Pincus said, kneeling down to look closely at his son.

Moshe frowned, and tears started to well up in his brilliant blue eyes. "When will you come back?"

"Very soon, Moshe, very soon."

Their voices woke Clara, Jennie, and Hymie. Sadie was probably awake too, but she didn't stir, and Pincus thought she would prefer to avoid the farewells.

Clara hugged Pincus tightly, her pregnant belly squeezed against him. She whispered into his ear. "Do not forget us, Pincus."

"I won't, I promise," he said.

They all gathered on the front porch and watched Pincus walk toward the train station. He looked back one last time and waved, just before turning the corner. Clara had one arm wrapped around Moshe's shoulder and the other cradling her belly. Pincus took a deep breath and took a step into his new life, leaving the old one behind.

CHAPTER 5

THE VOYAGE

S unny skies and calm seas greeted Pincus the next morning as he found himself lying on the open deck. Still woozy from the previous evening's orientation to sea travel, he realized he was not wearing his eyeglasses and could not focus on his surroundings. He patted the multiple pockets on his coat and found them tucked safely in a deep pocket on his right side.

Sliding his glasses back in place, he was annoyed at a layer of dirt on his lenses. He reached into the pocket where he kept his cloth and cleaned each lens. After replacing them on the bridge of his nose, he realized his spectacles were not at fault. The entire deck and its passengers, most of whom were still asleep in a tangle of curled-up forms, were covered in the thin coating of black soot that was gently falling from the sky.

Pincus followed the course of the black snowflakes to the ominous triple funnels towering above him. He then realized that the steerage passengers had been assigned to the portion of the deck downwind from the funnels, which meant that the ash would rain down upon them continuously.

With a thin black blanket of soot covering his clothes, he struggled to his feet and noticed Jakob still asleep beside him.

Looking more closely, he experienced a strange and baffling illusion. He could see no differentiation between the outline of Jakob's curled body and the flooring beneath him. It was if his body had fused into the metal deck of the ship.

Jakob shattered the illusion when he stirred from his slumber. He sat up and regarded Pincus with a smile. "Good morning, Pincus, how are you feeling today, and why do you look like a chimney sweep?"

....

On the afternoon of the second day at sea, the ship passed through the English Channel and out into the vastness of the Atlantic Ocean. Pincus and Jakob spent as much time as they could topside breathing in the crisp sea air. Although it intermingled with the falling black ash, it was far better than the stench and stifling conditions of steerage, and the seas had calmed down considerably.

Some days when the winds blew favorably, the steerage deck was ash-free, which meant that nearly everyone in steerage gathered for the refreshing relief. Pincus was amused by Jakob's ability to connect with strangers and marveled at how easy it was for him to casually approach people already in conversation and seamlessly engage with them.

From his perch against the railing, Pincus watched Jakob mingle like a farmer harvesting crops, gathering up the latest gossip. Finally, Jakob approached him with a satisfied grin.

"There's talk of a famous palmist on board named Dora Meltzer. She is emigrating to America, and the entire ship is talking about her. I hear she has given readings to many esteemed and wealthy people in Germany," Jakob reported.

Twisting his neck to look around Jakob and into the crowd, Pincus asked, "Where is she?"

"She's in first class, of course," Jakob said with a bit of exasperation. "But I hear she will give a reading to anyone who can pay," he added with a smile and a shifting of his bushy eyebrows.

Pincus recalled something about palmistry from Mendel, who had studied the Zohar, the main text of the Jewish Kabbalah—that the reading of wrinkles on the palm was not considered magic. Actually, it was mentioned several times in the Zohar and was deemed both an art and a science, which at times could be beneficial.

"I have money for a reading!" he said.

"So do I. But we will have to bribe an officer to get us into the first-class staterooms," he said, looking to Pincus for approval and receiving a nod and a raised eyebrow.

"Leave it to me," Jakob said and took off into the crowd with Pincus following closely behind him

The steerage deck was cordoned off with a railing to prevent the third-class passengers from wandering into the restricted sections reserved for the first- and second-class passengers. Pincus watched Jakob give one of the deck officers a smile that startled Pincus with its spontaneous charm. Once he had caught the young officer's attention, he approached, shook hands, and skillfully slipped him some money without attracting any unwanted attention.

"We want to see the palmist Dora Meltzer," Jakob whispered and planted a coin in the officer's palm with such deftness that Pincus was stunned.

"For the both of us," he continued with a cock of his head toward Pincus.

The next moment they were escorted out of the steerage corral and led into the first-class common area of the ship.

Pincus gawked as his world changed from the stink and sweat of steerage to the sweet fragrance and elegant luxury of the first-class lobby. The floor was carpeted with a plushness that made Pincus unsure of his footing as he walked gingerly across it. Large triangular glass windows that circled under a gold-leafed dome sparkled overhead. Suspended from its peak hung a crystal chandelier that projected prisms of rainbow light that washed over the flocked wall covering, reminding him of the soft green leaves of the forest surrounding Krzywcza. Pincus had never seen such beauty.

Moments later, Pincus and Jakob stood in front of Dora Meltzer's first-class stateroom as the officer gently knocked upon the door.

"Enter, please," a man's voice reverberated through the carved wood double doors. The officer twisted the fish-shaped brass doorknobs and pushed the doors open.

"I will escort you back to your quarters after your session," said the officer, who stood aside as the men walked into the darkened vestibule.

"Gentlemen, welcome to the mystical world of the renowned palmist, Madame Dora Meltzer," said a man so tall that his short-cropped hair brushed along the wood-paneled ceiling. The black suit he wore was buttoned snugly down his elongated slender frame.

"Please take a seat and allow me to introduce myself."

The waiting room was another marvel of luxury. The walls were paneled with wainscoting and stained in a walnut finish. Hand-carved wooden moldings wrapped around the ceiling's edge. Red silk veils were casually draped over lanterns to cast a soft rosy light.

Pincus and Jakob took seats in deeply tufted chairs upholstered in rich dark green velour.

Leading with his hand extended, the unusual man hinged at his waist, allowing his head to travel a long arcing distance from the ceiling to inches from Pincus's face. Pincus regarded his colorless eyes and translucent, smooth, hairless skin. "My name is Mr. Marcus," he said offering his frigid, skeletal hand.

Pivoting, he swung clockwise to offer a similar greeting to Jakob, and then unwound to a standing position. "Gentlemen, you will each have twenty minutes with Madame Dora. You may not write anything down during the session, but you may ask questions. Do not touch Madame and stay seated until your session has concluded. If you do not follow the rules, your session will be terminated."

Jakob stood up, gave his short waistcoat a tug from the bottom hem to smooth its creases, smiled and winked at Pincus, and said, "I guess I'll go first." He entered through another set of elaborate carved doors into the palmist's chambers.

Pincus waited nervously, trying to avert his eyes from the perpetual stare of Mr. Marcus, who sat across from him in what appeared to be a miniature chair, his giant frame folded down upon it. Pincus reminded himself that he shouldn't complain about the awkwardness of the company, as it was much better than his lodgings in steerage.

Twenty minutes later, the doors opened, and Jakob appeared. His emerald eyes sparkled with excitement, and he said, "She is incredible, Pincus." Then, looking over to Mr. Marcus, he asked, "How does she know?"

"She is connected to the spirit world, Mr. Jakob." Mr. Marcus rose like a marionette and motioned with a flutter of his long fingers for Pincus to enter the chamber for his session.

Pincus stood up and felt as if some kind of spirit had possessed his body. His legs seemed to be lifting of their own volition, propelling him forward even as he tried to remain rooted in place. With each involuntary footstep, he entered into Dora Meltzer's sanctum.

Burning incense rose from elaborately decorated glass jars that filled the room with spicy aromas. Then he heard her voice as softly as the swirling smoke of the incense.

"Come, Pincus, and sit down," offered Dora.

There she grew visible through a transparent curtain of misty vapors. As Pincus took a seat across from her, his eyes felt glued to her face. Her cheekbones were brushed with a reddish tint, and widely spaced in her young face were the most beautiful blue eyes Pincus had ever seen. Their color was highlighted by shades of blue makeup with sparkles twinkling across each lid and extending to the temples. Thick ringlets of blond curls framed her face, rolled down her shoulders, and fell upon her exquisite breasts.

"Give me your hands," she said, snapping Pincus out of his stupor. Careful not to knock over the numerous candles on the embroidered tablecloth, Pincus placed his hands in hers. The moment their hands touched, she closed her grip tightly as a signal that he was not to move them again until she had completed her reading.

She glanced at his palms and lifted her delicate chin to give him a catlike stare. The only woman with whom he had ever shared such an intimate moment before was Clara. However, Dora Meltzer was nothing like the pregnant wife he had left at home, where he always felt in control. Her stunning beauty left him feeling vulnerable to her charms.

"Pincus," she began, as she traced the lines in his right palm. "You are on a journey of discovery, where you will find great challenges and significant successes in your new life. I see that you are a craftsman . . . that you work with your hands." She gently stroked his calluses.

"Yes, I am a cobbler."

"You will open a business in America, and you will find great success."

Pincus nodded as if she had commanded it.

Digging her nails into the skin of his palm, she said seriously, "Pincus, you have a family you left behind."

He felt a sudden sense of shame and nervously tried to pull his hands away. But Dora held on tightly.

"Do not wait any longer than a year to return for your family. I sense real danger if you wait too long," she said, looking directly into his eyes. "You have a son?"

"I have two sons."

"Your eldest son, he is the special one."

"You mean Moshe? He is my eldest," said Pincus, surprised.

"Moshe, yes—he is the one. . . ." She looked again at the lines in his palm. "He is the one you must save. Do not forget him. Bring him to America," she said, and released his hands, breaking the spell. He rose quickly and left her chamber.

When he saw Jakob, he said meekly, "Let's go."

As they returned to steerage, Pincus shoved his hands deep into his pockets to hide how badly they were shaking.

CHAPTER 6

JAKOB'S STORY

"My name is Jakob Adler," he told the ticket agent with the Hamburg-Amerika Line. He was afraid he would need to provide proof of identify, but apparently, the ticket agents were so busy selling passages to America that checking such details was not considered important.

He shoved the receipt and boarding ticket into his coat pocket and ran a few blocks to his apartment building. Bounding up the steps two at a time, he climbed the five flights in a minute. Hastily and quietly, he unlocked the front door and entered his apartment. He gathered his essential belongings, threw them in his valise, and flew back down the stairs and out the front door. He was on the run.

Once inside Warsaw's Central Railway Station, he read on the large board that the train to Hamburg was leaving in a few minutes from Track 4. Cocking his hat at an angle to partially conceal his face, he walked slowly to the platform. After he'd waited only moments, the train arrived. He boarded, found his compartment, tucked his valise overhead, and took a seat by the window. Slowly the train pulled away from the station. He repositioned his hat to cover his eyes, rested his head upon the seat back and sighed with relief. *I think I'll make it*, he thought.

He was very fortunate that the ticket agent had allowed a casual change of name. Josef Horowitz was now Jakob Adler. Leaving his old identity behind was crucial for his escape and hopefully provided a guarantee that he wouldn't be tracked down by Fein's gang.

He had stumbled across the name when he'd read about the unfortunate drowning accident of a Jakob Adler a few days earlier in the obituary section of the newspaper. He was a good match, a twenty-five-year-old Jew, the same age as Josef.

He had been thinking about emigrating to America for several months. His life in Warsaw had little promise. He needed a fresh start, and he figured that stealing from a crook like Benjamin Fein was not a bad thing. Absconding with a few days of collections totaled about two hundred and fifty rubles. That should be plenty to begin a new life in America.

He had worked for Fein for years collecting debts for the gangster. The Fein gang worked the large Jewish communities in Warsaw, offering illegal, high-interest loans and providing merchants with protection for a price.

As a trusted gang member, he had the keys to the office and the combination of the safe. While Ben was out to some family event, Jakob had entered the office, and opened the safe, taken the bills off one of the stacks, and slipped them into his pocket. He was on his way out when the door opened, and Ben walked in.

After a few accusatory words, Ben pulled a handgun and fired it at him. The gun jammed and misfired. As Ben regarded the gun with disgust, Jakob quickly jumped him and tackled him to the ground.

Ben was a small, skinny man and no physical match for Jakob, who easily ripped the gun from his grasp and pinned Ben to the ground. As they struggled with the gun, it suddenly fired. The bullet went through Ben's neck and out through the back of his skull.

Shocked at what he had done, Jakob stood up and saw Ben lying in a pool of blood. He knelt down and placed the gun into Ben's outstretched right hand. Perhaps, with his reputation for not paying his creditors, the police would call it a suicide. Ben's gang, however, would certainly be more suspicious, Jakob realized.

....

Moments before the train was about to leave the station, a family with two young children joined him in the compartment. He raised his head and removed his hat to greet them. He had made a pledge to himself that he would not speak to anyone on the ten-hour train ride to Hamburg. There were many large cities along the way, and there was a risk that he might meet someone who knew him, as they made stops at Poznan and Berlin before arriving in Hamburg. But he couldn't resist the playful, innocent charm of the boy, whom he guessed to be around five years old, and who greeted him with a friendly smile.

He offered his hand to the little boy and tried out his new name. "I am Jakob Adler."

The boy turned to his father, who nodded his approval. "My name is Simon," he answered, putting his tiny hand in Jakob's giant grip.

"Very pleased to meet you, Simon," Jakob said and stood to introduce himself to the remaining members of the family.

Dressed in fashionable coats and hats, Simon's parents seemed well off. The father wore a closely trimmed red beard and greeted Jakob with a curt nod and a handshake. "Pleased to meet you. My name is Mr. Gorpatsch. Where are you headed?"

Sitting next to Mr. Gorpatsch was his wife, an elegantly slender woman wearing an elaborate hat decorated with a bright yellow sunflower that seemed perfectly suited to her beautiful face. On her lap perched Simon's sister, a younger girl, cute but shy, unlike her outgoing brother.

"I am going to Hamburg to sail for America," he said, and immediately regretted doing so. He had not planned to tell anyone where he was going.

"How exciting for you, Mr. Adler," said Mrs. Gorpatsch.

"Yes, I am very excited," he said, reacting a moment too slowly to his new name for the first time.

"Where are you from, Mr. Adler?" Mr. Gorpatsch inquired. "I am originally from Poznan, but I live now in Warsaw."

"What did you do in Warsaw?"

"I worked for a moving company, helping people move their belongings from their old home to a new one," he improvised, hoping the momentary pause before his reply didn't sound suspicious.

"Very impressive that you were able to save enough money for a ticket to America."

"Yes, well, I don't spend much, and this has been my dream for many years. Where, may I ask, is your destination?"

"We are going to Berlin to visit relatives. Perhaps one day we too will emigrate to America. But I have too many business interests in Warsaw to leave right now," Mr. Gorpatsch said.

The trip to Berlin took seven hours, and Jakob spent most of the time playing with the boy, Simon. Mr. Gorpatsch seemed to appreciate the attention to his little son and asked where he planned on settling in America.

"Most likely in New York City," he said. "I was told that's where most Jews settle, a place they call they the Jewish capital of America."

"Yes, that's true. It's called the Lower East Side. I've been there. You will find everything you need."

"You've been to America?" Jakob said in amazement.

"Yes, I do business there," Mr. Gorpatsch told him. "You know, I like you, Jakob. I can size up a man quickly, and you impress me. Perhaps I can help you get settled in America. You will need work and a place to live?"

"Yes, yes I will," he stammered. "That would be great."

Reaching into his pocket, Mr. Gorpatsch drew out a card and reached across to the opposite bench seat where Jakob sat with Simon.

"Here, call Manny when you get to New York. Tell him you met me and give him this card. He'll take care of you. The next time I come to New York, if you're still working with Manny, I'll look you up and see how you're doing."

Jakob looked at the card, which read:

MANNY PLOTNICK ENTERPRISES
210 DELANCEY STREET
NEW YORK CITY
TELEPHONE: OR7-1570

"Thank you, Mr. Gorpatsch," he said sincerely, tucking the card safely into his pocket with his most important documents.

As the Gorpatsch family gathered their bags and valises and disembarked at the Berlin Central, Simon jumped into his arms and gave him a big hug. Smiles and warm handshakes were shared as they said their farewells.

Through his window, he watched Mr. Gorpatsch call for a porter to help with their valises. A middle-aged man dressed all in black with an official porter's cap hurried over with a hand truck. As he attended to the luggage, Mr. Gorpatsch casually leaned over and mouthed some words into his wife's ear. Her expression turned cold as she quickly lifted her eyes toward Jakob's window.

What did he say to her? Shaking off the possibility of getting caught in an inconsequential lie, he settled back into his seat and closed his eyes. It was another three hours to Hamburg.

CHAPTER 7

SAILING TO AMERICA

Leaning on the ship's rail, Pincus watched the sun rise across the vast ocean. This quiet time offered him privacy from the crowds of the floating city of a thousand passengers plus crew. Except for the first night of the storm in the North Sea, the North Atlantic waters had been calm.

It was also a time to fight back his worries about Clara and the children, and in particular Dora Meltzer's strange remarks about Moshe. He wondered why she had said Moshe was special. He seemed like a normal nine-year-old boy, perhaps a bit more sensitive than most.

Clara had mentioned several times that she thought Moshe could understand when she was upset. "He has a keen sense of my feelings," she had said.

Pincus rarely noticed such things, though now he regretted not having paid more attention to his children.

He filled his days watching his fellow steerage passengers mingling topside. Couples were seen strolling along the deck reminiscing over stories of home, weaving dreams of their new life, sharing gossip, and playing cards.

Pincus thought most of the passengers in steerage looked honest and respectable. But he couldn't help his fascination with shady and questionable-looking characters, and steerage offered plenty to amuse him.

Most interesting were the single men, conversing and mingling among themselves, who, Pincus imagined, had left their homeland to escape the law. These were not like the men Pincus knew from the shtetl. They probably came from big cities like Warsaw and Krakow, he figured.

An unwashed man with a limp hobbled by him. His face featured a swollen scar that traveled down from his left eye and ended at his lip. Pincus watched him stop to speak to a larger and equally dirty man. Perhaps they were even now strategizing their criminal career opportunities in the New World.

He then observed Jakob speaking to two young, nefarious-looking men.

Finishing up his conversation, Jakob approached him. "Pincus, you know the card game quilok?"

"Yes, all the kids played quilok in my village."

"Great, I got a game with those two," he said.

Pincus followed the direction of Jakob's large hand pointing at the two young men who now stared back at them.

"Those men, Jakob? Why would you set up a game with them? They look um. . . ." He paused, stumbling for a way to describe them.

"They look fine, and I know they have money, and we are going to take it from them. Just play the game as you know it and leave the rest to me," he said with a slight smirk.

Play for money? I've never played for money, Pincus thought, but he reluctantly followed Jakob toward the unsavory-looking men.

Steerage passengers were not offered space in the grand salons that the two upper classes enjoyed. Instead, they assembled on assorted-sized wooden crates, which served as tables and chairs. Pincus sat down across from Jakob and watched their opponents take places next to them.

Finding a seat to his right was a man probably in his mid-twenties. He had dark oily hair combed back straight and flat and a disturbingly pockmarked face, the result of some childhood illness, Pincus thought. He introduced himself as Dovid and offered a cold and clammy handshake. His partner's name was Herschel, and his handshake actually compressed Pincus's bones. He was powerfully built and looked like he could give Jakob a good fight, something Pincus hoped would never happen.

Boys in the shtetl had played quilok in between their Torah studies. It was a quick, entertaining game that was played with twenty-four cards. The goal was to reach a threshold of points. Games lasted only minutes, and Pincus had been pretty good, winning more often than the other boys would care to admit. But he'd never played for money—that was not permitted or even considered.

The storage room was cramped with other groups of men playing cards. Cigarette and cigar smoke filled the quarters along with singing and laughing, which created an environment that bewildered Pincus but appeared to comfort Jakob.

Play moved fast, and Pincus kept up and won a few rounds. This pleased Jakob, who rewarded him with a subtle, proud glance. But it was Jakob who won the most games, perhaps too many, Pincus thought. He also noticed that Herschel and Dovid might be sharing a suspicion that Jakob was cheating.

As the wins and coins piled up in front of Jakob, a few nearby men were getting loud and rowdy from drinking the cheap whiskey they had smuggled on board. Moments later a fight broke out. A very robust and rather round man, his face reddened from the exertion of wielding wild punches, crashed down upon their crate, scattering the cards and coins all over the deck. A mad scramble ensued, with Pincus dropping to all fours to catch the coins before they spiraled away, as Jakob used his massive arms as a broom to sweep them into his possession.

"Quickly," Jakob instructed Pincus as they grabbed as much as they could and ran from the storage room while the bedlam continued.

Reaching the top deck, they found their favorite spot, next to the upper windows that peeked down into the first-class dining hall, and divided up their winnings.

"Were you cheating?" asked Pincus.

"What makes you think I was cheating?"

"You won too many hands."

Jakob gave his most charming smile, shook his head slowly, and said, "No, Pincus, I wasn't cheating."

Pincus looked into Jakob's gem-like eyes, smiled, and said, "Okay, Jakob."

....

Pincus had little time alone except just before the dawn while Jakob and nearly everyone else on board were asleep, except for a few members of the crew. He thought about Mendel and wondered how Sara was doing. Mendel was a good man, and the only man in the village he could have been friends with.

Pincus also thought about Jakob. Was he becoming a friend?

His companionship with Mendel had been cemented as children, which bonded their friendship for life. But the relationship with Jakob was different. He considered the probability that Jakob had been cheating, and how he wasn't feeling bad or ashamed of it. They had beaten those guys at a dirty game of cards, and he dared to admit to himself that he'd been excited. This stunning new emotion was creating a friendship with Jakob that filled a part of his life that he never knew existed.

....

The SS Amerika was on the final day of its ten-day voyage. Within a few hours, they would be docking at Hoboken Harbor in New Jersey, where the ferryboats would bring the steerage passengers to the greatly anticipated and revered Ellis Island for processing and entry into America. Pincus and Jakob leaned over on the ship's railing and quietly awaited the first sightings of the New World.

"Pincus," Jakob said, interrupting the silence.

Pincus turned his head toward his new friend.

"On the train from Warsaw to Hamburg, I met a man who told me he had connections in the Lower East Side. He said when I got to America, I should contact this man." He handed Manny Plotnick's card to Pincus.

"Delancey Street is in the Lower East Side, Pincus. We find this Manny and tell him that Mr. Gorpatsch referred us to him. Maybe he can help us find a place to live, and I am sure he can also find a good spot for your cobbler shop," Jakob said enthusiastically.

"Okay, let's find Manny Plotnick of Manny Plotnick Enterprises," Pincus agreed.

CHAPTER 8

CLARA'S STORY

Clara's fondest memories were of her teenage years, when she learned how to manage the Zieglers' traditional Jewish home. Clara's mother, Sadie, leaned heavily on her, as the only daughter in a household with five younger brothers. Clara was her assistant in almost every way, which included such tasks as preparing and delivering lunch to the boys at their Torah studies, tending the vegetable garden, managing the chicken coop, and preparing for Shabbat every Friday afternoon. Her mother boasted to her friends about what an amazing mother her daughter would become one day. Clara shared her mother's dreams and fantasized that she would marry a wealthy Torah scholar and raise a beautiful Jewish family.

Not only did Clara learn from her mother, she also became proficient behind the looms of her father's linen business. With growing demand for his product, Yisroel Ziegler made a nice living for his family, and Clara became a key part in its success. She was able—for a few hours a day in between the household chores—to work the looms and weave yards of linen fabric for her father to sell.

Clara had a few girlfriends who lived nearby, but they barely saw each other except for a few stolen moments as they criss-crossed the village during their daily chores. One of these days, as she was delivering the lunches to the boys, she ran into her friend Ruchel. Ruchel told her she was getting married soon and leaving to live with her fiancé in a village far away.

Clara thought it ironic that her best skills—keeping a home and helping with the family business—were the same reasons that at the age of eighteen she remained unmarried. She knew her parents would struggle without her, but didn't she need to marry and raise a family soon?

Clara shared her worries with her mother, who reassured her, albeit with a forced smile. "Clara, of course you will be missed. But your father and I will learn to manage."

They will "learn to manage," Clara thought. As always, her mother found a subtle way to instill a little guilt into her supposedly reassuring statements.

To Clara's surprise, a few months past her eighteenth birthday, her parents gave her the news that an arrangement had been made with the marriage broker. She was promised to a family in Krzywcza, which was about forty miles south of their village of Sanok. Her betrothed was the eldest son of a cobbler, Pincus Potasznik. Pincus was twenty-one years old and would inherit the family business. He had been apprenticing under his father's tutelage since his thirteenth birthday.

What a dream it would have been to be matched to a Torah scholar instead of a merchant! But she would never disrespect her father by verbalizing her disappointment. In addition, her father needed the dowry to offset the five dowries he had to come up with for the five boys in the family.

She thought back on that day when she sat outside the house for hours staring down the road as she waited nervously for the arrival of the family. Around noon, she caught a glimpse of the horse-drawn wagon transporting the Potaszniks. As it approached, she saw a couple who appeared to be her future in-laws. Pointing and laughing behind them were two boys and a little girl. The older boy, she would soon discover, was her betrothed, Pincus; the other boy was Lazar his younger brother, and the girl sitting in between them was his sister, Freidel.

The introductions were very awkward, as Pincus was painfully shy. During their chaperoned visit, he could barely look into her eyes and didn't say much except to utter the standard pleasantries. The farewells were just as clumsy. As they departed, she realized the next time they met would be on their wedding day.

That had been seventeen years earlier, and now here she was—about to give birth in a few months—with three small children needing constant attention, and a husband who had just left on a voyage across the ocean to America. Her eldest daughter, Jennie, now eleven, was becoming useful in the household. Fortunately, Clara's mother had moved in a year earlier, after her father had passed.

Before Pincus had left for America, they had discussed keeping the cobbler shop operational to provide income for the family. His goal was to set up shop in America, but it would probably take a while before he could send money home. Clara rarely stepped foot into her husband's cobbler business, but she knew enough about the tasks involved as a result of living with the shoemaker for many years.

They had hired Mendel Beck's son Shmuel to run the cobbler shop. Pincus had trained Shmuel for several weeks before his departure. Clara would make it a point to stop by twice a day to oversee and collect the day's receipts.

There were not many women in the shtetl who could raise a family, give birth, and supervise a business without a husband by her side, but Clara felt as if her entire life had prepared her for just such a challenge. She'd had expert tutelage from her mother, fortunately still by her side, and business savvy she had learned from her father. These teachers and her own life experience would provide her with the necessary skills. But it was her poise and wisdom that would prove to be the catalyst for her family's survival.

CHAPTER 9

ELLIS ISLAND

Pincus guessed that all of the thousand passengers plus the crew were topside watching the *SS Amerika's* approach into the vast openness of New York Harbor. An electric charge seemed to ripple along the length of the ship and through the crowd on deck. They first sailed past Governor's Island on the starboard side. When lower Manhattan came into view, Pincus joined in the collective gasp of amazement.

Then it began, first as a low murmur and then as a roar of excitement. On the port side they all saw it at last, the image of everyone's dreams, the Statue of Liberty. Standing tall and proud, she represented the American dream he heard so much about and was the most beautiful object he had ever seen. Pincus could not hold back his tears as he held tightly to the railing of the *SS Amerika* as it sailed right alongside the elegant lady that represented his and his family's future.

Upon docking at Hoboken Harbor, Pincus soon learned that the first- and second-class passengers would be quickly examined onboard for signs of contagious diseases such as cholera, smallpox, typhoid, yellow fever, scarlet fever, and measles. Once cleared, they were quickly processed through immigration at Ellis Island. But the steerage passengers would need to wait for hours until the barges transferred them for processing and a much more intensive health inspection.

Pincus and Jakob were waiting for what they understood were two cards they needed for immigration control. The first was a landing card, which was to be pinned onto their lapel of their coat and would list the name of their steamship, the manifest sheet number, and their passenger number. The other was a medical inspection card, which was a record of the examination by the ship's doctor.

Jakob leaned over to speak softly. "Most likely we'll get separated once we get inside. Whoever gets through first should wait for the other at the ferry before going into Manhattan."

"Okay," Pincus agreed.

As he stepped off the barge, Pincus was thrilled to be on firm ground. Carrying his valise and wearing his winter coat, he felt sweat trickle down his forehead and the back of his neck. It was the middle of summer, and he was either carrying or wearing all his clothing. He could feel his undergarments growing damp from perspiration.

He was led into the South Hall where the inspection process began. As he waited his turn, Pincus watched as doctors scribbled a chalk mark on some of the immigrants' lapels. He would later learn that the letters B, C, or F were codes that identified an illness that required further examination and would eventually be probable cause for refusing entry into America.

Pincus took a deep breath to calm his nerves when his turn came. The cooler interior of the hall had evaporated the sweat, but he was not the epitome of health. All was going well until the doctor, a young man probably just out of medical school, said, "This may hurt." He pinched Pincus's eyelids and yanked them up and over a metal buttonhook.

"What are you doing?" Pincus yelled in Yiddish.

It didn't matter what language was used, the entire medical staff knew what it meant. They were checking for a common eye disease in Southeastern Europe called trachoma.

Pincus apparently passed the medical inspection and was still rubbing his abused eyelids while he waited for his interview in the Registry Hall on the second floor. When he was called, he stood across a podium from a man with a nametag that read FIORELLO LAGUARDIA. Pincus stared at the Italian name as he waited for the young man to read whatever he was holding.

"You speak Yiddish?" asked LaGuardia, looking at papers in an open folder on his desk.

"Yes, I do," said Pincus, who was surprised to hear this Italian man speaking his mother tongue.

"Good," he continued in Yiddish. "I have a few questions to ask and then you can be on your way."

Pincus was pleased that he had spent many hours studying the questions with a group of single men during the voyage. Because of this, he knew what the Fourth of July was, how many stripes and stars there were in the American flag, and who was President of the United States.

"William Taft," he said with his very heavy accent.

An hour later, Pincus was walking down the stairs and out into the sunlight on a path that led to the ferry to New York City. To his great delight, there stood Jakob with a huge smile, his arms spread wide, and announcing, "Welcome to America!"

CHAPTER 10

THE LOWER EAST SIDE

On the voyage, Pincus learned many things about the so-called Jewish Capital of America, the Lower East Side. A few seasoned travelers told him how Eastern European Jews had overwhelmed this small area of southern Manhattan. Not only were there many Jews, there was also tremendous overcrowding with large families crammed into small living spaces.

But none of the stories prepared Pincus for what he and Jakob saw as they walked with their valises in hand along Delancey Street. Pushcarts lined the boulevard with merchants selling fruits and vegetables, pickles, meats, and popular household items.

Pincus stopped in front of pushcart selling cold borscht with a chunk of a boiled potato. "I am so hungry," he said.

The merchant working the cart was a young teenage boy, who spoke to Pincus in Yiddish, asking "They are a nickel for one, how many do you want?"

Pincus dug into his pocket for the American coins he had obtained on the ship.

"Two, please. We just arrived in America, and we are hungry," Pincus told the boy, who just smiled and handed over the cups.

Using his valise as a seat, Pincus sipped the cup of borscht and bit into the boiled potato. "This is good," he said to Jakob, who nodded in agreement.

Pincus marveled at the swarm of people making their way between the pushcarts and horses that clogged the thoroughfare. He gawked in amazement at the dilapidated tenement buildings that were squeezed into place between alleys and streets that appeared either unpaved or in great need of repair. *Is this really to be my new home? How will I start a business and find lodgings and eventually bring my family over?*

"Okay, Pincus, time to get on with our new lives. Let's go find Manny." Jakob's voice interrupted his friend's daydreaming. "He can't be far—the card says 210 Delancey Street."

In a few minutes, Pincus and Jakob found themselves in front of a six-story apartment building with the number 210 on a large, oval, white ceramic sign centered over the pair of wooden doors. Lining the block on either side of the entryway was a variety of stores, each one draped with a worn-out, faded fabric awning. Pincus watched as Jakob took the six steps up to the vestibule in three leaps. He might have expected Jakob to be so bold, but he himself took one step at a time.

The sign by the door advertised the same name as the card in Jakob's hand. The stairs were barely wide enough for Pincus and his valise and definitely not wide enough for Jakob, who had to carry his bag front of him as he would a small child. The old, dilapidated staircase tilted sharply to the left, which was disconcerting for Pincus, who had to fight the pull of gravity in two directions as he climbed to the fourth floor.

Moments later they stood in front of a door with the name MANNY PLOTNICK ENTERPRISES neatly printed on it. Jakob knocked boldly, and a voice from within shouted, "Come in."

After a quick glance and a reassuring wink, Jakob turned the doorknob and entered with Pincus right behind him.

Pincus saw someone hunched over a desk, his back toward them as they walked in. Dust particles floated by in the streams of daylight dancing their way across the room. Pincus couldn't identify the odor, but it appeared to be something rotten that should have been thrown out weeks ago. The man spun around on a swivel chair and, without losing any momentum, hopped out of it to face them.

"Good day, gentlemen. My name is Manny Plotnick. How may I be of service?" he said, offering a handshake to the first taker.

"I am Jakob Adler, and this is Pincus Potasznik. Mr. Gorpatsch of Warsaw gave me your card and recommended that we contact when we arrived. He said you could help us."

"Oh, Mr. Gorpatsch, my good friend," Manny said enthusiastically.

Pincus had heard the story from Jakob about how they had met on the train from Warsaw. He was skeptical that this would turn into anything helpful, but maybe he was wrong. Manny seemed as disheveled as his office. He obviously shaved and bathed infrequently, which probably accounted for some of the offensive smells in the office. It appeared that he lived here as well, perhaps sleeping on the lumpy brown sofa and in the same wrinkled clothes he was wearing. But he seemed friendly, and his brown eyes sparkled as he shook hands.

"Good to meet you, Pincus. You are both from Warsaw, I assume?"

"No, I am from a small village in the southeast called Krzywcza, and Jakob is from Warsaw."

"Good, good. Tell me how can I help?"

"We need a place to live, and I need to find a spot for a store. I'm a cobbler."

"Wonderful, I can certainly help. What about you, Jakob, what do you do?"

"I'm going to work with Pincus and help him out with the business."

"That's good, but I imagine that a man of your stature," Manny said, looking at him from head to toe, "has certain skills that Mr. Gorpatsch recognized, and that's why he sent you to me. But we can have that conversation later. Let's get you settled."

He reached into a drawer and pulled out a key with a wooden block attached with a twine. "Ninety-seven Orchard Street, apartment six-E. You will both be very comfortable there."

"How much is it?" Pincus asked with concern.

"We'll work that out after you get settled," Manny said as he handed Pincus the key.

....

Walking many flights of stairs was something new to Pincus. Back in Krzywcza, the tallest homes had two or at most three flights to climb. Lumbering up the five flights at 97 Orchard Street was not only exhausting but also precarious. Scattered on almost every step were pages from old newspapers, half-eaten and rotting fruit, and oil-stained rags—or perhaps old shirts, Pincus couldn't decide.

With his valise in one hand and steadying himself with a grip on the rickety wooden railing, Pincus reached the first landing of the dilapidated building. Laid out in the entry to the two hallways that led to the apartments were battered and stained mattresses, pillows, and clothing.

"Are people living here?" Pincus whispered, turning to Jakob, whose face showed equal disbelief at the sight.

"Apparently so," Jakob replied, as he pointed at several children and adults milling around the two hallways leading to the apartments on this floor.

Pincus saw more evidence of overcrowding on each floor until they finally reached the sixth. Walking down the long hallway required some zigzagging around tossed garbage, sleeping people—though it was midday—and an assortment of household items used for daily living.

Apartment Six-E was tucked away down a small alcove at the end of the hallway. Pincus unlocked the door and was knocked back by the overpowering stale stench that greeted him. He glanced over his shoulder at Jakob who signaled with a nod that he should enter the dark and dank space.

With no windows, the room was pitch black. Pincus heard a short scrape and a flicker of light appeared, as Jakob held up a lit match. He could now see the room was very small. Scattered on the stained wooden floor was an assortment of trash and old clothes.

"This is it?" Pincus asked, looking at the small ten-by-ten room. "Where do we sleep? Where's the toilet? There are no windows!" he lamented.

"Pincus, we'll figure it out," Jakob said. "I think I saw a toilet down the hall."

....

Though he was exhausted, Pincus could not sleep that first night. Jakob, on the other hand, feel asleep quickly and snored incessantly. In addition to finding the floor very uncomfortable, the noises from the adjacent rooms and hallways were never-ending. He heard mothers yelling at their children, husbands yelling at their wives, and babies crying inconsolably. Since their room had no windows, the time of day was undeterminable. Eventually, he figured it must be morning when the myriad of voices and sounds outside the door and through the walls sounded like people getting ready for the day.

He reached over and jostled his friend. "Jakob, wake up."

By Pincus's third wake-up call, Jakob had begun to stir.

How can he sleep so soundly in this hideous, smelly, noisy place? Pincus wondered.

A few moments later, Jakob sat up. Pincus had found a light switch that lit up a bulb that dangled off an electrical cord tacked to the ceiling. It buzzed with a low hum. The room looked no better by lamplight than it had the night before. It was small, dark, and dirty, and it smelled worse than steerage.

"We can't stay here. This place is terrible."

"It's not so bad for a few days until we can find a better place. Let's go see Manny and ask him where we can open your shop," Jakob suggested, trying to sound optimistic.

....

Pincus sighed happily as he stepped out into the street and inhaled the fresh morning air. As they walked from Orchard Street to Delancey, they passed Yonah Schimmel's Knishery. The smell coming from the open front door of this bakery reminded Pincus how hungry he was.

"Jakob, let's buy a knish," Pincus said.

"Yes, great idea," Jakob agreed.

Walking into the crowded bakery, they saw a dazzling, mouthwatering display of freshly baked, large, round knishes. They each handed the boy behind the counter five cents.

Pincus bit into the dumpling of dough stuffed with potato. "This is wonderful," he said.

Jakob said nothing, but demolished the knish in two enormous bites.

....

Pincus and Jakob sat in two flimsy chairs, separated from Manny by a large wooden desk littered with papers, empty coffee mugs, and uneaten leftovers. Manny seemed less friendly than he had been the day before.

"You two are back already. Is there something wrong with your room?" Manny asked, obviously perturbed.

Pincus jumped at the question, "Actually yes, there is—"

"No, what Pincus means," Jakob interrupted, "is that the room is fine, but we'd like to find a place that maybe has beds and a window, if that's possible."

"I see," Manny said curtly. "Anything else you two need?"

"Well, yes, we need a place for my cobbler shop," Pincus said. "We don't want handouts. We have money for rent. Can you help us?"

Manny looked at the men and shook his head. "Pincus, why don't you wait downstairs, let me speak to Jakob for a few minutes."

....

Manny turned and faced Jakob, who sat comfortably in a swivel chair with one leg crossed over the other.

"So, Jakob, you are an interesting fellow. You bring me my card from Mr. Gorpatsch," he said while displaying the card between two fingers.

Jakob nodded slightly.

"I imagine that Mr. Gorpatsch was impressed with you, which is why he gave this to you."

"Yes, I think he was impressed," Jakob said cheerfully.

"Do you know what I do, Jakob?"

Jakob shook his head.

"I am a banker of sorts. Let's say a banker without a bank," he said, using his arms to display his unkempt office.

"Okay," Jakob said, glancing around the place.

"I lend people money. You probably know what I am talking about, don't you, Jakob?"

"I think so. You lend money with very high interest, and when they can't pay, you send very persuasive people to collect."

"I'm impressed that you know about such a business."

"I did similar work in Warsaw," Jakob confessed.

"That's what I thought. If you work for me doing collections, I'll set you two up in a better apartment and give your ornery friend a storefront. You'll work with Pincus. People won't be suspicious of you, and we can use the shop as a place to drop off payments," Manny said with a smirk and a raised eyebrow.

"I might be interested," Jakob said, not ready to commit.

"I appreciate your caution. Tell me about your work experience in Warsaw."

Without mentioning the name of Benjamin Fein, he told Manny about his years in the so-called "banking business," and gave him an account of his basic routine.

The first visit was a friendly reminder that the loan was about to become due. Usually, most paid on time, and he had a drop-off location in the back of a butcher shop behind the trash that collected the rotting cutoffs of meat that the butcher would accumulate throughout the day. This was a great spot to hide money, as no one would be snooping around.

Then there were the late payers. Jakob told how he would begin to ratchet up the pressure. Of course the interest rate would start to increase, and the threats of physical harm would creep into the conversation. As a large, muscular, and imposing man, his words had an impact, and most paid.

But still there were the ones who refused or couldn't repay their loans. This, Jakob explained, would be most unfortunate because he would need to inflict some more persuasive ways to collect his money. He offered some examples of breaking bones, cutting off fingers or toes or both, and even threatening other members of the deadbeat's family with similar injuries.

"So you know the business," Manny said with a smile, as Jakob finished his verbal resume.

"I can see why Mr. Gorpatsch offered you my card. He is very skilled at recognizing talent. So what do you say, Jakob? I can offer you a place to live, a place to work, and a chance to make some good money. Not so bad since you only arrived in America yesterday."

Jakob darted down the stairs and out onto the sidewalk, where Pincus stood waiting for him. Any doubts he had getting his life started in America were gone. With his arms spread wide, he hugged Pincus and shouted, "The American dream!"

CHAPTER 11

CLARA GIVES BIRTH

"Childbirth is easy for my daughter. She has wide hips," Sadie announced proudly to the midwife, who had just assisted in the birth of her new granddaughter, Anna, which took a mere twenty minutes.

"Mom, can you stop boasting about my wide hips?" Clara said before turning her attention to the midwife cleaning her baby girl.

Clara could barely lift her head off the pillows propped up behind her. Even with her mother's help, between caring for three children, running a household, and overseeing a business, she had been exhausted these past two months, since Pincus had departed for America. And she had just given birth!

Fortunately, the cobbler shop was doing well. She was grateful that they had found Shmuel, the youngest son of Mendel Beck, Pincus's only friend in Krzywcza. Shmuel didn't have the aptitude for being a Torah scholar like his father, so learning a trade provided him a valuable opportunity to make a living, and it helped ease Clara's burdens as well.

Now that she had the baby, Clara would make a point to stop by the shop at least once a week, instead of her previous daily visits to see how he was doing. She liked Shmuel and trusted him. She was still required to count the receipts, pay the bills, pay Shmuel his salary, and take home what was left. It was just one more major responsibility that had fallen on her shoulders. But this was something she liked doing, and she would discuss ways to improve the business at her weekly visits with Shmuel. One of the first improvements she made was to have Shmuel bring some order to the shop.

"This place needs a good cleaning," she'd told him on his first day. Together they had spent a few hours throwing away years of accumulated trash that Pincus had collected or simply ignored. She'd instructed Shmuel to keep the storefront clear of clutter. "When a customer walks in they need to see a neat, well-organized place."

She had a head for commerce. The years of working for her father in his weaving business had proved to be both helpful and enjoyable.

Sadie complained that she was spending too much time at the shop and not enough time at home, and even more disturbing was that she was being talked about in the village. Clara told her that she didn't care about gossip and she enjoyed making changes and seeing positive results.

Clara liked being active. It was unusual for the children to see their mother lying in bed at all. Every night when they went to sleep, Clara was still busy catching up with the housework, and when they arose in the morning she was already up and about, preparing for the day, her life full to the point of bursting.

Every few weeks her mother would start with the endless nagging questions about Pincus. "When do you think he will come back?" she would ask.

"Pincus says a year. Finding a home and a place for a business won't be easy," she found herself repeating to her mother.

"I don't understand why he left you," Sadie complained. She didn't understand the growing problem of political and religious persecution the Jews were facing. Clara, on the other hand, knew that it would be best to leave their homeland.

"It's best for the sake of the children," she reassured her mother.

Clara had lived with anti-Semitism her entire life. She could recall from childhood her father being harassed many times by local government officials over some minor issue with his textile business. The men in the gray uniforms wearing funny hats with badges sewn onto them had made sure that her family knew they were not welcome in the village—the same village their family had known and lived in for generations.

She remembered each and every moment she first looked into the eyes of her newborn children. The birth of her oldest, Jennie, was over eleven years ago, but she could still feel the overwhelming emotion of that moment. Then came Moshe and Hymie, her two little boys, she thought as she gazed into Anna's clear blue eyes. That was the name she and Pincus had selected, based on the first letter of her grandmother's name, Ahuva. Clara remembered her grandmother telling her that her name meant *beloved*.

Any joy she felt breastfeeding Anna vanished instantly once her mother started up again with her complaining.

"Do you really think Pincus will be able to start a new business in America? Where will you live? Do you think he found a nice place? Will it be big enough for the family?"

Clara wanted to scream. She didn't have answers for her mother's relentless questions. But it was true that so much of their future depended on Pincus. He had a tall task ahead of him.

Will he be successful in America? she wondered. *I do believe in him*, she reassured herself.

CHAPTER 12

THE COBBLER SHOP

Pincus paced the sidewalk in front of 210 Delancey Street. *So this is the Lower East Side*, he thought as he observed the vibrant Jewish community. Signs and announcements in Yiddish advertising special deals in local stores lined the street.

Stepping off the curb and onto the cobblestones, he maneuvered his way around the many pushcarts selling an assortment of things. He was amazed at the variety of items for sale. One pushcart offered the most wonderful ripe bananas while another sold pretzels loaded with salt crystals that sparkled in the bright sunlight. A plump woman wrapped in a white apron had repurposed a baby carriage as a pushcart, which she had loaded up with red apples. Pincus felt his stomach growl with hunger.

He carefully crossed the street as horse-drawn wagons made their way down the boulevard. Just as he was about to reach the other side, he stepped into a steamy pile of horse dung. His right shoe was thoroughly covered with manure. Quickly he hopped to the curb on his clean foot and then realized that he only was on the center mall of Delancey Street. There was an entire second lane for the traffic going in the opposite direction. The mall itself served as a small park with trees and grassy areas and benches. He immediately sat down on one, found a cloth in his pocket, and cleaned off his shoe.

Children were playing along the mall, and men and woman sat on the other benches. Some, he noticed, were watching him and were apparently amused at his predicament. He was quick to offer a snarl to anyone who cared to make eye contact. *Sure, make fun of the cobbler with his shit-covered shoe*, he lamented.

Tossing the cloth away, he gathered his wits and once again took in his new surroundings. Delancey Street was a wide boulevard, as he could see, yet it seemed small. Perhaps, Pincus thought, it was because of the hundreds of people living within the confines of the tall buildings that lined the street.

Allowing his gaze to go beyond the facades of the apartments and storefronts, he could make out activity through the open windows and imagined the intimacies of so many Jews making a new life in America. He thought of Clara. Could she and the children thrive here? Certainly, the opportunities seemed plentiful.

The sight of families walking together caused him to wonder how many other men had left their wives and children behind in order to first secure a new life. *What if I made a mistake?* This thought frightened him so much that he pushed it forcefully to the back of his mind.

The condition of his shoe suddenly became a welcome distraction. He decided to return to the room that he shared with Jakob, where he could properly clean his shoe and give it a good polish from the bag of tools and supplies he had brought with him from home.

As he made his way back across Delancey, the front doors of number 210 swung open with a pounding force that nearly tore it off its hinges, and out popped Jakob.

"Pincus, we're all set. In a few days, we'll have a new place to live with a window and a toilet, and there's more good news." He paused to hand Pincus a key. "We have a place for your cobbler shop, too."

Pincus looked at the key, which was attached to a block of wood with 95 Ludlow burned into it.

"I know Ludlow Street," he said enthusiastically and pointed. "There, it's the next corner." Too excited to be slowed down by details, Pincus was nearly in a full run.

"Slow down, you don't even know where you are going," pleaded Jakob.

"Yes, Ludlow is right here," Pincus yelled as he rounded the corner.

By the time Jakob caught up, Pincus was standing in front of 95 Ludlow Street. The empty store was squeezed in between a tobacco shop on the left and an optometrist on the right.

Pincus took one step to the landing and inserted the large metal key into the keyhole. The old door swung open on its rusty hinges, and he stepped inside. As the sunlight streamed into the dark, dusty space, Pincus could see what had once been a news-stand and bookstore. Old pages from the Yiddish newspaper, *The Forward*, were scattered on dark wooden shelves and spilled across the dirty tiled floor. A few random books remained from the previous shopkeeper.

"This will be perfect!" Pincus announced. "Let's get to work."

CHAPTER 13

THE LANDSMAN SOCIETY

I t took nearly a full day for Pincus just to clear the garbage from his new shop. Occasionally he would pause to read a headline or an article from *The Forward* dated several months earlier. He learned in a story about the Lower East Side that there were now over half a million Jews living there, supported by over 500 synagogues. Many of these were places of worship hastily organized in cramped tenement apartments.

As he was washing the years of dirt off the storefront window, Jakob walked in and said, "Come with me."

"Why, where are we going?"

"Just come, I'll show you."

Pincus put down the dirt-covered rag and followed Jakob out the front door and into the door right next to their entrance.

Jakob led Pincus up four flights of stairs and opened the door to an empty apartment.

"Welcome to our new home," he said, sweeping his arm wide.

This was indeed an improvement over where they had slept the past three nights. Although it was still a one-room apartment, Pincus was very pleased with the fresh air breezing past him from the single window that also offered a great view of Ludlow Street.

Pincus and Jakob spent the next few days building shelves and a wall that would separate the entrance of the store from the workplace in the back.

This is how my father set up his cobbler shop, Pincus thought proudly, as he arranged the tools of the trade in precise order. *I wish he were alive to see how I've made it to America.*

"What are you doing?" Jakob asked as he watched Pincus placing small piles of salt in the corners of the room.

"Keeping away evil spirits. They like to hide in the corners," Pincus said emphatically.

Looking around at their progress, Pincus said, "We need a sign for the front of the shop. I saw a sign maker over on Orchard. I'll stop by this afternoon and see how he can help us."

Orchard Street was a short walk from the store. As Pincus entered the store, the proprietor greeted him warmly.

"How may I be of assistance to you this fine day?"

"My name is Pincus. I've just opened a cobbler shop on Ludlow, and I need a sign."

"Wonderful! My name is Murray. This is my shop, and I'd be happy to make a beautiful sign for you."

After Pincus and Murray agreed on the design and cost of his sign, the conversation shifted to each other's stories. As a fellow Jew, Murray asked Pincus if his village had established a Landsman Society. He told Pincus how he had joined one as soon as he'd arrived in America.

"I'm from Plock, a shtetl fifty miles west of Warsaw. The Landsman Society of Plock was established over five years ago," he said.

As if he'd just been told he'd won a prize, Pincus explained that his rabbi had instructed him to form the Landsman Society of Krzywcza. But he didn't know how to begin. "What does your group do?" he asked.

Murray explained that he was very involved with his society. "Coming to America can be traumatic. There is so much to learn and adjust to. But we agreed that leaving our homeland was what we had to do to protect the future of our children and of our children's children. Do I not speak the truth?"

Pincus nodded.

"Of course, this is true. But we come from fear of what we left behind, and we live in fear of what is yet to come. That's why we formed the Landsman Society of Plock. We are a support group for families emigrating from our village. When they arrive, we greet them and arrange for housing and a job. We can help them find relatives or friends. In emergencies, we can even provide some money. When people are sick, we call on our committees to visit, and when they die, we bury our loved ones in our own cemetery."

Pincus knew that a proper Jewish burial was important for the people of Krzywcza. He remembered as a child going on the first Sunday of each month to the cemetery with his family, which included his grandparents, when they were still alive. His mother and his sister would prepare food to bring with them. It was a family outing to visit the dead. Pincus would hear the same plea each week from his grandfather: "Don't forget us, Pincus. Make sure you and your brother and sister visit us when it is our time."

"Come meet the founders of our society," Murray offered. "They can guide you on how to start yours. You can be the founder of the Landsman Society of Krzywcza."

"Yes, I'd like to meet them," Pincus agreed with enthusiasm.

....

Seated with Jakob at a table near the window of the Katz Delicatessen, Pincus took another large bite of the soft, steamy corned beef sandwich.

"This is good," he said, as he pulled a swollen pickle out of a glass jar.

Jakob smiled but waited until he'd swallowed before he added, "Great place."

After washing down his meal with a long drink of seltzer water, Pincus leaned over the small table covered with white craft paper and said, "I need to find my cousin Hersch. He's living here with his father, my uncle Benjamin. They are carpenters. Hersch can help me start the Landsman Society of Krzywcza. Will you help me locate him?"

Scratching his stubby, unshaven chin, Jakob suggested, "Let's ask Manny—that's a good place to start."

"Okay. Let's go see him in the morning," Pincus said as he knocked twice with his knuckles on the wooden table. It was a superstition they both believed would bring them good luck.

....

The next morning Manny was not in his office.

"Where is he?" Pincus asked.

Jakob and Pincus had no luck knocking on doors or asking neighbors. Finally back on the street below, next to the main entrance at 210 Delancey Street, they found a tailor shop. A sign, hanging off a black iron bracket slightly swinging from the gentle breeze, read:

BERLINER'S TAILORING & CLOTHIER

MEN'S SUITS $5.00

"Manny told me he owns the building. Maybe the shop owner knows him and can tell us where he is," Jakob said as he opened the door, allowing Pincus to enter first.

"Gentlemen, quick come in, let me show you the latest in sewing technology." Standing before them was a man waving a long pair of scissors, with a cloth tape measure draped around his neck, and pointing to a sewing machine.

Pincus turned and shared a puzzled look with Jakob.

"Good day, are you Max Berliner?" Jakob asked the man.

"I am—the one and only," he said.

"Do you know Manny Plotnick?"

"Manny, sure I know him. But let me show you my new Singer sixty-six sewing machine. It's amazing. It can out-sew any machine. I can sew through six layers of fabric, and not just linen or wool, mind you. I can even sew through horse blankets. Imagine that. Let me show you." He sat down and skillfully pushed some fabric through the foot of the machine, now quickly bobbing up and down.

"Sir, please, we have no time. Do you know where Manny is?" pleaded Jakob.

Max stopped the action of the machine, looked up over his glasses and said, "Haven't you heard? He was arrested this morning."

"Arrested? For what," Pincus asked.

"There was a fire at the Triangle Shirtwaist Company. They say over a hundred and forty workers burned to death." He leaned over to whisper. "I hear they lock the doors from the outside until the shift is done. All of them trapped, many teenage Jewish girls. They didn't stand a chance," Max finished sadly.

"What does that have to do with Manny?" Pincus asked.

"He owns the building. He's being charged with murder."

CHAPTER 14

CLARA STRUGGLES

When Clara received the first letter from Pincus, Anna was already two months old. She waited till the children had been put to bed before she sat down to read it.

Reaching into her apron pocket, she lifted the slightly worn envelope and brushed off the flour that stubbornly clung to it. Her eyes swelled with tears as she ran her fingers across the canceled stamps from America.

"Finally, a letter!" she said aloud.

Planning to save the envelope, she delicately sliced it open with a paring knife. She removed a single page of words in his sloppy handwriting.

October 15, 1910
Dear Clara,

After a difficult voyage, I have made it to America. In only a few days of my arrival, I opened the shop and found a place to live above the store. My address is 95 Ludlow Street. The area is known as the Lower East

Side. I have never seen so many Jews. Hopefully soon I can launch the Landsman Society of Krzywcza, and we will be able to help our people when they arrive here.

I hope all went well with the birth. Write to me and tell me if I have a son or a daughter. Are you doing okay? Tell Jennie, Moshe, and Hymie that I miss them. Hopefully your mother is helping you. How is Shmuel doing in the store? I will send money soon.

Zei gezunt,
Pincus

Shaking her head she muttered, "Pincus." She folded the letter and slid it back in its envelope. Tapping it twice against her left palm, she placed it in between the tin storage cans on the shelf under the window looking out onto the street. With darkness approaching, she could see candlelight flickering in the neighbor's windows.

It had taken nearly two months for the letter to arrive, and all she'd learned was that Pincus had made it to America. *He may be a man of few words*, she thought, *but couldn't he have told me more about his new life or when he will he be able to come back for us?*

She turned as a door closed behind her. Her mother entered and sat down at the table, covered with a coating of flour and holding a nicely shaped round dough that looked ready for the oven.

"The children are sleeping," Sadie announced.

"Thank you, Mother."

She sat down at the table across from her mother and said, "I received a letter from Pincus."

"What does he say?" Clara told her the good news without revealing her disappointment with its brevity. But Mother was not easily managed, especially when she started complaining about Pincus.

"All is well. Soon he will start sending money from the store. In the meantime, I should go see how Shmuel is getting along. I haven't visited with him since Anna was born," she said, skillfully changing the subject.

The next morning, after she'd cleaned up from breakfast, Clara called out to Moshe, "Are you ready?"

She had promised Moshe a trip to the village for his tenth birthday.

"Yes, Mama." His blue eyes sparkled, and he wore his best outfit that he normally saved for shul visits with Papa.

She smiled—such a bright and happy boy. Taking his hand, she turned to her mother. "We'll be back in a few hours."

"Mama, can we go to the bakery?" Moshe asked.

"Yes, I told you we would, but first we must stop and see how Shmuel is doing. He's taking care of the shop while your papa is in America."

Along the packed dirt road, Clara held tightly to Moshe's hand. She sensed danger, watching the wagons maneuvering their way into the village square. The horses were jumpy and unpredictable on market day.

In the center of the village square stood the cobbler's shop. Clara pointed it out to her son. "There, Moshe, that's it."

He stood on his tiptoes to see through the gathering vendors setting up their pushcarts. As they entered the square, Clara pointed out the fruits and vegetables displayed in colorful arrangements along the way.

"Here we are," she said as they entered the front door.

"Clara, what a pleasant surprise," said Shmuel as he looked up from his worktable.

The shop looked busy. Clara saw many pairs of shoes lining the shelves waiting their turn for the cobbler.

"Good day, Shmuel. Do you know my boy, Moshe? Today is his tenth birthday."

"Moshe, what a big boy you are. Happy birthday! I am so happy to meet you."

Letting go of her son's hand, she said, "Stay here. I am going into the back room with Shmuel to talk for a few minutes."

"Okay, Mama," Moshe said with a smile. "Can I just look out the window?" "Yes, of course. I'll be right back."

"Everything looks very good," Clara said, returning to the front of the shop. "I'll try to get back to you with some ideas on how to find some new places to buy hides." As she turned her attention to where she left Moshe, he was gone.

"Moshe," she said. "Moshe, are you hiding?"

Shmuel looked under the counter and behind a crate leaning against the wall. "He's not here."

"Where is he?" Clara was frantic.

"He must have walked outside."

"Shmuel, help me find him," she pleaded.

Her heart sank as she opened the door. The activity in the square seemed to have multiplied tenfold in the past few minutes. Wagons drawn by horses and mules crisscrossed in every direction. Children ran under and around the pushcarts. Could one of them be Moshe? She ran into the square, but he had disappeared.

Shmuel insisted they go to the police station for help.

"They won't help us, Shmuel."

"We have no choice, we must go," he insisted.

After a curt reply from the desk sergeant, she resigned herself to the hard wooden bench against the wall in the police station, buried her face in her hands, and cried.

"Thank you for staying with me."

"Of course, Clara. He'll turn up. You'll see," Shmuel offered unconvincingly.

Abruptly she stood and again approached the sergeant who was busy with paperwork at his desk.

"Sir," she interrupted the officer at the desk. "How much longer must I sit here?"

Without pausing to look up, he said, "For as long as it takes Captain Berbecki to finish his current business."

A half-hour later, a door swung open, and Captain Peter Berbecki walked through it. Planted firmly between the edges of his lips protruded the stump of a cigar. Trails of smoke found its way among the knotty wood beams supporting the ceiling.

"Are you Mrs. Potasznik?" he asked, looking directly at Clara.

At first she sat there, unable to answer. She had never seen such a strikingly handsome man. *What a perfect color his blue suit is*, she thought, as the translucency of his clear blue eyes disarmed her.

"Mrs. Potasznik, can you hear me?"

"Clara," Shmuel said, placing a gentle hand on her shoulder.

With that, she snapped herself out of her reverie. "Yes, I am Mrs. Potasznik. I am looking for my son Moshe," she said, suddenly moved by guilt at allowing herself to be distracted.

"Moshe is fine, come with me," he said, and with a sweeping gesture of his long arm, offered an invitation to enter his office.

Shmuel lifted Clara up from her chair by her elbow and escorted her in.

"Mama," Moshe yelled, jumping off the chair and wrapping his arms around her legs.

"Sit back down," instructed the captain.

"Mama?" Moshe looked at her fearfully.

"It's okay, Moshe. Listen to the captain. We'll be going home soon."

"Your son has caused a great disruption, Mrs. Potasznik," the captain said.

Shmuel helped Clara into a chair that seemed tiny compared to the imposing desk Captain Berbecki stood behind.

"What did he do? He's a good boy, never a problem."

"Is that so?" He picked up a report from his table. "He was caught stealing an apple from a pushcart. Then he ran away from two of my officers. One of them twisted his ankle," he added, pointing out the door as if to identify the man.

"No, Mama, I didn't do it," Moshe protested.

"Quiet that boy or I will," the captain threatened.

"Moshe, please don't say anything," Clara warned. "Captain, I am sure this is a big misunderstanding. My boy is not a thief. Please let me take him home."

The captain took a seat in his large swivel chair and swung around to look out the window that offered a view of the market square.

"Perhaps, Mrs. Potasznik, you can provide some service that would allow me to forget the incident."

"A service? What could I offer someone like you, Captain?"

With a motion that startled Clara and Shmuel, he spun back around, lifted his legs, and slammed his boots on the desk, releasing a cloud of dust that mingled with the cigar smoke swirling in the air. "I understand that you are the wife of a cobbler."

"I am," said Clara.

"I would like a pair of new boots made."

"I would be happy to do that for you, sir, but my husband is in America, and Shmuel is running the shop. He can repair shoes, but he has no skill in making them."

The captain fixed his eyes on Shmuel. "You had better learn fast. I expect a fine pair of new shiny black boots by the end of the month."

"Yes, Captain, you will have the most beautiful pair of boots," Shmuel said, clearly trying not to let his fear show.

"Very good. You may take the boy. Do not disappoint me," he said, staring at Clara and Shmuel.

Clara looked at Shmuel with surprise, thinking, *He's never made a pair of boots—or even shoes, for that matter. What will the captain's retribution be if he doesn't approve of the finished product? Will he take it out on Moshe? And why would a man of his status bully people like us?*

She stood up and intentionally avoided eye contact with the handsome captain as she grabbed Moshe's hand.

"Moshe," the captain said, stepping around his desk and leaning over to shake a massive finger in the boy's face. "No more stealing."

CHAPTER 15

JAKOB MEETS NITA

The fire killed 146 women and men. Most were women between sixteen and twenty-three years old, Jakob read on the front page of *The Forward*.

"Tsk, tsk, tsk," he overheard a man nearby. "They were jumping from the tenth floor because the managers locked the doors to prevent unauthorized work breaks."

Jakob lifted his eyes from the newspaper to realize that others were also reading about the disaster at the Triangle Shirtwaist Factory. There were dozens of men and women lining the benches on the Delancey Street mall, reading and talking about the deadliest industrial disaster in the city's history.

What about Manny? He wasn't mentioned in the article. Would the owner of the building be held liable for the deaths?

Jakob folded up his newspaper, tucked it under his arm, and walked in the direction of Manny's office. Someone there must know what is going on.

When he arrived at Manny's office, the door was open. Jakob could see Manny looking through his large dirty glass window onto the street below. He knocked on the doorframe to get his attention. "Manny," he called.

"Hello Jakob, come sit. I'm glad you're here," he said, motioning to the chair.

"I heard you were arrested—what happened?"

"I was, but I was released this morning. It's good to have friends," he said with a glimmer in his eye. "And I am not responsible. My tenant is. I hope he has friends—he's going to need them."

"Oh great. I'm happy to see you're okay."

"Yes, I'm fine. How about you and Pincus? How is the space for the store? Do you like the apartment?"

"It's perfect. Pincus is very happy. He's started cleaning and organizing, and he's already ordered a sign."

"Excellent. Now let's talk about you."

He moved around to the front of his desk and leaned against it. "Here's my idea. My clients will bring in their shoes for a shine or a repair, and they'll drop off what they owe inside their shoes. One of my associates will visit you at the end of each day to collect. Very easy."

"I see. Umm . . . that seems okay, but I'd rather not tell Pincus. He wouldn't understand."

"That's fine with me, as long as he doesn't interfere with the day-to-day business."

Jakob stood up to face Manny and asked, "Will this arrangement provide something for me?"

"Yes, yes." Manny laughed. "You'll be paid based on how you do. I take care of my people." He smiled, leaned forward and shook Jakob's hand firmly.

....

The long wall of Katz's Deli provided a good place to post announcements. While patrons waited their turn for a table, they browsed the wall. Jakob stood in the line with about a dozen other people. Hungry for a quick bite to eat, he stood staring at a large poster with a photo of a white-bearded man singing. The poster announced that Yoselle Rosenblatt, the world's greatest cantor, would be performing that Sunday night at The Grand, a Yiddish theater at the corner of Grand and Chrystie Street.

The words "excuse me" startled Jakob as he turned his attention to a waiter pointing out an open stool at the counter. "Do you want it?" he asked.

Jakob took the stool and opened the enormous food-stained menu. He was searching the assortment of overstuffed sandwiches when someone caught his eye. At first he could see only her long red hair, which swirled down her straight back. She sat perfectly upright, which encouraged Jakob to stop slouching. She was looking for a waiter. As the waiter moved in her direction she raised her hand to attract his attention.

Using the motion of her bar stool, she spun to follow his path closer and closer and then sadly farther and farther away. Disappointed, she let her summoning hand drop to the counter.

"Dammit!" she yelled, now face to face with Jakob. "Oh, excuse me."

"That's okay. Let's see if I can help."

He stood up, took a step around the counter, leaned over to the waiter, and slipped a coin into his palm. He nodded and was taking the young lady's order moments later.

"Wow, that was amazing. What did you say to him?"

"I just told him that we were on our first date and I wanted to impress you."

"Is that so?" she said, trying to hold back a smile.

"My name is Jakob Adler."

"Nice to meet you, Jakob."

"And you are?"

"I am not in the habit of giving my name to strangers."

Jakob offered his most charming smile. "Very wise. A girl so pretty should be careful."

"You are a charmer, Mr. Adler."

"Please call me Jakob." He was devouring every detail of her exquisite face. He had never seen eyes so blue or skin so pale.

"Okay, Jakob," she relented.

"I have just immigrated here from Warsaw. Where are you from?"

"Ireland. Have you heard of it?"

"No, where is Ireland?"

"It's an island in the Northern Atlantic not far from England."

"Oh, yes, I've heard of England," Jakob said. "So, then, you are not a Jew?"

"A Jew, no," she chuckled. "Like I said, I am from Ireland—that makes me Irish."

Jakob looked around and then leaned in to whisper, "I've never met an Irish person before."

"And you won't, if you never leave the Lower East Side. There's a world beyond these few blocks where you'll find many Irish, Germans, and Italians."

As he searched for some witty reply, she rose from the stool. "I must go. It was nice meeting you, Jakob. Perhaps our paths will cross again one day."

Jakob watched her saunter away, her hips swaying enticingly. *As Hashem intended*, he thought.

....

As Yoselle Rosenblatt took his final bow that Sunday night, Pincus and Jakob, along with the rest of the audience at The Grand Theater, jumped to their feet in a standing ovation.

"So what did you think, Pincus?" Jakob asked.

"Remarkable—what a voice. He's as good as advertised. The world's greatest cantor."

Surrounded by hundreds of people exiting the theater, Jakob directed Pincus down the wide staircase.

"Pincus," Jakob shouted, "come to the center, it's less crowded."

A few steps from the main level of The Grand, Jakob noticed a crowd gathering. "What's going on? Let's look."

Jakob used his strength to maneuver through the pack, with Pincus in tow.

"It's Nita Naldi," people buzzed.

"She's an actress on Broadway," said others.

"Oh my god, I know her," Jakob said.

"Who is she?" asked Pincus.

"I met her at Katz's Deli a few days ago. Isn't she beautiful?"

Skilled at working her adoring fans, she smiled and posed for their pleasure.

With Pincus following, Jakob powered his way through the crowd and tapped Nita's shoulder. She turned around and gave Jakob a smile that nearly melted him.

"Well, hello, Jakob. Don't you look nice this evening? Did you enjoy the performance?"

Jakob was suddenly sharing the spotlight with the Broadway actress Nita Naldi. "Who is he?" the spectators buzzed.

"Yes, we liked it very much."

"We, Jakob? Please introduce me to your date."

"Oh, you mean Pincus? He's not my date, he's my friend," he said and awkwardly pulled him forward.

"Nice to meet you, Pincus."

Pincus smiled and said nothing.

"Nita, please tell me how I can find you again," Jakob said.

A moment later, someone grabbed her wrist, pulling her into the crowd and toward the exit.

"Come to the Winter Garden Theater on Broadway," she shouted and was gone from sight.

CHAPTER 16

MENDEL ARRIVES

Pincus took a few minutes from his busy morning to read a favorable review of Yoselle Rosenblatt's concert two nights earlier. When he heard his name shouted from the street, he folded the paper, set it down on the counter, and walked out to the sidewalk. Murray was admiring his handiwork. He pointed to the sign swinging in the gentle morning breeze:

P. POTASZNIK
COBBLER
REPAIRS & SHINE
95 LUDLOW

"That looks wonderful, Murray," Pincus said, admiring the simple black-lettered sign.

"Yes, I must say that I agree." Murray looked pleased with himself.

"Murray, perhaps you can help me with something else," he asked as they walked into the shop. "I am looking for my cousin Hersch Rubenfeld. He's a carpenter and should be living here in the Lower East Side. Any idea how I can find him?"

"Sure, I know Hersch—we work on jobs together. Sometimes I use him for large signs that need a carpenter. Would you like me to take you to his workshop? It's only a ten-minute walk."

Pincus thanked Murray for his directions, but he wanted to surprise Hersch. Before stepping in through the front door that was propped open with a tree stump, Pincus looked up to read the sign:

H. RUBENFELD

WOODWORKER

FURNITURE AND FINISHING

110 HESTER

Pincus stepped through the door and onto a carpet of sawdust. Hersch stood only a few feet away, busy sanding a tabletop, and didn't notice the visitor.

"Hello, Hersch."

Hersch looked up and smiled. "Pincus Potasznik, is that really you?"

The cousins embraced.

"It's so good to see you, Hersch."

"This is wonderful, Pincus, let's go celebrate."

....

"They serve the best Vishniak in the city," Hersch said, walking into the New Bridge Liquor Store. Besides selling bottles, they also provided a few tables for patrons to congregate and drink.

"*L'chaim!*" the men toasted.

"It's so good to see you, Hersch."

"Yes, yes, you too."

After a few drinks, Pincus grabbed Hersch's hand, which rested on the table. "I'm starting a Landsman Society for our village. Would you be able to help me?"

"I don't know," Hersch said, slipping his hand out of Pincus's grip and running his fingers nervously through his thick, curly black hair. "I'm so busy with my business. I don't think I have the time."

"I'm busy too, Hersch, but this is important work. Remember when you first immigrated? It's not easy. We can make a big difference in our people's lives. Help them find a job and a place to live, and most important, provide a Jewish burial."

"Yes, I'm aware of what these societies do. But I must say no. Please understand. You can find someone else to help you, I'm sure."

"Really, you think it will be easy to find someone from our village to help me? You're the only person I know from Krzywcza, and you're my first cousin."

Hersch said, "I'm sorry, but my answer is no."

Pincus stared at Hersch in disbelief. "This is outrageous," he said, slamming the bottle of Vishniak on the table, which startled the nearby patrons.

He knocked his chair over as he rose, causing even more of a disturbance. "Goodbye, Hersch."

....

Pincus walked home, the flickering lamps along Delancey Street lighting his way. By the time he arrived at the apartment, he couldn't even remember how he got there. Jakob had left the door open and was seated in one of the two chairs at the kitchen table as Pincus entered.

"My damn cousin said no. Can you believe that?" Pincus closed the door and sat down in the empty chair across from Jakob.

"I'm sorry. Maybe someone else will arrive here soon from Krzywcza who can help you," Jakob said.

"I hope so. This is too much work for one person to do alone."

....

Still reeling from his cousin Hersch's betrayal, Pincus thought he should find a synagogue to attend on Shabbat mornings. With over 500 synagogues to choose among, Pincus found himself at the nearby Congregation Chasam Sopher at 10 Clinton Street, a few blocks north of Delancey. Thoughts of Hersch's disloyalty distracted him from the rabbi's service.

A few men rose for the *Yizkor*, the prayer for the dead. Pincus scanned the mourners, curious to see who had lost a loved one, when his eyes fell upon someone he thought he knew. Was that Mendel Beck?

Pincus sat through the rest of the evening service with his knees bouncing in excitement. The moment it ended, he forced his way down the center aisle and put his hand on the man's shoulder. "Mendel, is that you?"

"Pincus, I've been looking for you," Mendel said and hugged him.

As they pulled apart, Pincus asked, "When did you get here?"

"I've been here for two weeks. There was no longer a reason to stay."

"Sara passed?" Pincus said.

Mendel nodded. "Yes, she never improved after the last time I saw you. She died in my arms."

"I am very sorry, Mendel. Sara was a lovely woman and a good mother. How are your boys doing? Did they come with you?"

"Yes, Dovid and Hersh are here. We found a room over on Broome Street." In a whisper he continued, "It's terrible—no running water, no heat, and a single toilet down the hall for over twenty people."

"What about Shmuel? He didn't come?"

"No, Pincus, he wouldn't leave. He said that Clara and your children needed him to run the cobbler shop. He wants to wait for you to return for your family. Then he'll come."

"He's a good boy," Pincus said.

"Yes he is. We need to help each other."

"Come with me. I want to show you something," Pincus said, leading the way down the center aisle and out the front doors to the shul.

....

"Is this really your place?" Mendel asked, as they stood in front of the shoemaker's shop.

"Look at the name," Pincus said, pointing to the sign swinging gently in the evening breeze.

"How did you manage this so quickly?"

"Come upstairs, I'll show you where I live."

"You've done very well in such a short time," Mendel said as they walked into the empty apartment.

Pincus told Mendel about the voyage on the *SS Amerika* and how he had met Jakob. He continued with the story of how Jakob had met a man on a train who'd given him the name of a man here in the Lower East Side, and how that man had set them up in this apartment and the shop downstairs.

"Why would he do this?" Mendel asked, bewildered by his friend's good fortune.

"I'm not too sure. Maybe he thinks we will be good tenants and pay the rent on time. Anyway, tell me more about yourself, Mendel. What are your plans?"

"I need something to do. Apparently, there is no work in America for a scholar of the Torah. All of those years of study mean nothing now. What was respected back home is laughed at here. Would you have ever imagined that our way of life would be turned completely upside down?"

"This is true, and it's why we need a way to help our people when they arrive in America. I want to start the Landsman Society of Krzywcza. I asked my cousin Hersch, who refused me. Can you imagine the nerve?"

"I'll help you with the Landsman Society," Mendel blurted out.

Pincus looked up into his friend's eyes. "That would be wonderful. Would you really do that?"

"Yes, I want to. It will give me a purpose, and I can help our fellow Jews make a life here in America."

"This is wonderful news. Just a few hours ago I was feeling hopeless about this. You've answered my prayers."

CHAPTER 17

JAKOB MEETS GORPATSCH

Jakob poked his head into the workroom and found Pincus busy replacing a leather sole on a boot and humming one of Yoselle Rosenblatt's songs, the one that had brought down the house at the previous week's performance. He noticed how Pincus's mood had improved since seeing his cousin Mendel yesterday. With the lunchtime rush over, Jakob thought it okay to take off for a short while.

"I'll be back in a few hours," Jakob said, capturing a quick glance from Pincus before walking out the front door.

With resolve in his heart, he found his way to the Winter Garden Theater on Mercer Street. *She did invite me to visit*, he thought.

The theater took up an entire block. The building offered a white limestone facade with large windows and black painted wooden shutters. A small group of four or five people stood examining a poster on the wall. Jakob approached to see what had captured everyone's attention. He couldn't believe his eyes—there she was.

"Glorious," he whispered.

Nita Naldi, tall and elegant, had struck a perfect pose for the photo. Jakob would swear that the breeze blowing down Mercer Street caused the embroidered lace scarf draped off her delicate shoulders to flutter a bit.

The large letters along the top of the poster read:

STARRING NITA NALDI AS THE YANKEE GIRL.

"What's a Yankee?" Jakob asked aloud.

A skinny teenage boy with pimples standing behind him replied, "A Yankee is a real American, and Nita Naldi is a real American dream girl."

"Yes, she is," Jakob agreed.

....

With the next performance scheduled for later that evening, the theater's main entry doors were locked. *There has to be another way in*, Jakob thought. He ran around the corner and down to the rear of the theater where an alley led to an open pair of doors. Surveying the scene, he saw a small sign posted above:

STAGE DOOR—ACTORS AND STAGE HANDS ONLY

He cautiously took a step inside, stopped, and caught a glimpse of the inner workings of the theater.

"Sir, are you coming in or going out? Rehearsals are about to begin, and I need to close these doors," said a young man carrying a clipboard.

"I'm coming in," Jakob said.

The doors slammed shut. It took a few seconds for Jakob's vision to adjust to the sudden change from the natural daylight to the few swinging gas lanterns. Looking up into the cavernous space, he saw what reminded him of a sailing ship. He followed the path of the thick ropes that snaked their way through pulleys and ended at boards supporting velour curtains towering above him.

Muffled sounds of indistinguishable musical instruments filled the space. Unsure of their source, he walked along a series of the staggered long curtain panels. The sounds of the strings, brass, and percussion instruments lured him to the edge of a giant stage. Straining for a peek without being caught, he leaned in just far enough to see the orchestra assembled in a deep well below the edge of the stage.

Just at that moment, Nita Naldi glided onstage. She spun to face the hall and smiled. Jakob leaned out a little farther this time, craning his neck to see her.

A tap-tap-tap from the conductor's baton silenced the musicians. Then, at once, the sounds of a well-rehearsed orchestra rose from the pit. On cue, Nita burst into song. Jakob stood mesmerized, stunned by the beauty of her voice. The conductor acted as the conduit between the singer and the musicians, following Nita's lead as she glided across the stage. She ended the song a cappella, and left Jakob teary-eyed. *From this day forward, I will never love anyone as much as I love this woman*, he proclaimed silently.

A few claps from a lone audience member ended the rehearsal. Nita smiled, offered a dramatic full curtsy, and exited stage left, directly into Jakob, who was applauding silently.

"Jakob, how did you get in here?" Nita whispered.

"I walked in through the stage door."

"Come with me," she said. She grabbed his hand and led him off the stage.

Moments later they stood before a door adorned with a sign that read: NITA NALDI.

"That's you," Jakob said, surprised.

"Yes, that's me, this is my dressing room. Come inside quickly," she said, closing the door behind them.

Nita turned and looked up into his eyes. "You have to leave. You can't be here."

"I wanted to see you. You invited me. Don't you remember?"

"Yes, I remember, but this is not a good time."

At that moment someone tapped a few times on the dressing room door. "Nita, open up, it's me, Leo."

"You have to hide," Nita whispered. "Here," she said, pointing to a rack of costumes standing along the wall.

Jakob squeezed in through the colorful array of dresses on wooden hangers. He crouched down and waited.

"I'm coming, one moment," Nita said.

She took a brief look in the mirror and opened the door.

"Leo, it's so nice to see you. Were you watching the rehearsal?"

"Yes, my dear, and you were amazing."

"Oh, thank you," she said with a smile.

Jakob heard what sounded like a kiss. *Who is this Leo? Is he Nita's lover?* He stuck his head in between a burgundy velour gown and red sequined dress. The small gap he created allowed him to see Nita's back and the man she called Leo. She moved slightly to her left and Jakob could see his face. *I know this man,* Jakob realized. *I know this red beard. This is Mr. Gorpatsch, the man I met on the train from Warsaw with his family. He told me that he does business in America, but what are the chances that I would ever see him again?*

"Leo, please, you can't stay. I need to be back on stage in a few minutes."

"Okay, Nita, but I must see you tonight, after your performance," he said.

"Yes, that would be nice. Now please go. I need to change."

"I'm going, but kiss me first," he said, grabbing her at her waist.

Jakob watched his hands slide down to her back as he pulled her close for the kiss.

"I'll see you tonight, Leo," she said as the door closed.

Jakob emerged from the rack of costumes. "I know that man. That's Mr. Gorpatsch. I met him on my way to Hamburg," Jakob said.

"Yes, that's Leo Gorpatsch. He is my benefactor."

"Benefactor. Does that mean lover?"

"No, it doesn't mean lover," she said sarcastically. "He helps me with my expenses. I need to maintain a certain lifestyle to support my career. He provides me with a nice monthly stipend that supplements what I make from these performances."

"Does that include being his lover as well?"

"That's not your concern," she said, turning her back to him and sitting in a chair facing the large mirror.

Jakob stood behind her, looking down at her reflection. He placed his hands on her shoulders. "Nita, I don't want you to see him."

Her eyes expressed outrage as she rose from her chair. "How dare you? Get out now," she said, pushing Jakob toward the door.

Instead of leaving, Jakob embraced Nita. They paused for a slight moment looking at each other, and then Jakob kissed her. Her mouth opened to accept his lips and tongue. Her hands reached up, her delicate fingers fondling the curls of his chestnut hair. Jakob responded, pulling her tight against his body.

"You must go," she said, breaking the embrace.

"When will I see you?"

"I'll come find you. Tell me where."

"Come to the cobbler shop on 95 Ludlow. It's where I work with Pincus. I'm there every day."

"Okay, Jakob. Now leave, please."

CHAPTER 18

NITA NALDI'S STORY

Leo took the elevator down from his office in the Flatiron Building. He was running late, and trouble at one of his establishments needed attending to. He knew that Nita would be waiting, but he had no choice. *Business always comes first*, he reminded himself.

His mustachioed chauffeur was waiting by his motorcar and opened the back door the moment he stepped out onto Fifth Avenue. He nodded his thanks and climbed in. As the motorcar pulled away from the curb, he thought about the first time he'd met Nita.

It had been nearly two years since he'd first heard Nita sing, at McSorley's Ale House. Although the venue was a hole in the wall, he had always found its grittiness and musical acts amusing—until Nita came onstage and showed him real magic.

He had never seen such a beautiful woman. Her red hair transfixed him, like a crown amplifying her bright blue eyes. Leo was not the only one mesmerized by her looks and her voice. The other patrons in this men-only establishment were transformed from a subdued buzz of lowlifes into a rowdy drunken mob at the sight and sound of Nita singing and dancing on the small wooden platform. Soon, Leo couldn't even hear her beautiful voice over the catcalls.

Only minutes into her performance, the men wanted more from Nita.

"Take something off," someone yelled.

"Yeah, show your tits," another patron barked.

Nita stopped singing and stepped off the stage, looking for a way out, but a few of the aroused and inebriated rabble pushed her back to the platform.

"Let me go," she pleaded.

Leo knew what these men were capable of. He pushed his way through to Nina, grabbed her wrist, and led her through the pack.

"Don't let go of me," he said.

Leo knocked away the hands trying to grope at Nita as they squeezed through the crowd. Moments later they were out on the street.

"Thank you, sir," she said.

"Let me take you away from here. It's still not safe," Leo said.

He stuck two fingers in his mouth and whistled for his motorcar.

His driver stopped in front of the pub. Quickly he opened the door to the rear two seats of the vehicle.

"Madam," he said, offering his hand to assist Nita.

"I'm not getting in. Thank you for rescuing me from that mob in there," she said, pointing with her thumb over her shoulder. "But I don't know you."

"Very wise, my dear. My name is Leo Gorpatsch," he said, removing his elegant black felt hat. "I am a gentleman, Miss Naldi. Please allow me to escort you to a more elegant establishment for a drink before I have my driver take you home."

"Very well, Mr. Gorpatsch," she said, lifting her skirt out of the way and exposing a long shapely leg in order to step into the motorcar.

Once they were seated, the vehicle accelerated, startling Nita. "Oh, my!"

"No need to worry, my dear; it's perfectly safe, and Rocky is an excellent driver."

Rocky turned for a quick glance, tipped his hat, and said, "Ma'am."

Leo noticed Nita staring at him with a curious expression. "Is something wrong?" he asked.

"Oh, quite the contrary. I don't think I have ever seen such an elegant man before. You look like a model from a catalog."

Fifteen minutes later they pulled up to a building with a large black door adorned with polished brass hardware. The sign next to the door, also in shiny brass, read:

THE PLAYER'S CLUB
PRIVATE—MEMBERS ONLY

Leo smiled as he watched Nita expose her leg once more as she stepped from the motorcar. *Aha*, he thought, *she's preening for me. My irresistible charm is working.* A few other people turned their heads to admire the beautiful woman emerging from the 1910 Buick 10 Touring Sedan. He offered his arm, and Nita took it as they approached the front door. Leo pushed the large black door open, and they stepped inside.

A maître d' approached. "Good evening Mr. Gorpatsch, and welcome to the Player's Club, madam. Right this way, sir, we have your table ready for you."

Nita smiled when he turned to look at her. The path to their table took them right down the center of the main salon floor. Groups of couples sat around small cocktail tables with white cloths and flickering candles. Cigar smoke filled the air. Nita and Leo made their way to a table right in front of center stage.

"What is this place?" she leaned in to ask Leo the moment they took their seats.

"It's a private club—you know—members only," he said.

"And I assume you are a member?"

"I'm a member, and I'm also the owner," he said with a satisfied smile.

"Is that so?"

He nodded.

"Tell me Leo, what brought you to McSorley's tonight?" she asked.

"I came to see you. A friend saw you perform and thought that I should come to see for myself. I'm glad I did."

The house lights dimmed, and the stage lights came up.

"I'm going to make you a star," he said, sitting back in his chair.

CHAPTER 19

MURDER IN THE FOREST

Moshe couldn't sit still. He didn't like being squeezed in between his friends on the long bench listening to the teacher go on and on. But this was the daily torture of sitting in the *cheder*. Moshe knew that many of the other boys found the Torah lessons equally tedious.

His thoughts wandered from running through the fields to exploring the back alleys of the village with his friends. Max, who sat next to him, gave him a few pokes with his elbow.

"Moshe," he said.

"What?" Moshe asked his best friend.

Max cocked his head to the front of the room. Moshe looked up to see the teacher staring at him.

"Moshe, are you with us?" the tall lanky bearded man with yellow teeth asked.

Moshe looked at the teacher and then at the classroom of boys staring at him.

"Yes, I'm sorry," he said, blushing. The other boys laughed.

"Quiet," demanded the teacher. "I was asking you, Moshe, if you know what a *kohen* is."

Moshe sat up straight, placed his hands on his lap and replied, "*Kohen*, yes, I am a *kohen*."

The classroom broke out in laughter at Moshe's announcement.

"*Shtil*," shouted the teacher trying to restore order. "Yes, Moshe, you are a *kohen*. Do you know what that means?"

Moshe shook his head. "No, not really. My Papa has told me, but I'm not sure what it means."

"It means, Moshe, that you, as a *kohen,* are a direct descendent of Aaron, the brother of Moses," instructed the teacher.

The fascinated students listened to the mysterious tale of the ancient priests known as the *kohen* who had presided over animal sacrifices in Jerusalem's Holy Temple.

"Moshe, I am a *kohen* too. My papa told me when I was little," said Max as the boys ran from school and out into the market square.

"We are *kohen* priests," Moshe joyfully announced. "We need to perform a sacrifice, Max. Let's go to the woods and catch a squirrel or a bird."

"Yeah, great idea," Max agreed and off they bounded through the wagons, horses, and villagers, who were busy buying for tonight's Shabbat meal.

....

All the boys Moshe and Max's age knew about the woods. A twenty-minute run from the center of town, the woods provided a secret place where the boys could escape the ever-watchful eyes of the townspeople.

Beautiful silver fir trees spread across the lands northwest of Krzywcza. Moshe and Max found themselves chasing after squirrels without success.

"We need to build a trap," Max announced and dropped on all fours, pushing away the pine needles carpeting the forest floor as he looked for appropriate materials.

"Aren't you going to help?" Max asked Moshe.

"I'm not feeling so good, Max," Moshe said, as he felt himself breaking out into a sudden sweat. He sat down against a fallen tree.

"You don't look so good, Moshe," said Max.

"Did you hear that?" asked Moshe. "Quiet," he said, putting a finger to his lips.

Moments later a few more voices caught the wind. The boys slid down further to hide themselves.

Max poked his head up for just a second before Moshe grabbed his coat collar and pulled him back. "Stay down," he whispered.

Nestled behind the log and completely out of sight, the boys could hear the voices draw near.

"Keep him quiet," said a man's voice. "Tie him up to that tree."

"Okay, but you need to help me. Hold him while I bind his wrists," said another.

Max looked at Moshe with horror expressed in his eyes.

"Let's cut his throat," whispered the first voice.

A muffled yelping sound came from a third voice that Moshe figured was the man they'd tied to the tree.

"Okay, let's do it," agreed the second voice.

The boys could hear the desperation from the bound prisoner. Then they heard a sound of choking and gurgling.

Before Moshe could stop Max, he'd leapt to his feet and shouted, "Don't do it!" with his arms stretched out and fingers extended in all directions.

Oh no, Moshe thought and rose to his feet alongside Max. There he could see two large men dressed in dirty old clothes, their faces unwashed. One man held a bloody knife, while the other had a grip on the nearly dead man's hair. All three men stared at the two ten-year old-boys.

"Grab them, Alex," shouted one man, as he let go of the victim, whose head fell forward in death.

Moshe overcame his nausea and pulled Max by his wrist. "Let's go, Max," he yelled.

The boys took off through the woods as fast as their legs and fear could carry them. Moshe looked back and could see that the two men were in pursuit.

"To the caves," Max said breathlessly.

Darting sharply to their right, they scampered down a sharp incline. They wove in and around the trees until they made it to the entry of the caves.

Moshe knew they could lose their pursuers here. Many times the boys had played hide and seek in the labyrinth, and even his playmates, who knew the caves well, would eventually give up looking.

Terrified for their lives, Moshe and Max ran into a cave barely visible through a scattering of large boulders and shaded by thirty-foot-tall pine trees.

They knew exactly where to hide. They ran directly to a corner of the cave and, as expertly as mountain climbers, scaled the twelve-foot wall in seconds. The boys curled up, bringing their knees to their chests and fully disappearing in the darkness.

CHAPTER 20

MOSHE IS MISSING

Clara smiled with relief at the sight of Mordecai the Shabbat knocker, banging his fist on the wooden shutters. Standing outside the front door of her home, she glanced to her left and saw the sun only moments away from setting in the western sky.

"*Shabbat shalom*, Mordecai," Clara said.

"*Shabbat shalom* to you and your family," replied Mordecai, moving on to remind the village of the pending day of rest. She smiled as she watched him continue his task of knocking on the shutters of all the Jewish homes.

"Clara, where are you," shouted her mother from inside the house.

"I'm coming," she replied.

"Have you seen Moshe? He hasn't come home," Sadie said.

Stepping inside, Clara saw Jennie and Anna fussing with Hymie, who refused to move his schoolbooks so the girls could set the kitchen table.

"Girls, have you seen your brother?" Clara asked.

"Not since this morning," Jennie answered.

"Mother, stay here with the children. I'll go look for him."

"Why does he do this to me?" Clara muttered as she marched down toward the center of town. Perhaps she could find one of his friends still out before sunset that had seen him. She saw a few stragglers hurrying home and moments later she found herself alone in the middle of the square, as the dusk turned to darkness.

"Moshe!" she yelled.

Not knowing where to search for her son, she frantically looked behind wagons now emptied of their contents, their long handles resting on the ground. She looked down the alleyways and inside abandoned buildings. Then she saw Shmuel locking the front door of the cobbler shop.

"Thanks to Hashem, Shmuel," she said rushing toward him.

"Clara, why are you out so late? It's already Shabbat."

"Moshe never came home. We haven't seen him since early this morning," Clara said, as she clasped her hands together to prevent them from shaking.

"Okay, Clara, calm down. We'll find him."

They searched the entire marketplace, and then Clara suggested, "Let's try his friend Max's house. Maybe he is at the Gorens."

"Great idea, Clara," Shmuel agreed.

Walking down the street toward the Gorens' home, they saw two people walking toward them.

"It's the Gorens," she said, now running toward them. "Have you seen Moshe?"

"No," said Helena Goren. "Have you seen Max?"

Oh no, Clara thought. *They're together.* Both boys had pushed the limits of getting home in time for Shabbat before, but they'd always made it.

"We need to go to the police," said Janusz, Max's father.

CHAPTER 21

MENDEL TAKES CONTROL

"I cannot believe the difference in you, Pincus. You're not the same man who left Krzywcza," said Mendel.

"What do you mean?" asked Pincus.

"You just told Mrs. Schwartzman how lovely she looked."

"Oh right, I suppose some of Jakob's charm is rubbing off on me," Pincus said.

"Maybe, but what about the fuss you just made with Mrs. Cohen's boy Stanley, saying how he reminded you of Moshe?"

"It's good for business, that's all."

"Oh, never mind. It's good to see you like this," Mendel said with a brief wave of his hand.

Pincus shrugged his shoulders and said, "I've got work to do," pointing to the boots and shoes that filled every shelf. Even the workspace in the back had footwear sitting in piles waiting their turn. Business was good. His shop in Krzywcza had provided an adequate living for Pincus and his family and continued to do so, even now with Shmuel running it. But the shop here on Ludlow Street did double or even triple the business.

While Pincus worked, Mendel reported his progress on setting up the organizational structure of the Landsman Society of Krzywcza. Pincus listened as Mendel told him about his difficulties researching what needed to be done, until he'd found his answer: the shul.

Unlike Pincus, who went to shul only on Shabbat and High Holidays, Mendel, a former Torah scholar, attended the Congregation Chasam Sopher every day. Pincus also knew that Mendel felt obligated to offer the *Yizkor* prayer for his beloved, recently deceased wife, Sara.

Mendel told Pincus about some of the men he had met.

"You know how, after services, the shul puts out a small snack?" Pincus looked up from his work and nodded.

"So I was noshing on a piece of almond cake and chatting with a few of the men. Most come from villages just like ours, and they have started Landsman support groups," Mendel said.

This time Pincus put down his knife to listen.

"I've learned what we need to do. In fact, I've written a mission statement. Here, read this," Mendel said, handing Pincus a paper.

Pincus took a clean cloth from his pocket and polished his lenses. He placed the spectacles on the bridge of his nose and read:

The Landsman Society of Krzywcza will provide:
- *A social structure and support system for all immigrants from Krzywcza.*
- *Assistance in finding a place to live and work.*
- *A search service for locating family members and friends.*
- *Education on the politics and government of the United States.*
- *Financial and/or emotional support to the families in need.*
- *Proper Jewish burials in a duly organized cemetery.*

"This is excellent, Mendel. How do we get started?" Pincus asked.

"If it's okay with you, I'll write a letter to Rabbi Shapira back in Krzywcza with information for families planning to emigrate to America. I'll provide details instructing them that, after passing through customs at Ellis Island, they should make their way to the Lower East Side and find the cobbler shop at 97 Ludlow Street and see either Pincus or Mendel."

"This is brilliant, Mendel. Yes, please proceed."

....

Six months after its inception, the society had over twenty families as contributing members. Now that the Landsman Society of Krzywcza was financially sound, Pincus no longer needed to subsidize Mendel's salary, since the dues provided enough income to pay him and cover some administrative expenses as well.

Mendel took the role of treasurer and administrator, while Pincus became the president and the public face of the society. Pincus cherished his role as the man welcoming the anxious families upon their arrival to the New World.

"I'm an important man now, Mendel," Pincus would remind Mendel more than once.

When the Torah scholar Saul Bloch and his family arrived in America, Pincus relished telling Saul that such a learned man might have trouble finding work in America.

"After all," Pincus said, "what can you do?"

Pincus knew Mendel felt sorry for Saul, but he did not.

"Perhaps I could ask for a few favors and try to find work for you," Pincus offered.

Saul said he was grateful.

Pincus smiled and said, "I'm happy to help."

....

One day a letter from the rabbi came congratulating Pincus on his hard work in getting the society organized. His landsmen owed him recognition for such an achievement. And he should expect more members of the community to emigrate soon.

"We need to buy land for the cemetery," Mendel said. "I was talking with someone at shul who said we should look in Queens. We can buy a quarter-acre plot for very little money."

Soon Pincus, Mendel, and several other founding members of the Landsman Society announced the purchase of a plot of land inside the Beth David Cemetery in the town of Elmont.

A few weeks later, a contractor was hired to build a wall to enclose the plot. At the main entrance, a beautiful black wrought-iron gate hung off two stone columns. On these columns were installed brass plaques that would forever proclaim the names of the Landsman Society's founding fathers. And at the top of the names was that of the society's president, Pincus Potasznik.

CHAPTER 22

CAPTAIN BERBECKI

Clara sat alongside Shmuel and the Gorens waiting impatiently to see the police captain.

"Please, Sergeant, our boys have not come home. It's way past sundown," Clara said to the officer behind the desk.

"I apologize, Mrs. Potasznik, but Captain Berbecki is finishing up a few things. I am sure he will be out to speak with you soon."

Clara rose and approached the desk. "Tell me, Sergeant, do you have children?" she asked with a sudden surge of poise.

"I have two daughters."

"How would you feel if one of your daughters hadn't come home last night?"

The sergeant leaned over his desk to speak in a voice not to be overheard.

"Mrs. Potasznik, you must understand something about the captain. Have you ever heard of a Russophile?" he whispered.

"What does that mean, he's Russian?" Clara said.

"It's a political party that supports the Russians," he said with disdain.

Just as Clara was offering a grateful smile for the sergeant's unexpected honesty and explanation for the long wait, the door to the captain's office opened.

"What's the commotion?" Berbecki asked.

"Captain, this is Mr. and Mrs. Goren, and I believe you know Clara Potasznik and Shmuel Beck," the sergeant said.

"Indeed I do. So, Mrs. Potasznik, is your boy in trouble again?"

"We don't know, Captain," Clara replied. "Moshe and his friend Max have not come home. We've looked everywhere for them," Clara said with tears now streaming down her face.

"This is not a police matter," the captain said firmly. "You can file a report here with the sergeant. We will alert our men when they arrive on duty in the morning. Now please go home. I'm sure these boys will eventually turn up."

"Captain, please, we need your help now, not in the morning," Clara pleaded.

"There's nothing that can be done now. Go home, and I will have an officer stop by in the morning to see if the boys turned up," Berbecki said.

Just as Clara, Shmuel, and Goren turned to leave, the doors to the police station swung open and in burst Moshe and Max.

"There has been a murder!" Moshe yelled.

The boys stood in the doorway, wide-eyed and red-faced, waiting for a reaction.

"Moshe, where have you been?" Clara asked. "We have been searching for you."

Max's mother grabbed onto him and hugged him tightly. "Max, are you okay?"

"Yes, we're both fine," Moshe assured them. "We were in the woods playing after school, when we saw two men tie someone to a tree." Moshe paused. Tears filled his eyes.

"What happened to the man tied up?" the captain asked.

The boys looked at each other and Max said in a whisper, "They slit his throat."

The mothers gasped.

"Did the murderers see you?" asked the captain.

"Yes," Moshe said. "We ran and hid in the caves. They searched for us but we had the best hiding place."

"Caves, what caves?" asked Max's father.

"Yes, I know the caves," Berbecki said. "Very clever place to hide."

Clara wrapped her arms around Moshe, pulled him in tight against her, and asked, "What do you plan to do about this, Captain?"

He looked at Clara and the boys before shaking his head and walking back into his office. He slammed the door shut, leaving Clara standing there, stunned.

CHAPTER 23

GORPATSCH RECRUITS JAKOB

Jakob spent every day, except Shabbat, working at the cobbler shop. With Pincus working long hours in the back, Jakob had the front end to himself. This worked out quite well for his side business with Manny.

A few times throughout the day, a "client" would make a drop. The shop provided a perfect cover for this illegal activity. The money easily hid inside the shoes, and along with a receipt for the repair or shine, Jakob provided a receipt for the cash as well.

The extra traffic offered more work for Pincus. Sometimes shoes came back after being done just a day or two ago. Pincus would ask, "Didn't I just repair these shoes?"

Jakob told Pincus, "Yes he just wants it buffed out a little more. He knows he has to pay."

Pincus did not ask many questions as long as the money kept coming in. The cobbler's shop on 95 Ludlow became the busiest one in the Lower East Side. Both men enjoyed their sudden wealth.

Pincus allowed Jakob to take care of the money, which he did happily. He arranged a weekly wire transfer of funds to go to Clara through the Jewish-owned Jarmulowsky Bank on Canal Street.

A few weeks later, Jakob decided that he would figure a way to casually meet up with Nita. Since she was worried that Gorpatsch would catch the two of them together, he needed to find a way to see her without detection. The only place he knew where she would regularly be was the theater.

So one evening, he tucked himself into the shadows of an alleyway directly across from the stage door and waited for the performance to end. The street flooded with light the moment the large doors swung open, and out stepped Nita. She exchanged kisses with a few fellow performers and stagehands and wished them a good evening. As she turned to walk in the opposite direction, Jakob emerged from the shadows and called out her name.

Startled, she looked over and saw him. "You frightened me. What are you doing, lurking around?"

"I'm sorry, but I didn't know how to find you," he said as he approached.

"Congratulations, you'll make a fine detective. Why don't you work for the police?"

"Don't be mad at me, Nita. I just want to see you," he said, putting his hand around her waist and pulling her body against his.

"Is that so?" she asked.

"Yes," he said, kissing her.

She pushed him away. "Not here, Jakob. Meet me tomorrow after the performance and take me out. I don't like being accosted in the street like this."

Every night since, Jakob had waited for Nita outside the stage door. Sometimes they would share a sandwich at Katz's or a drink at a pub. But he wanted to do something special, take her to a fancy place. One of Manny's clients had told him to take her to Luchow's. He said it had an indoor tropical garden room with giant palm trees. Jakob never heard of a palm tree, but it sounded perfect.

He decided that he needed a new suit to impress Nita. With Gorpatsch as his competition for her heart, Jakob needed to look good. In the newspaper, he had seen an advertisement for men's suits. The headline read: "The Edwardian Fashion Sack Suit." Four drawings of men in brown, black, and gray suits filled out the full-page ad. They called the style double-breasted, a term Jakob did not know. But he intended to find out.

After closing the shop, Jakob told Pincus he had something to do. He walked down Ludlow and turned west on Delancey on his way to Walter's Men's Clothing Store. The store windows had mannequins dressed in the same Edwardian-style suits he had seen in the paper.

....

Jakob made the thirty-minute walk to Luchow's feeling like a peacock dressed in the latest men's fashions. He sensed all eyes turning toward the handsome man in the double-breasted gray tweed suit, over a crisp white shirt, a black tie with white polka dots, and a gray suede hat wrapped with a two-inch band of black satin.

They decided upon dinner at seven. Nita told Jakob that she would meet him there.

"I can come pick you up," he suggested.

She insisted on meeting him. Even after several weeks of dating, she still had not disclosed her home address. Jakob suspected this was because Gorpatsch had her place under surveillance.

He paced the sidewalk in front of Luchow's, looking for Nita in each motorcar that pulled up to the curb. Elegant guests emerged, all in fancy dress, and entered the restaurant. Jakob pulled on the chain attached to the gold watch he had just purchased to check the time again. It was 7:20. Was she coming?

The glare from the setting sun prevented Jakob from seeing the vehicle at first. Blocking the sun with his palm, he noticed the white Buick Model 10 Touring Sedan, and waving from its back seat was Nita. Jakob swallowed hard at the sight.

The motorcar pulled up to the curb. Jakob stepped up to open Nita's door before the driver could jump out to perform the task.

Nita smiled at Jakob. "Don't you look handsome?"

Jakob could only mutter a meager, "Thanks."

"Well, Jakob, how do I look?" she asked.

Nita wore a silk outfit in navy blue accented with white borders that cascaded in alternating layers. The tailoring of the fabric crossed dangerously low, nearly exposing the upper portion of her breasts, then draped down to follow the curves of her hips and tapered to a narrowing at the ankles.

Jakob stood staring, his jaw hanging, saying nothing.

"Jakob, I asked you a question."

"Oh, oh, you look amazing! I mean beautiful, elegant," he stammered.

"Thank you, Jakob. Please take me inside now."

With Nita on his arm, Jakob nervously observed the eyes of the room taking in the handsome couple. The maître d' escorted them to their table next to one of the palm trees Jakob had heard about.

....

Jakob woke the next morning, alone in his bed. The only sound he heard was Pincus's snoring a few feet away. *What a night—but she still refused to let me go back to her place*, he lamented. But the kiss they'd shared, right in front of Luchow's, had provided compensation and a smile.

Jakob dressed and walked down the four flights of stairs and out the front door. As he looked down at his chain for the shop's key, he felt a strong hand shove him from behind. Before he knew what was happening, he was in the carriage of a black, horse-drawn wagon.

Jakob found himself sitting next to two large men. In the passenger seat sat a mustached man with black eyeballs who turned his head and said, "It's best to sit still, Mr. Adler."

"Where are you taking me?" he asked, but got no reply—not had he expected one.

A half-hour later, Jakob found himself being lifted twenty-two stories in an oversized birdcage his abductors called an elevator. The loud, clanging contraption squeaked and groaned its way to a halt, and the men stepped off. Jakob felt the hand of one of the goons pushing him down a hallway toward two large doors with a small sign that said:

GORPATSCH INVESTMENTS

Ah, Gorpatsch. I should have known, thought Jakob.

"Take off your shoes," the mustached man instructed, pointing to a chair.

The men removed their shoes and then walked across a plush white carpet. Jakob smiled taking a careful step on the soft floor covering. The pushy hand found its place again between Jakob's shoulders. This time, he turned and swatted it off.

"Enough of that," Jakob warned.

A young brunette with beautiful brown eyes sat at a desk next to another set of closed doors. She looked up at the men and said, "Go right in. He is expecting you."

"After you, Mr. Adler," offered the mustached man.

Sitting behind a magnificent, wood-carved desk sat Leo Gorpatsch. He looked as dapper as ever, even without his suit jacket. The black suspenders and tie over a crisp white shirt outlined his slim torso. His neatly trimmed red beard was the only color in his black-and-white attire. The wall behind provided a dramatic backdrop, a series of large windows with an amazing perspective looking up Broadway. As he admired the view, Jakob found himself wondering how many men Leo Gorpatsch had threatened in this room.

"Ah, Jakob. It is so good to see you again. It has been a while since we first met back on the train on my way to Berlin," said Gorpatsch rising from his desk.

"You can leave," Gorpatsch told the mustached man and the two goons.

As the men exited, Gorpatsch continued. "Quite a view isn't it?"

"Yes, it's amazing. This is the tallest building I've even seen."

"It's one of the tallest buildings in the city," boasted Gorpatsch. "Did you also notice the building's unique architecture?"

"I didn't really get a chance. Your men were in a hurry to get me here."

"Yes, they're a bunch of morons. They take everything I say so literally," he lamented. "They call this building the Flatiron because it looks like a clothes iron."

"What do you mean?" asked Jakob.

"It's in the shape of a triangle. See how the walls taper in behind my desk?" He gestured. "This is the top part of the triangle," he explained.

"Oh yes, I see. That's interesting."

"Sit down, Jakob. You are wondering why you're here," Gorpatsch said with a smile.

Jakob nodded and took a seat.

"When we met on the train, you impressed me, at first," Gorpatsch said.

What does he mean, at first? Jakob thought.

"I appreciated your attention to my son Simon. That's why I wanted to help you, and I gave you Manny's card." He paused and looked directly at Jakob. "Now I understand that you and Manny have met, and you have an arrangement."

"Yes, we met," Jakob said cautiously.

"That's very good. But there was something that you said to me back on that train that got me thinking. You said you were from Warsaw and you had worked for a moving company. Is that right?"

Jakob nodded.

"Moments before boarding the train in Warsaw, I received a message. One of my guys ran to the station to catch me before the train left. He told me that Ben Fein had been murdered." He paused. "Some sort of disagreement had led to a fight in his office with someone named Josef Horowitz, who killed Ben and fled."

Jakob felt his face flush and thought, *There's no way I can deny this. He sees right through me.*

"I didn't mean to kill Ben, it was an accident," he confessed.

Gorpatsch stared at Jakob but said nothing.

"I'm guessing he worked for you," said Jakob.

"Yes, he did."

"So now what?" asked Jakob nervously.

"So now you work for me, Jakob. You actually do already. I know about the arrangement with Manny. But I need more from you," Gorpatsch said, leaning against his desk. "I don't blame you for Ben's death. Things happen. Let's turn the page."

Yes, let's, Jakob thought, though he knew Gorpatsch would want more in exchange for his forgiveness.

"The first time we met, I liked you, Jakob. The way you played with my son gave me a sense of your character. I need men like you in the organization." Gorpatsch now took his turn at the bank of windows wrapping around the north end of the office.

"You will work for me, Josef Horowitz." He turned around with a smile. "I mean, Jakob Adler."

CHAPTER 24

CAPTAIN CHARLES BECKER

For two days in a row, Jakob had been forcibly shoved into a wagon, although this time it was the police disturbing his morning routine. He had been brought to the police station and escorted through large double wood doors. Once inside, he'd been told to sit and wait.

With its door open, everyone could hear the voices coming from the office. Jakob read the nameplate on the door:

CAPTAIN CHARLES BECKER

He could not only hear what was going on in the smoke-filled office, but he could also see who was doing the talking, since the wooden blinds were tilted open.

"You've been investigating Leo Gorpatsch for three months, and you tell me you have nothing?" asked the large, cigar-smoking man whom Jakob assumed was the captain.

"That's not exactly true, sir," ventured a skinny man. "We know that Manny Plotnick works for him. He's the guy that owns that building that burnt down, where the Triangle Shirtwaist factory was."

"Yeah, Kelly, I know about that, what else?" Becker asked impatiently.

"Well I followed a few of his henchmen. They picked up some guy who works in a cobbler shop on Ludlow and brought him to Gorpatsch's office in the Flatiron."

"Okay, who is this guy?" asked Becker.

"Don't know sir, but we brought him in," he said, pointing at Jakob through the glass window.

"Bring him in here," Becker said, squinting through the glass.

The skinny detective looked though the open doorway and addressed Jakob. "Let's go, the captain wants to talk to you."

Jakob walked in to the smoky room and was greeted by the captain's warm smile.

"Please take a seat. Kelly, that will be all," the captain said, dismissing the detective.

As Kelly left Becker extended his hand. "My name is Captain Charles Becker."

Jakob shook his hand. "I am Jakob Adler."

"I understand you had a visit with Leo Gorpatsch yesterday."

Jakob nodded and said, "I did, but I'm surprised you know about that."

"I know everything that's worth knowing in my precinct. Can you tell me what Leo wants with you?" the captain asked, lowering himself into his worn leather swivel chair.

"Nothing really. He asked me if I wanted a job. I told him I already had one."

"Is that so?" said the captain with a cooler smile.

Jakob nodded.

"You're new here, Jakob. I know how it is. It's a struggle getting started in a new world. You need friends. I can be a good friend, Jakob. Would you like to be friends?" The captain blew out rings of cigar smoke.

"Maybe."

"Good. That's good," the captain said, rising from his chair. He walked over to the dust-encrusted wooden blinds and looked out into the busy police station.

"I've been chasing Gorpatsch for too long with nothing to show for it. The commissioner will be calling me into his office again asking for something tangible to show. I have nothing."

He turned to face Jakob.

"Do you know anything about me, Jakob?"

Jakob shook his head.

"I'm famous in this city. A few years ago, I arrested a prostitute named Ruby Young, a.k.a. Alice Whitmore. She happened to be the daughter of Clarence Whitmore, a prominent financier. As expected, this caused a huge uproar. My name and photo made the front page of the papers," he said, pointing to the framed newspaper article hanging on the wall.

The captain sat down and continued his story.

"Later on I made some enemies in the department when I led a special unit probing police corruption. My team uncovered bribes and payoffs at very high levels, including the police commissioner. Eventually, I realized that the man behind my investigation was Deputy Police Commissioner William McDougal. He'd used me to do his dirty work in order to clear a path for him to become the new commissioner."

Jakob sat quietly, listening to the story and wondering why the captain was sharing this with him.

"On the day he was sworn in, I was summoned to the new commissioner's office. He told me he had heard a lot of good things about me, and how he wanted me to take down Leo Gorpatsch."

The captain paused to take a puff on his stub of a cigar.

"So that is why you're here, Jakob. You'll be my man on the inside. You'll help me take down Leo Gorpatsch. You're my new best friend."

"It's good to have a friend, Captain. But if you don't mind, may I ask what Leo Gorpatsch has done?"

The chair wobbled as the captain rose. He walked across his cluttered office and closed the door. "Let's have some privacy," he said softly and took a seat next to Jakob.

"Gorpatsch runs a division of an organized crime syndicate. On a larger scale, it's connected to the Italian mob. Locally, it's the Jews controlling the Lower East Side. The Gorpatsch gang members are racketeers. Are you familiar with the term, Jakob?"

"Racketeer, yes I know what that is. They offer protection for businesses for money and if they don't pay, they get beat up," Jakob said.

"Yes, that's right Jakob. But it's much more than that. They fence goods, which means they steal them and resell them to bargain-seeking customers at tremendous profits. Then there is loan sharking, money laundering, kidnapping, bribery of police and politicians, and murder for hire."

Jakob asked, "Okay, what do you want from me?"

"As you can imagine, Leo Gorpatsch is very smart. He has created layers of protection. The only way we can get to him is to have someone on the inside. We need someone who can give us a heads-up about where he is going, who he is speaking with."

"You want that someone to be me?" Jakob asked.

"You're quick, Jakob, I like that," Becker said sarcastically.

"Why would I do that?"

"You'd be a paid informant, Jakob. I assume you could use some extra cash. Working in a cobbler shop can't be very lucrative."

"Will you give me some time to think about it?" Jakob asked.

"Of course, Jakob. I'm sure you want to have me as a friend."

"Indeed I do, Captain."

....

The fifteen-minute walk back gave Jakob some time to consider the captain's offer. Apparently, Becker didn't know about Manny and how he was using the shop as a cash drop. *I'm already in deep. I don't want the police snooping around and learning about these activities. But if I can work both sides, maybe this is a good way to protect myself.*

Then it occurred to him: *Nita. If I can get Gorpatsch put away for a long time, I'll have Nita to myself. This is good*, he thought.

CHAPTER 25

BERBECKI AND MURDER

"Here it is," Clara said, picking up the local newspaper with resignation. It had been four days since that fateful Shabbat evening. Both Moshe and Max were under the watchful eye of every Jew in the shtetl. She knew enough not to expect any protection from Captain Berbecki or anyone else on the police force.

The journalist had insisted on interviewing Moshe and Max separately. "It's more reliable," he'd assured Clara and Max's parents.

Clara knew that once the article appeared in the newspaper, the story would spread quickly. Probably for the best, she hoped. The more eyes on these boys, the better.

Before heading home, they stopped by the police station for news. The desk sergeant shook his head before she could even pose her question.

"I'm sorry, but there's nothing new to tell you, Mrs. Potasznik," said the sergeant.

"Is the captain in? Can I speak with him?"

"I'm sorry, but he asked not to be disturbed. Maybe come back tomorrow," he suggested.

Once back home, she sat down with her mother and Moshe at the kitchen table and placed the newspaper on it. "Front page," she said.

"Read it, Clara, what does it say?" asked her mother impatiently.

"Yes, Mama, read it," Moshe said.

Clara put on her reading glasses and began.

Murder in the Woods

This past Shabbat evening, Moshe Potasznik and Max Goren, both age ten, witnessed a gruesome murder in the forest area northwest of the market square. The story began when the boys failed to came home for Shabbat. Moshe's mother, Clara Potasznik (the boy's father Pincus Potasznik is in America), along with Max's parents, Janusz and Helena Goren, went to the police station after searching for hours without success.

The quiet night for Police Captain Peter Berbecki ended when the frightened parents arrived at the station. After twenty minutes of describing the circumstances of their missing children to the captain and the sergeant on duty, both Moshe and Max ran into the police station looking for help.

The boys told the captain, sergeant, and the relieved parents about their adventures of that night. Their corroborated story is as follows:

After Torah studies, Moshe and Max ran into the woods just northwest of the village market, an area where the boys often played. Just before they heard voices, Moshe felt ill and needed to lie down.

As they hid behind a large log, they peeked and saw three men walking in their direction. The boys say that one of the men had his hands tied and a gag in his mouth. He looked tired and beaten. Now only a few feet away, they could hear one man tell the other to tie him to a tree.

According to both Moshe and Max, interviewed separately, one man said, "Let's slit his throat." That was done.

Max Goren, upon hearing that, jumped out to yell for them to stop. His plea came too late, as both boys witnessed one of the two men holding a bloody knife. The boys ran in fear for their lives deep into the woods.

With good knowledge of the area, they knew where to hide. A series of caves, known to many of the residents of Krzywcza who enjoy exploring our forests, became the boys' salvation.

The two men chased the boys into the caves, but they were well hidden. Wisely, the boys remained in the caves for hours before venturing back out into the village and finally to the police station.

According to Captain Berbecki, the police found the murder victim the next morning. He has been identified as the well-known Jewish journalist, Yitzhak Cohen. Mr. Cohen gained notoriety with his controversial essays about the government's anti-Semitic policies.

As of the writing of this article, the two suspects are still at large.

"Yitzhak Cohen," Clara repeated placing down the newspaper.

"You know the name?" asked her mother.

"Yes, I've read his articles and pamphlets. He writes about Jewish oppression and government policies. He has apparently made a few enemies."

"Mama, they said my name in the newspaper. Are Max and I famous?" Moshe wanted to know. He was smiling.

"Yes, you're famous, but not in a good way, Moshe. These men will come looking for you and Max. We need to find a way to keep you hidden until they find these men," Clara said.

"Captain Berbecki will protect us," Moshe said.

"Moshe, we can't rely on the captain. He's not Jewish, so he's not on our side. Do you understand?" Clara asked.

"Yes, Mama," said Moshe.

Turning to Sadie, she said, "These boys need to find a place to hide."

"We can hide in the caves. They'll never find us there," Moshe suggested.

"You're not going to live in a cave like an animal," said Clara firmly. "I'll go talk to the rabbi. Your father said before he left that if I needed help I should ask the rabbi. Moshe, you stay here. If anyone comes while I'm gone, hide in the cellar. I'll be back soon," said Clara putting on her coat.

....

Clara walked briskly to Rabbi Shapira's house. Just like Clara's home village, the shul provided the rabbi and his family a house to live in. She thought about the daily requirements of the rabbi. He had such a burden as the community's spiritual leader.

Will he speak to me without my husband? she wondered. Most likely the rabbi's wife, the rebbetzin, would be present for proper protocol.

With the front door in sight, she heard a voice shout, "Clara, wait."

She turned to see Shmuel running toward her.

"Where are you coming from?"

"I just read the paper. I stopped by your house to talk with you, and your mother told me you were heading over to speak with the rabbi."

"Why don't you come with me," said Clara.

"Yes, of course."

Moments later they stood at the front door of the rabbi's home. Shmuel knocked gently on the wooden door. There was no answer. Clara looked at Shmuel, sighed, and took a turn knocking so hard with her knuckles that she rattled the door in its frame.

"I'm coming," a voice said from inside. Clara rocked back and forth impatiently until the door opened.

"Good evening Clara, good evening Shmuel," said Sara, the rebbetzin. "The rabbi and I were just reading the newspaper. I am so sorry about what happened. Please come in."

Sara escorted them into the rabbi's study.

The rabbi rose from his desk. "Clara, come, my dear. Please sit down."

"Hello, Rabbi, thank you for seeing us," said Shmuel.

"Shmuel, it is good you are here," said the rabbi, returning to his chair on the other side of his desk.

"Rabbi, what am I going to do? The killers are out there. My Moshe and Max are in danger."

The rabbi leaned forward, his elbows on the desk.

"Clara, yes, the boys are in grave danger," the rabbi agreed.

Clara felt suddenly faint. She slumped in her chair, her chin resting on her chest. Then, just as quickly, she inhaled and shot back up with an erect spine. "We need to hide the boys until the police capture the killers," she stated.

"Clara," began the rabbi. "We will find a good place to hide the boys. They will be safe, but only for a while."

"The police will eventually find the murderers, Rabbi. Then the boys can come home," she said.

"You need to understand something. Captain Berbecki already knows who the killers are."

"They already know? What do you mean, Rabbi?"

"The murder victim, Yitzhak Cohen, was very controversial. He wrote about government abuse toward Jews and its anti-Semitic policies. They wanted him silenced."

"So does that mean because he wrote about controversial topics, the police will do nothing?" asked Clara.

"That's exactly what it means. Captain Berbecki will not be investigating the murder. He may go through the motions for our benefit, but don't expect any arrests to be made."

"So what about Moshe and Max? They won't be safe. The killers know what they look like. They'll come after them," Clara said in a near panic. "I need to speak with the captain. The police are here for our protection."

"No, the police will do nothing to capture these men," the rabbi insisted.

Clara started to weep uncontrollably. Sara moved around the desk and placed an arm around her.

"Clara, the police may do nothing, but that doesn't mean nothing can be done," said the rabbi with a small smile.

CHAPTER 26

A LETTER FROM CLARA

I n the evenings, Pincus often stayed behind after Jakob closed the front end of the shop. With the door locked and the CLOSED side of the sign hanging in the window, he had some time to clean up and organize for the next day. Business had been good, very good.

He liked working with Jakob, and apparently so did the customers. From the time they opened the shop until closing time, people came. Sometimes Pincus saw the same pair of shoes he had repaired or shined just a week earlier. When he asked Jakob why, he replied, "People in America like their shoes looking their best."

Pincus really didn't care as long as they paid, and they did. He had enough money to eat in restaurants when he wanted and still plenty to send home to Clara once a month.

Today Jakob told him there was a letter from Clara in the mail. He found it on the front counter and took off his spectacles to polish the lenses, as was his habit before sitting down to read.

My dearest Pincus,

All is well here at home. The children are growing every day. You won't recognize them as they change so fast at their young ages. Anna is now three years old and is a beautiful sensitive child. Jennie has become a big help at home taking over the chores of bringing lunch to Moshe at his Torah studies. Hymie is a good boy, still at home, always getting in my way as I do the household chores. Mother is fine too. She sends her regards and hopes you're doing well.

Thank you for your last letter which, while brief, does give me comfort in knowing you are well. The money you are sending is more than I expected. You should know that Shmuel does an excellent job running the cobbler shop. So between you and Shmuel, your family is well taken care of.

But please tell me when you're coming for us. I realize I ask you this in every letter, but it's been three years now. I know you're busy with the shop and the Landsman Society, but Pincus, don't forget us. We belong there with you.

All my love,
Clara

Pincus folded the letter, placed it back in its envelope, and added it to the stack of her previous letters. All of them pretty much said the same thing: all is well, and when are you coming to get us?

Pincus rubbed his hands together, pondering the letter. He was mindful of his promise to return in a year. But things were going well. If he left now, he'd be gone for a month. This would be very bad for business, and things were picking up steam with the Landsman Society. He had to admit that observing families arriving together made him long for Clara and the children. It would have been a wonderful moment sharing the experience of arriving together. But he knew that the joy of many of these people was short lived.

Moments after setting foot in the Lower East Side, they were confronted with the reality of finding a place to live and securing a job. Therefore, the creation of Landsman Societies grew in popularity because they could ease the immigrants' many burdens.

The Society had welcomed nearly three hundred men, women and children over the past few years. Mendel did an excellent job running it, greeting each family, and orienting them to their new life in America.

Pincus reserved his participation in the Landsman Society of Krzywcza to presiding over the monthly meetings, making decisions concerning the cemetery, and—most important— greeting the Torah scholar families himself.

He shared his vengeful glee with Jakob. "You should see the look in their eyes when they see me now. How the world has turned upside down!" he boasted.

Maybe it *was* time to plan the trip back. *I could travel first class now, never again in steerage,* he thought cheerfully. *I will arrive back home in triumph. The rabbi will be very proud. I am sure to get a special recognition at the shul. Maybe even a plaque in my honor.*

CHAPTER 27

SHMUEL'S ADVENTURE

"Good evening, Shmuel. You're right on schedule, please come inside," said the rabbi.

"Good evening, Rabbi," Shmuel replied, shaking the extended hand of the eighty-year-old rabbi.

Rabbi Shapira was the only rabbi Shmuel had ever known. This was true for most residents of the shtetl, since he had been the only rabbi of Krzywcza for the past fifty years. Shmuel could only imagine the amount of wisdom, guidance, compassion, and sympathy he had provided for his people. Now with the shtetl in an uproar about Moshe and Max, the rabbi had something to deal with that was more complicated than saying a prayer for an ailing loved one.

With the door to his office now closed, the rabbi gestured for Shmuel to sit.

"The boys are safe, Rabbi. They have been very well hidden," Shmuel whispered.

"Good, that's good. But we can't hide them forever. Captain Berbecki will do nothing to bring these men to justice, so we must take action."

The rabbi leaned toward Shmuel, grasped his hands, and said, "We need to find these men before they find Moshe and Max."

"I understand," said Shmuel. "I will find them. But what then?" he asked fearfully.

"Not so fast, Shmuel," the rabbi said patting his cheek in a fatherly way. "You can't find these men on your own."

"What do we do then, Rabbi?"

"You will need to go to the capital city of Lviv, where the government that makes our laws is located. We have influential friends in Lviv whom I have called on from time to time for special favors. These are good men who understand the plight of our people.

"When you arrive at the train station, you need to find this address," he continued, handing Shmuel a piece of paper. "It's a short walk. On the outside of the building there will be a directory of businesses. You will look for The Galician Life Insurance Company. Go to the office and tell the receptionist you are there to see Antoni.

"When you meet with this man, tell him the events exactly as the boys told us. That's all, nothing more," the rabbi instructed. "This man has connections and will find out who issued the order to kill the journalist, Yitzhak Cohen. He will also know the names of the killers." He paused.

"Wait in Lviv as long as it takes for him to return to you with the names. Then take the train back here and report to me," the rabbi said.

"I will," Shmuel agreed. "When should I leave?"

"The first train tomorrow leaves at six a.m. And one more thing, Shmuel," the rabbi added as both men rose from their chairs. "You must stay very alert. You may be followed. The government has eyes everywhere," he whispered. "I want you to take this with you," he said, handing him a long hunting knife in a leather sheath. "Just in case."

....

Shmuel didn't sleep well at all. His bed in the rear of the cobbler shop had provided him with many restful nights, but not this night. The rabbi's instructions kept playing over and over in his mind, alongside his responsibility for saving Moshe and Max.

He thought about his father and brothers in America. Just a few days earlier, he had received a letter from his father. He sat up, lit a candle on the shelf next to his straw mattress, and reached for the letter that he'd tucked into a book he was reading by the writer and historian Wilhelm Feldman, who believed that Jews had no future in Galicia.

Father's letters typically were very long and detailed accounts of his new life in America. Shmuel read about how he had found Pincus and how well he was doing. He described with joy his involvement in organizing the Landsman Society of Krzywcza. "This is the most important work of my life," he wrote.

The letter finished with his father reminding Shmuel to visit his mother's grave often. "Place stones upon her gravestone for your brothers and me," he asked.

Shmuel paused for a moment, allowing his mind to drift to thoughts of his mother. Her last few years, he had watched her suffer and wither to a thin, frail woman. When death came, it was a welcome relief. Shmuel smiled at the thought of her. She had taught him not only how to live, but how to die.

....

Shmuel found himself ready and pacing the empty station floor well before the six o'clock train. Just as he heard the whistle of the approaching train, a man joined him on the platform. The man wore a long dark coat. A similarly dark hat shadowed his eyes, and both hands were buried deep into his pockets. He carried no luggage.

Shmuel nervously boarded the train and walked through the connecting cars. He paused and stuck his head out to look over the platform but saw no one. The stranger must have boarded. *The rabbi did tell me that I might be followed*, he reminded himself.

The train slowly left the station for the two-hour journey to Lviv. He settled in to a rear-facing bench. Better to see anyone approaching, he figured. He thought of how his life had taken some dramatic turns in the past few years, and of the task at hand. For assurance, he nervously ran his fingers over the rabbi's hunting knife that was now tucked into his pocket.

The journey ended uneventfully, and the train pulled into the Lviv station right on time. Shmuel adjusted the brown coat that his mother had made for him. He brushed his long hair back with his fingers, musing that if his mother were still alive, she would be urging him to get a haircut.

He stepped off the train and onto the platform. Unlike the station at Krzywcza, Lviv station had dozens of travelers stirring about. Shmuel looked for the stranger, but no one else seemed to have disembarked. *Maybe I'm worried over nothing*, he thought. He asked a ticket agent for directions into the city center.

This trip to Lviv was the first time he had ventured outside the village of Krzywcza. Under the circumstances, he knew not to get too excited, but he couldn't help feeling in awe of his surroundings. He followed the directions from the train station, walking along the cobblestone streets lined with the tallest buildings he had ever seen. He nearly bumped into people clogging the sidewalks as he gawked in amazement.

"This is it," he said looking at the paper and then again at the sign on the building: THE GALICIAN LIFE INSURANCE COMPANY. He entered the building and stood before a wooden staircase the likes of which he had never seen. The ones he knew back home were narrow and warped. But the staircase leading up to the Galician Life Insurance Company was wide and grand, with carved mahogany handrails. He could feel the solid wood with each step. *These stairs don't creak like the ones in my Dad's old home*, he thought.

Upon reaching the landing, he turned the large brass doorknob and entered. A woman sitting at a desk looked at him and asked rudely, "What do you want?"

"I am here to see Antoni," he said softly.

"Antoni?" She seemed startled. "One moment, please. Take a seat," she said, pointing to a chair against the wall. "What is your name?"

"Shmuel Beck."

"One moment please," she said as she rose to open a door behind her and went inside.

She reappeared in a few seconds. "Mr. Beck, please come in."

He got to his feet, took a deep breath and entered the office.

"Hello Shmuel," said a deep baritone voice.

Sitting at an elaborately carved wooden desk sat a very plump man with a round face and deep-set light blue eyes. The largest collection of books that Shmuel had ever seen covered the entire wall behind him.

"You made my assistant nervous when you said you were here to see Antoni," the man said.

"Oh, I am sorry sir, I was told to ask for Antoni when I got here. Are you not Antoni?"

"There is no Antoni." The man laughed. "Let's just say it's a name that opens my door. My name is Mr. Chmura. Now tell me Shmuel, why are you here? Who sent you?"

"Sir, Rabbi Shapira sent me here to ask for your help." His voice shook as he revealed his secret to this stranger.

"There's no need to be nervous, Shmuel. I've known the rabbi for over forty years. I am probably his best friend who is not a Jew." He smiled again. "So tell me, why has the rabbi sent you to see me?"

....

Shmuel discovered that, in addition to large buildings, Lviv also provides its residents with a beautiful park in the city center. Once he had told Mr. Chmura his story and explained the reason for his visit, Mr. Chmura had told him to wait in the park by the fountain. It might take several hours, Mr. Chmura had warned, but once he knew something, he would send someone to fetch Shmuel and bring him back to his office.

Shmuel amused himself by watching the geese scuttle their goslings around the grassy areas. A few unsuspecting pedestrians were hissed at by the overly protective birds if they walked too close.

The hours passed and the sun started to set over the buildings to the west. He hoped someone would come soon, so he could learn the names of these men and catch the evening train back home.

Shmuel was sitting on a bench watching some boys around his age playing a game that involved knocking down the player carrying the ball. He had never seen this game played before, but it looked like fun.

He became so focused on the game that he didn't notice a man had joined him on the bench. Shmuel looked over and to his shock he recognized the coat and hat. He had completely forgotten the suspicious man on the train this morning.

The man turned his face, which featured a long pinkish scar on his left cheek. His wide-set eyes had the devastating effect of paralyzing Shmuel. He leaned over and said, "Stand up slowly and walk with me."

Too frightened to speak, Shmuel rose and walked out of the park with the stranger.

CHAPTER 28

LUCHOW'S

"**W**here have you been? Seeing that redhead?" Pincus asked with a little smirk.

"Actually, yes. Sorry I'm a little late."

"You had a very interesting visitor stop by."

"Already? It's only eight thirty."

"He was waiting for me when I came down at eight to open. He asked for you directly. Looked very well off to me. Came in a motorcar with a driver. Here, he gave me his card," Pincus said handing it to Jakob.

Jakob didn't need to look at the card, but he did anyway. He didn't want Pincus to suspect anything, not that he thought it would matter much. Pincus must have had some idea of the illicit activities going on in his shop on a daily basis.

"Leo Gorpatsch," he read. "Are those his shoes?" he asked pointing to a shoe bag lying on the counter.

"Yes, he wants me to make him a new pair of shoes. He said just to copy the style of these," Pincus said, excitedly removing the shoes from the bag. "I haven't made a new pair of shoes in years."

"That's great, Pincus," he said, patting him on the back and watching him disappear with the shoes in hand into his workroom in the back. Jakob appreciated his ignorance of the obvious. *As long as he is making money, he just doesn't care*, Jakob realized.

Jakob settled in for another day in the shop. But he couldn't shake the mystery of why Leo Gorpatsch would come here. *We haven't seen each other once since that first meeting in his office. Not even a visit from the mustached man or one of his goons. Perhaps I am doing his bidding through Manny. But I do need to get inside. Captain Becker will be asking for information sooner or later.*

Still holding the card, he flipped it over, and hand written across the back he read: *Luchow's tonight 9:00.*

"Luchow's," he whispered. "Why there?"

Just then, the front door opened and a gentleman entered. Jakob tucked the card in his pocket and greeted the man.

....

As he turned the corner that evening, he spotted Luchow's and smiled at the scene of the luxury motorcars dropping off glamorous patrons who milled on the sidewalk before entering. *Just long enough to be seen.*

He stepped into the gaggle of the city's elite with confidence. *I may not be rich, but I look good,* he thought, adjusting his suit jacket. He smiled, thinking of the last time he'd wore his suit, just a few weeks ago when he had met Nita here.

Squeezing through the crowd, he entered the smoke-filled establishment. The maître d' greeted him. "Yes, sir, how may I be of assistance?"

"I am here to see Mr. Gorpatsch," he said.

"Mr. Gorpatsch is dining here, yes. But why would I disturb him?" asked the maître d'.

"Because Mr. Gorpatsch is expecting me," he answered. Jakob produced the card and turned it over to show the note on the back.

After disappearing for a few minutes, the maître d' returned. "Right this way, Mr. Adler," he said smiling.

Jakob followed the man through a zigzag of many tables. He saw the table where he had sat with Nita. Now an older couple sat there, sipping Champagne.

"Sir, please," the maître d' instructed Jakob to enter a private dining room.

"Thank you," Jakob replied and stepped in.

A large round table filled the room. Smoke billowed in large clouds. *Who are all these people?* he wondered. At first glance he couldn't see Gorpatsch. Then he heard him.

"Jakob, you came," said Gorpatsch turning around in his chair. "Please take a seat next to me. I'm pleased you are here."

Jakob sat in the empty chair. He scanned the table, nodding greetings.

"Jakob, let me introduce you to my date. This is the fabulous singer and star of Broadway, Nita Naldi."

Gorpatsch leaned back in his chair so Jakob could see her sitting on his other side. Her red hair was swept up in an elegant bun, and she had allowed a few curls to fall along either side of her beautiful face. Her full red lips were moving, saying something.

"It is very nice to meet you, Jakob," she said, offering a slightly limp, delicate hand.

Jakob took her hand, leaned awkwardly across Gorpatsch, and kissed it gently.

"Enough of that," Gorpatsch boomed, slapping Jakob on the back.

Leaning back in his chair, Jakob took another peek at Nita. Her neck and shoulders were exposed with her hair pinned up. While she made his blood boil with passion, Gorpatsch made it boil with hatred. There he sat, blocking him from the woman for whom he would do anything.

"Jakob," Gorpatsch said, turning to look at him. "Thank you for coming. I need to speak with you. Come, there is an office in the back where we can talk quietly." He stood up and signaled with his hand for Jakob to follow.

As they crossed the restaurant, many people greeted Gorpatsch with waves and nods, and a few men stood up to shake his hand.

Does he own this place too? Jakob wondered as he followed Gorpatsch through a door marked PRIVATE.

After closing the door, Gorpatsch sat on one of two chairs positioned in front of a desk. "Sit, Jakob," he said pointing to the other chair. "This is my friend's office. He lets me use it."

Jakob looked around the office and saw nothing unusual, except there were no windows. *One way in and out,* Jakob observed. *Let's hope I don't need to make a forceful exit.*

"Okay, you're probably wondering why I asked you to come here, of all places."

Jakob nodded and smiled.

Gorpatsch took out a cigar and offered one to Jakob.

"Here, allow me," Gorpatsch, said taking back the cigar. He pulled out a shiny chrome cutter, lopped off its end, and handed back it to Jakob. A silver lighter appeared in Gorpatsch's hand, and, with the deftness of a magician, he made it glow with a blue flame. Jakob leaned in, took a few quick puffs, and the cigar lit. Their smoke intermingled as they exhaled silently.

"That's a beautiful lighter," Jakob said.

"It's from Paris. Look how they engraved my initial," Gorpatsch said, showing Jakob the stylized *G* emblazoned on each side.

"Elegant," Jakob added.

"Jakob, I like you. You're smart and resourceful," he said.

Jakob looked at him with open palms and shrugged shoulders. "We only met once."

"I get reports from Manny. He tells me you are doing very well."

"That's good to hear," said Jakob.

"I have a job I need done, and I believe you're the right man." He paused to take a drag on the cigar and leaned back to blow the smoke into the clouds swirling above them. "Jakob, have you heard of the Eastman Gang?"

"I have not."

"The Eastman Gang is led by Edward Eastman, a Jew. He came here a few years ago from a small town not far from Warsaw. His men call him the Monk. Don't know why, doesn't matter. What does matter is that he is a pain in my ass."

Jakob sat quietly, listening and wondering where this would lead.

"The Eastman Gang runs a few rackets, just like me. You would think that there is enough business for all of us, but not the Monk. He has been making some aggressive moves lately. There have been some . . . let's say, some physical encounters between my men and his. What I would like you to do is to reach out to the Monk. Set up a meeting, so we can talk."

"You want me to set up a meeting between you and someone called the Monk?" Jakob asked, bewildered.

"Sounds crazy, yeah, I know." Gorpatsch laughed. "But, yes, that's exactly what I want you to do."

"Suppose I agree to do this, how would I find him? I have no idea where to start."

"That's the easy part. You just ask around. Try the men making drops in the shop. I bet some of them would know. Listen, you're a clever guy. I'm sure with a few questions here and there, you'll find him, and when you do, set up this meeting in a neutral place. Each of us can bring one man, no more, and no weapons. He'll agree just out of curiosity."

"Okay, I guess I can do that. But what's in it for me?"

"I'll give you a hundred dollars now and another hundred after we have the meeting. Is that acceptable?" he said, handing Jakob an envelope.

"That's acceptable," Jakob said, taking a peek at the cash and hoping he would not regret it.

CHAPTER 29

CLARA AND THE CAPTAIN

The rabbi had told Clara about Shmuel's mission to identify the killers. He'd said that he should be back in a day or two at the most. She paced the kitchen slapping a wooden spoon against the open palm of her left hand, over and over.

"It's been five days now. Something is wrong. Why would the rabbi send Shmuel? He's just a boy," she told her mother.

Sadie rocked back and forth in her chair, as nervous as her daughter. "I'm worried about Moshe, stuck in the basement day and night. It's not good, Clara," she lamented.

"It's better than being dead, Mother," she screamed and walked into her bedroom, slamming the door behind her.

She fell onto her bed, buried her face in the pillow, and wept. Her body heaved uncontrollably. Flipping over onto her back, she realized she was still holding on to the wooden spoon, which she now flung to the floor.

I need to figure this out, but how?

She didn't trust the rabbi's judgment anymore. *What if I plead to Captain Berbecki for help? Why would he allow harm to come to Moshe and Max? They are innocent boys.* She stood up, straightened her dress, brushed her hair, and told her mother she would be back soon.

During the ten-minute walk to the police station, she had a flood of thoughts. *I'll beg him to help us. There must be some humanity in the man.* But as she stepped through the front door of the station, she had no idea what she would say.

"I'm here to see the captain," she said to the sergeant.

"Hello, Mrs. Potasznik. This is not a good time to see the captain. Please come back tomorrow."

"I must see Captain Berbecki," she demanded and walked past the sergeant to the captain's office door.

"Mrs. Potasznik, please, you cannot just walk in," he pleaded.

Ignoring the sergeant, she opened the door and saw Berbecki sitting at his desk staring at her. The sun, low in the afternoon sky, filtered in through his window and fell on his face, giving his blue eyes a disarming sparkle.

"Welcome, Clara. You look upset. Please sit down and tell me, what's the problem?"

"What's the problem?" she stammered. *Did he just call me Clara? Perhaps I've been too forthcoming with my behavior. I don't want to give him the wrong impression.*

Gathering her wits, she continued, "You know all too well what the problem is. I need to know how you plan on arresting those two men who are still out there."

"Not to worry. We are investigating the murder and following some good leads now. I would expect to have the murderers in custody soon."

"Oh, is that true, Captain?"

"Of course, it's true, Clara," he said with an unusual smile.

She took a breath to calm herself. But the captain's uncharacteristic demeanor disarmed her, and she wanted to leave. "Oh, that's very good news," she said, turning to the door.

"Wait, Clara, where are you going so fast? Please sit down, relax, have a drink with me."

A bottle of Vishniak sat on his desk. He poured some in an empty glass, stood up from his desk, and handed her the drink as he offered her a chair.

He's been drinking, she realized. *That's why he is calling me Clara.*

"No, I can't stay. I left my mother alone with the children, and Moshe is not safe. I need to go back right away."

"Clara, stop worrying. I can help you," he said, walking to his office door behind her and closing it. "With your husband gone, you must be lonely for a man," he said with a slight slur.

"No, Captain. You have been drinking. I must go home."

Berbecki took a step closer. She could now smell him, his sweat, his breath, and his lust. "Give me a kiss, Clara. No harm comes to the boys."

"No!" she screamed and shoved him. The inebriated captain, taken by surprise, tripped over a table piled high with files. He crashed to the floor along with the contents of the table. Clara watched in horror, then turned to the door, opened it, and fled the police station as Berbecki called her name. She ran home, now fearing for her own life as well as Moshe's.

CHAPTER 30

SHMUEL'S PLIGHT

He couldn't stop staring at the man's scar. In the bright sunlight it looked pink, but here in the darkened room it took on a more sinister brownish color. Shmuel imagined the man had earned it in a knife fight.

"Listen carefully, Shmuel," said the man, who sat in an identical chair across from him, their knees almost touching. "Let me tell you what is going to happen."

Shmuel, his hands and legs bound to a wooden armchair, asked, "Are you going to kill me?"

"It all depends on you," said the stranger.

Tears welled up and cascaded down Shmuel's flushed cheeks.

The man now leaned in, his hands clasping his bony thighs. "Shmuel, we know everything. We know Rabbi Shapira sent you to meet with Mr. Chmura and find out the names of those two men accused of the murder of that Jew journalist. But this will not happen. You will take the train back home with me. Then you will go to the rabbi and tell him that Mr. Chmura couldn't help you."

"But I need to know the names. They want to kill Moshe and Max," he protested.

"You don't seem to understand who you are dealing with. There are powerful men involved here, and they need to be protected. These accused men can lead back to them, and that can't be allowed to happen," he explained. He stood up, walked to the corner of the room, and grabbed a hammer lying on a table, as Shmuel watched in fear.

"Shmuel, tell me, do you write with your right or left hand?"

"Why do you want to know that?" he asked, looking at the hammer in the skinny man's hand.

Shmuel tried shaking his bindings loose. *If only I could free myself, I could run away and escape*, he thought. But the ropes were too tight, so he had no choice but to resign himself to the inevitable. "Right hand," he answered.

"I'm not a cruel man," said the man with the scar as he smashed the hammer down upon Shmuel's left hand, shattering flesh and bones.

Shmuel screamed. He could see his blood pooling in the round indentation caused by the hammer's violent impact. He tried again but was unable to loosen his bonds, and the man was still talking.

"I want you to know this is serious. If you want to live, you will do what I say. Moshe and Max are most likely dead already. Why risk your life too?" he said, wiping the blood off the hammer with an old cotton rag.

Shmuel felt no pain in his numb hand. He watched in horror as his blood continued to flow and drip on the floor. A wave of dizziness washed over him. Then he was unconscious.

....

From far away he heard the words, "Shmuel, wake up."

A sharp slap across his face brought him back. He opened his eyes and there stood Mr. Chmura. "We need to get you out of here."

Shmuel watched as Mr. Chmura released his restraints and wrapped a bandage around his injured hand.

"Can you stand?" he asked.

"Yes, I think so." He looked down and saw the man with the scar lying on the ground with a growing puddle of blood around his head. "What happened?"

"He's dead," said Mr. Chmura. "I shot him. We must go. Quickly now."

Mr. Chmura turned to another man. "Get rid of the body." The man nodded.

Once outside in the bright sunlight, Shmuel saw a wagon waiting for him. Mr. Chmura motioned him inside.

Shmuel gingerly stepped into the cab. Mr. Chmura followed and shouted to the driver, "Let's go."

Once underway, Mr. Chmura said, "I am taking you to a doctor. He will look at your hand. You will stay with me for a few days."

Shmuel could feel the pain now. His hand throbbed under the blood-soaked gauze wrapped around it. He winced. "Did you get the names?"

"You are a brave young man, Shmuel," Mr. Chmura said, offering a comforting smile. "I got the names. I'll tell you more in the morning. Right now, you need to see a doctor and then get some rest."

CHAPTER 31

LEO'S STORY

"I'm testing him," Leo Gorpatsch told his wife, Freida. "I could have any one of my guys set up a meeting with the Monk, but let's see how he does."

Leo liked bouncing ideas off his wife. She had proven to be a good listener as well as having a steel-trap memory. She was like a living file cabinet, he boasted.

They'd had had a good marriage over ten years and produced two fine children. As he had built his career in Warsaw and then Berlin, and eventually here in New York, she understood her role. In particular, he appreciated that she never questioned his numerous infidelities—though the latest one with the singer Nita Naldi had become scandalous. The gossip columnist Blanche Sweet had seen the two of them at Luchow's more than once. When Freida had discovered this particular indiscretion, she had communicated her distress by leaving the newspaper open to the gossip column in plain sight for him to see when he sat down for dinner. He, of course, dismissed the affront by casually folding the newspaper and pouring himself a glass of wine.

It was true that the Eastman Gang had been challenging his business interests in the Lower East Side. There was indeed cause for concern. The Monk had raised the level of violence even beyond Gorpatsch's notorious methods. Of course, Leo would need to respond in kind.

It had started with a disagreement over some territory. Edward "the Monk" Eastman, looking to expand his operation north of Hester Street, had sent his men to make the rounds on Grand Street. These businesses had complained to Gorpatsch's men, resulting in some beatings of the Monk's men. The Eastman Gang had retaliated by setting fires to stores on Grand Street.

Such was the cost of doing business, Gorpatsch knew. Then again, he did admire the Monk, about twenty years his junior. Leo liked the upstart's ambition. His spunk reminded Leo of his younger days.

His career had begun over thirty years earlier in Warsaw. He'd gotten his start working for the Tsvi Midal, an outfit that lured Jewish women from shtetls with offers of a chance to work for wealthy Jews in Argentina. Once they arrived in Argentina, they were forced into prostitution.

As a young, well-dressed, handsome, young Jewish man, Gorpatsch traveled from village to village, placing posters in local synagogues advertising a rosy future for young Jewish girls. Frightened parents, many financially desperate, would send their daughters away with Gorpatsch in hopes of a better life for them.

Gorpatsch brought the girls back to Warsaw where their training as prostitutes began. Next, they were taken by train to Hamburg where they were boarded on a steamship for Buenos Aires, Argentina. Once they arrived, they were brought to brothels, some housing as many as sixty to eighty sex slaves.

After a few years, and with some money to his name, Gorpatsch moved on from the Tsvi Midal to start his own business. The idea came to him after speaking with several of the merchants along the shopping boulevard in his Jewish neighborhood in Warsaw. They had a common complaint. The local police demanded weekly payments in exchange for their so-called protection. But when they called on the police for help, they never came.

"I will start a Jewish merchant protection business, Freida," he said, pointing out his apartment window to the street below. "They need my help. For a modest monthly fee, I will offer real protection. Jews protecting Jews."

"How will you protect them from the police?" she asked with concern.

"That's easy. I'll pay off the captain in our precinct. He'll make more money this way with no effort. I'll be doing him a favor," he said, gesturing with open arms.

CHAPTER 32

JAKOB MEETS THE MONK

I t didn't take long to meet the Monk. Jakob followed Gorpatsch's suggestion and asked some of the shadier characters
making their drops. He struck gold with Michael Malone.

"Hey Michael, would you happen to know a guy they call
the Monk?" Jakob asked.

"The Monk? I may know him. Why do you ask?" Michael
asked suspiciously.

Jakob leaned over the counter filled with tagged shoes ready
for repair and whispered, "I've been advised by a business asso-
ciate that we ought to meet. The cobbler business is no road to
riches, if you know what I mean."

"Sure, Jakob, I know what you mean. I can introduce you to
the Monk. He buys liquor from my uncle for his establishments.
You know, those private clubs with the girls," he said with a sly
smile. "I do the deliveries. The Monk is there sometimes. He
counts the cases and pays me. Why don't you tag along next time?
Maybe you'll get lucky."

His opportunity came a few days later, when he was instructed
to meet Michael at the warehouse on 22 Orchard Street.

"Come tonight at ten. There's a side door that says Malone & Sons. Knock hard on the door. It's hard to hear anything inside."

Later that evening, Jakob stood on a dark street in front of the warehouse, banging on a heavy metal door. As it opened, light flooded the sidewalk and Michael's head poked out. "Come in. We're just about ready."

Jakob stepped inside. Liquor bottles in wooden crates filled shelves that wrapped around the cavernous warehouse space.

"Hop in," Michael said, pointing to a truck that had been loaded with crates.

"This is beautiful," Jakob said, admiring the truck.

"This is a Ford Model T panel truck. Brand new. My uncle just bought it," he said as he climbed in.

Soon they were headed north on Broadway. The warm evening provided a comfortable breeze through the open cab. Thirty minutes later, the truck pulled into an alleyway and stopped. Michael got out and bounded up the three steps to the landing. A sign read:

DELIVERIES ONLY—SATAN'S CIRCUS

He knocked a few times until the door opened. A brief exchange took place between Michael and a man wearing a newsboy hat.

"Let's go, Jakob. He tells me that the Monk is here."

"What about the crates?"

"His men will take care of them," Michael said.

They walked down a long, smelly corridor. Muffled sounds of music and talk vibrated around them.

"Why do they call this place Satan's Circus?" Jakob shouted.

Michael turned and smiled. "You'll see soon enough."

As the door opened, Jakob felt he'd walked into a dream world. Dozens of women dressed in white frilly undergarments mingled with men in suits and sat on their laps, while the men blew puffs of cigar smoke around them. Long legs in stockings crisscrossed here and there. A man played popular tunes on a piano.

The working ladies took note of Jakob as he entered.

"Hey, handsome, come sit with me," a voice called out.

Michael led him to a deeply tufted banquette upholstered in burgundy velour. Between two lovely ladies sat a thin man with a severely receding hairline, wire-rim spectacles, and a bushy black mustache.

"Who's your friend, Michael?" asked the Monk.

"This is Jakob Adler. He's helping me with deliveries tonight. Jakob, this is the Monk."

"Ladies, please give us a minute here," the Monk said, indicating the women should vacate the booth. As they left, they gave Jakob flirtatious glances.

"They like you, Jakob. Perhaps you might like to enjoy some of the fruits here tonight?"

"They are very beautiful," he stammered, "but I'm here just to help Michael."

The man with the newsboy hat appeared at the table and nodded at the Monk, perhaps confirming the delivery to be the correct amount.

"Gentlemen, please sit."

Jakob and Michael took seats on either side of the Monk in the half-round banquette. The Monk placed a small leather case on the table. He unclasped the straps, opened it, took out an envelope, and handed it to Michael.

Michael nodded, said, "Thank you," and glanced around nervously before stuffing the cash into his pocket.

Perhaps Michael was only boasting about knowing the Monk before this, Jakob thought. *This looks like the first time he's ever dealt with the mob boss.*

"Don't worry," the Monk said, patting his hand. "This is the one place in the city where you won't get robbed."

"So, Jakob, what do you think of Satan's Circus?" the Monk asked with a sweeping gesture of his scrawny arms.

....

As he climbed the stairs to his apartment after Michael dropped him off, Jakob couldn't imagine how someone as unassuming as the Monk could become so powerful. He had seemed charming and not at all the monster Gorpatsch had described. But the stories that Michael shared had described a man who had no qualms about using violence as a means to an end. The accounts of cutting off fingers, gouging out eyes, and breaking bones made Jakob tread carefully when he broached the subject of a sit-down with Gorpatsch.

"Leo wants to make peace?" The Monk had smiled. "It's about time. Sure, set it up."

This is way too easy, Jakob thought. He sat quietly at the kitchen table to remove his shoes. Pincus, who had probably been asleep for hours, was snoring loudly on a mattress lying on the floor in the corner.

Jakob rose from the chair and walked up to the single window to look out upon Ludlow Street. The Monk had also agreed that the meeting be held in a neutral location. Without thinking it through, Jakob had proposed the cobbler shop.

If Gorpatsch would agree, the meeting would be set for tomorrow at midnight. It looked like all of the obstacles had been removed. Then a loud snore from Pincus reminded him that he couldn't be here. *How can I make Pincus disappear for the evening?*

⋯⋯⋯⋯⋯⋯

Jakob awoke to an empty apartment. Pincus usually left early on Shabbat morning to attend services at the synagogue. Jakob had three items on the agenda for the day.

The first was to inform Gorpatsch of the meeting he had set up with the Monk at midnight.

The second was to get Pincus out of the apartment. He planned to have him picked up in a motorcar and brought to the Asser Levy Public Bathhouse. Then he'd be taken to the Player's Club, where he would enjoy an evening of cigars and Vishniak. Jakob would also arrange for Pincus to have a room at the club with a real bed and private toilet for the night.

The third item on the agenda was to pay a visit to Captain Becker and inform him about the meeting between the two of the city's most notorious crime bosses.

CHAPTER 33

SHMUEL RETURNS

He took a window seat looking out onto the platform and waved goodbye to Mr. Chmura with his good hand. This is how he would refer to his hands from now on, he thought: his good hand and his bad hand. The bad hand, wrapped in gauze, had many broken bones. The doctor had done what he could.

"I'm sorry to say that the fingers on your left hand, except for your thumb, will never function properly again. But you will adapt to your handicap," the doctor had told him.

As the train pulled away from the station, he thought about what Mr. Chmura had told him the night before in his office.

"The journalist wrote some provocative articles criticizing several government officials by name. Usually they are tolerant with general anti-government comments. But naming names crossed a line," Mr. Chmura said, pausing to take a puff on his cigar. "What I learned is that two men were sent from Warsaw to murder Yitzhak Cohen."

"What do you mean, *sent?*" asked Shmuel.

"These men are part of a gang in Warsaw run by a man named Leo Gorpatsch. Gorpatsch is involved in many illegal activities, one of which is murder for hire." "Someone paid these men to kill?" Shmuel asked.

"That's right."

"What can we do then? We need to stop these men from hurting Moshe and Max," Shmuel said.

"That may be a problem. If we kill them, more will come. Leo Gorpatsch is not a man who would let such an act go without retribution."

"What do we do, Mr. Chmura?"

"I thought about this. I can arrange passage for the boys to go to America. You told me that Moshe's father is already there," he said.

"Yes, he has opened a cobbler shop in the Lower East Side."

"I have heard that Gorpatsch has expanded his business to New York, but with over half a million Jews now living in Manhattan, there will be little chance for them to cross paths."

"Aren't they too young to travel alone?" Shmuel asked. "Clara would never allow Moshe to go unaccompanied."

"I thought so too. That's why you will take the boys."

"Me, go to America?" he said with a grin.

"Yes, you can be reunited with your father and brothers."

Shmuel shook his head as he thought about it.

"You're a good boy, Shmuel, and you've sacrificed enough," Mr. Chmura said, pointing to his mangled hand.

....

The train pulled into the station at ten. Shmuel moved with care through the car and onto the platform. He had learned that the slightest bump of his hand, even against soft surfaces, would hurt. But he wanted to tell Clara the news right away.

Approaching the house, Shmuel noticed it was well lit. At this hour, Clara would have only a single lamp burning. He walked up to a window and took a peek.

Quickly he darted out of view. Clara, her mother, and the children sat closely huddled looking warily at two men. He stealthily took another look. His eyes did not deceive him. *These men must be the killers looking for the boys.* The women had their arms wrapped around the terrified children.

Shmuel held his breath to listen.

"Tell us where the boys are, and no harm will come to you," said the larger one, who wore a long black coat.

"They are not here. I've sent them away," Clara said.

"Is that so?" said the other man, who bounced nervously. "That's fine, we'll kill these little ones then," he threatened, pointing at the children.

The children shrieked and huddled closer.

Shmuel moved his hand down to the knife the rabbi had given him. He unsheathed it, gripped it with his good right hand, blade facing down. Then he moved to the front door, hesitated for a moment, and shoved it open. The killers turned in surprise. Shmuel charged in, lifting the blade high above his shoulder and driving it deep into the neck of the taller man.

Blood gushed from the wound as he fell to the ground. The children screamed. The other man jumped at Shmuel, knocking him off his feet. He lost his grip on the knife as he tried to use his good hand to break the fall.

"You little shit!" yelled the man as he jumped on Shmuel and punched him over and over in the face. Shmuel lay defenseless on his back in a pool of the dead man's blood. He closed his eyes, resigned to taking a beating. Then it stopped. The man fell off him. When he opened his eyes, he saw Clara standing above him holding his bloody knife.

"Shmuel, are you alright?" she asked.

"I'm okay," he said and let out a gut-wrenching groan as he stood up gingerly, touching his bruised and swelling face. At his feet lay the dead men, drenched in a pool of their intermingled blood. The children and grandmother looked at Shmuel and Clara in utter horror.

"Clara!" her mother shrieked, pointing at the doorway.

All eyes turned to the open doorway where Moshe and Max stood gawking. "Mama?" Moshe asked. "What happened?"

Moshe looked sick.

"Moshe, you don't look well," Clara said.

"I got sick right before the men came. But I'm feeling better now," he said, looking at the dead men on their living room floor.

"Mother, put the children to bed," Clara said, placing the bloodstained knife on the kitchen table.

She looked at Shmuel, who stood hunched over and looking bewildered. "Shmuel, boys," she called out. "Let's go see Captain Berbecki."

CHAPTER 34

THREE YEAR ANNIVERSARY

Mendel shook Pincus's hand and took the seat of honor next to him on the dais. On Pincus's other side sat Benjamin, an old friend from Krzywcza who had arrived a few months ago. He had provided Mendel a great deal of help with the growing responsibilities of administrating the Landsman Society.

While the assembly mingled and chatted among themselves, Benjamin leaned behind Pincus to address Mendel. "How's your eldest boy?"

"Very well, according to the letter Pincus just received from Clara. He's running his cobbler shop."

"Why didn't he come to America with you and the boys?"

"When his mother died, Shmuel was heartbroken," Mendel said. "He refused to come with his brothers and me to America. So, I left him there. He's a sensitive boy. Maybe he will toughen up being on his own. I'm praying when Pincus goes back to collect his family, he will convince Shmuel to come."

"I hope so too," Benjamin said.

"Simmer down, gentlemen. I'm about to start," announced Pincus.

Pincus approached the dais, took off his glasses, pulled a cloth from his pocket, and polished the lenses, a familiar ritual that signified he was about to speak.

"Good evening, my friends," he began, looking out onto a packed house with over two hundred men from his village—*and not a stranger among us,* he thought proudly.

"I am happy to see such a large turnout."

"Tonight marks our three-year anniversary." He paused to allow for applause.

"To date, the Landsman Society of Krzywcza has received a hundred and forty-three families. This includes over a thousand men, women, and children." More applause.

"We have offered assistance to many of you," he said, making a sweeping gesture with his right arm. "This includes finding jobs and housing. Our sick fund has provided support for those in dire need. I am especially proud of our exclusive section in the Beth David Cemetery where we have laid our beloveds to eternal rest."

....

Pincus and Mendel stepped down from the dais together and walked into the crowd, mingling and chatting after the evening's presentation.

"Good evening, Mendel, Pincus," said Saul Bloch extending his hand.

"Good evening, Saul. How are you?" Mendel said, shaking the hand of his childhood friend.

"Hello, Saul," said Pincus with less enthusiasm.

"We're managing," Saul said. "It hasn't been easy finding work. I've been teaching at the shul a few days a week. But you know how it is in America for men with our skills. You have done well, I see."

"The Society takes a lot of work. I don't know what I would have done without it," Mendel said.

"I'm happy for you both," Saul remarked.

"Thank you," Pincus said. "I know how tough it can be for intellectuals who hope to find meaningful work here."

"I appreciate that," Saul replied.

"Maybe we can help you find a position more suitable for your skills," Pincus said, looking at Mendel, who nodded his approval.

CHAPTER 35

JAKOB MEETS THE COMMISSIONER

Jakob waited as Captain Becker wrapped up his meeting with Police Commissioner McDougal.

"Can I get you a coffee?" asked the detective whose desk Jakob was sitting at.

"No, I'm good. Thank you. Can you tell me why the commissioner is here? Does it have anything to do with me?"

"Sorry, buddy, I wish I knew," said the detective, dropping his cigarette butt into a nearly empty coffee cup.

Just then the captain's door opened, and he asked Jakob to come in.

Jakob stood, smiled, nodded to the detective, and entered the captain's office.

"Jakob, this is Police Commissioner McDougal."

"Nice to meet you, sir," he said, shaking hands with the commissioner.

The commissioner exhaled a long puff of cigar smoke, creating a silver cloud around his large head.

"So, you're the guy who set up the meeting with Gorpatsch and the Monk?" he asked.

Jakob nodded. "Yes, sir."

"I understand that you set this meeting up at the cobbler shop where you work."

"I did. Is that okay?"

"The captain and I were just discussing it. Is there a place in the shop for two men to conceal themselves while the meeting takes place?"

Jakob thought for a moment before answering. "Under the counter, there's room to hide from anyone who comes in the front door."

"Perfect," the commissioner said.

Captain Becker stepped around his desk and spoke to Jakob. "Wait outside for me. I'll be back as soon as I address the men."

....

Jakob sat alone in the room filled with desks and empty chairs while the captain briefed his officers. Perhaps this wasn't such a good idea after all, he thought. Things could easily go wrong.

Just as he was considering changing his mind, the captain returned. Following closely behind was a man wearing a blue suit and red tie. He had premature gray hair, which gave him a more dignified appearance than the captain, who always seemed to look as if he had just woken up from a nap.

The captain flicked his finger, indicating Jakob should follow him into his office.

"Jakob, this is District Attorney Whitman."

"Hello, sir," Jakob said as they shook hands.

"In order to prosecute Gorpatsch, we need to have a witness to the incriminating conversation. So the DA and I will take up positions under the service counter during the sting operation," the captain said.

"You want to be in the cobbler shop during the meeting?" Jakob was surprised.

"This is how police work is done. Go now and prepare yourself. We'll meet up with you later."

As he walked home from the police station, Jakob thought

about turning back and telling the captain that he'd changed his mind. But he realized that perhaps things had gone too far. If he backed out now, he would have not only Gorpatsch's wrath to deal with, but that of the Monk, the captain, the DA, and the commissioner as well.

....

When evening finally came, Captain Becker and District Attorney Whitman met Jakob a few blocks away from 97 Ludlow at thirty minutes before midnight.

"Is Pincus out for the evening?" asked Becker.

"He won't be back until tomorrow."

The three men walked down the dark empty alleyway and entered the shop through the back door.

"This way," Jakob whispered. He directed the men through Pincus's workroom to the customers' part of the shop. "You can hide here," he said, pointing to the small space under the counter. "We'll enter through the front so you won't be seen."

The D.A. took off his jacket and folded it carefully. He bent down to look in the cramped space that Jakob had cleared out earlier that day. "Both of us in here?"

"We'll be okay, Whitman." Becker smiled. "You better hurry, Jakob. You're meeting them in a few minutes."

Jakob nodded and left through the back door.

CHAPTER 36

THE MEETING

Jakob leaned against the wall, his hands in his pockets, watching the coroner place the third corpse into the wagon. It had taken hours for the police to complete the crime scene investigation. The sun would rise soon, and Pincus would be coming home. How would he explain the blood and the pieces of skull and brains now splattered across the walls and floor of the cobbler shop?

Everything had happened so fast. Gorpatsch and the Monk seemed to be having a productive conversation. It looked like they had agreed to a mutually beneficial arrangement of merging their organizations. Just as they were about to shake on the deal, a miniature pistol suddenly appeared in Gorpatsch's right hand, and he shot the Monk in his forehead. The bullet went right through his skull, leaving a gaping hole in the back of his head.

Outside the front door where each man's second was waiting, Jakob heard another gunshot. The mustached man had killed the Monk's man. Then, rising from behind the counter, Becker and Whitman appeared. Without surprise or hesitation, Gorpatsch put a bullet though the District Attorney's right eye.

Jakob had stood there gaping at Gorpatsch. "What are you doing?"

Gorpatsch slid the small revolver back into his jacket pocket. He stepped over the corpse of the Monk, walked around the counter, and regarded the crumpled body of the former DA.

Jakob continued to gape. Gorpatsch merely patted his cheek in a fatherly way. He tipped the brim of his hat to the captain and slipped out through the back door.

Jakob looked at the captain, puzzled. "Aren't you going to stop him, arrest him?"

The captain shook his head. "Well done, Jakob. You did exactly what we wanted."

"*We* wanted? What does that mean?"

"You think Leo Gorpatsch would walk into a police ambush?"

Jakob looked at the captain for a while before saying, "You work for Gorpatsch?"

"Don't we all, Jakob?"

CHAPTER 37

WAR

"It's been nearly four years. Get it through your head, Clara—he's not coming back!" her mother squawked from her usual perch at the kitchen table, as she peeled potatoes.

"I refuse to believe that. His last letter promised me he would come before year's end," she insisted as she put on her shoes.

"Where are you going?"

"I'm going to see Shmuel. The same thing I do every Wednesday morning, Mother," she answered.

"If he was coming back, he would have done so already," her mother insisted.

What if Mother's right, she lamented? *Why would Pincus pick up and leave America? He would need to be gone at least a month.*

"I'm sure he loves his work as chairman of the Landsman Society. Finally he has reached a level of respect from his peers that he could never have achieved here," she admitted with one hand on the doorknob.

"That's right and that's why he's never coming back."

"There's no way he would abandon us," she insisted and walked out the front door.

When he left, I was pregnant with Anna, who will have her fourth birthday in a few weeks, and he's never laid eyes on her. Meanwhile, Jennie has blossomed from a shy little girl into a vibrant young lady of fifteen. Hymie, only two years old when Pincus left, has no memory of his father except what we tell him. Then there's Moshe. When Pincus emigrated to America, Moshe had just turned eight. In the past four years he has grown up without a father and along the way has had some harrowing experiences. Maybe next year we can all celebrate his bar mitzvah together in America. . . .

She stopped a few feet from the cobbler shop. The CLOSED sign hung in the window permanently now. Since Shmuel had lost the use of his left hand, he couldn't do the work anymore, and she couldn't find a replacement. So she had decided to close the shop for good. Pincus had been sending money regularly, which provided for the family, but that didn't have the same honor as a long-standing family business. On the day Clara had cleaned out the shop, she'd taken one last look around. Her eyes had blurred with tears as she took in the details of this space that was so familiar to her, and on which so many families had relied for the fifty-plus years that Pincus and his father before him had operated the business. *But where are they now? While Pincus has been in America all this time, I'm the one who's borne the burden of overseeing the shop for him. And now that Shmuel's gotten himself hurt, what choice do I have?* She'd nodded firmly to herself, as if to approve her own decision, and then she had shut the doors on the past for the last time.

....

The rabbi hired Shmuel to do scribe work for the shul. After all, he could still write. "The community owes it to him after what we put him through," the rabbi had told her.

Turning the corner, she headed for the shul where the rebbetzin greeted her. "Come in, Clara, it's so nice to see you. Shmuel is working in the back today. We are having a wedding tonight, and he is writing the marriage contract," she said excitedly.

Clara smiled and walked through the kitchen, down a

hallway that connected the home to the shul. As she entered, she saw the rabbi standing at the bimah, his back to her.

"Good morning, Rabbi," she said.

He turned and said, "Oh, hello, Clara. It's so nice to see you."

"I came to see Shmuel. Is he here?"

"He's in the back office," the rabbi said, pointing to the door.

....

"Good morning, Clara," Shmuel said, setting down his quill. "How are you today?"

"I'm well," she said, taking a seat in front of his desk that was covered with parchment paper.

"I'm working on a marriage contract for the Benders. Their youngest son is getting married."

"Are you enjoying your work, Shmuel?"

"It's good, and it's something I can do," he said, lifting his disfigured left hand. "What I truly love is working for the rabbi. He's taught me so many things." He continued in a whisper. "Clara, I need to tell you something."

Shmuel rose from his chair and walked over to close his office door.

"What I am about to tell you no one in the village knows. The rabbi shared some news with me late last night from a friend who just arrived from Warsaw." He paused and sat down.

"A few weeks ago the Archduke Ferdinand of Serbia was assassinated in Sarajevo. This caused the Austro-Hungarian Empire to declare war on Serbia, which moved Russia, an ally of Serbia, to mobilize its army to intervene against Austro-Hungary. Then, only three days ago, Germany, an ally of Austro-Hungary, declared war against Russia."

"Shmuel, what does this mean?" Clara asked, stunned.

"We should expect that our beautiful Galicia will soon become a bloody battleground between the Austrians and Russians," Shmuel warned.

"Does this mean that Pincus cannot come for us? He promised me this year."

"I'm afraid not. The borders have been closed. All of Europe is affected. We are all stuck here until the end of the war."

Clara placed a palm on her cheek, rocked her head back and forth, and asked, "How can this be possible?"

"For now we need to prepare. Soon the news will spread through the village, and there will be a run on food and supplies." He looked directly at Clara. "Buy what you need for your family now, today, before the news reaches the village and it's all gone."

Clara couldn't speak. She stood up, turned and walked away, stunned. Shmuel called after her, but she heard nothing. The walk from the shul back home was a blur. The challenges of the past years now seemed small. How could she protect her family from war?

CHAPTER 38

THE TZADDIK

Moshe couldn't sit any longer. He rose and walked over to the hundreds of old books in the rabbi's study. He had never been in here before, and the musty smell of old leather and decay filled his nostrils. The first book that caught his eye was the largest book on the shelves. In large gold-leaf type, the title on the binding read: *The Atlas of the World*. He carefully slipped it out and placed it on the large wooden desk.

Where is America? he wondered, gently turning the large crisp pages.

"Good morning, Moshe," the rabbi greeted him. "What are you looking at?"

"Oh, hello Rabbi," Moshe said, startled. "I found your atlas, and I'm trying to find America. Is that okay?"

"Of course, Moshe. Let me help you."

Rabbi Shapira stood next to Moshe and flipped the pages to the section titled North America. "The atlas is divided by continents. America is here," he said. "Now let's find where your father is. He's living in New York City, isn't that so, Moshe?"

Moshe nodded his head. "In a place called the Lower East Side, his letters say."

The rabbi found the pages for New York State. "Let's see, here it is. New York City."

Moshe leaned in as the rabbi pointed to the southeast corner of the island of Manhattan. He imagined his father working in his cobbler shop and wondered if he missed him or even thought about him.

"Moshe," the rabbi said, closing the giant book. "Come, sit. I need to speak with you."

Moshe sat down in an old upholstered chair with horsehair stuffing escaping from worn and torn splits in the fabric. It poked sharply at Moshe through his lightweight pants, causing him to shift uncomfortably.

The rabbi explained to Moshe about a conversation he had with his mother about his "episodes."

"What's an *episode*?" Moshe asked, unfamiliar with the word.

"It's those times when you feel sick right before something bad happens. She shared several events with me," he said. The rabbi counted off each instance starting with his index finger. "The first time she recalled was right before you and Max stumbled upon those men in the woods, and shortly thereafter in the basement with Max. Are all these true, Moshe?"

"They're true, Rabbi," he answered, feeling ashamed.

The rabbi put his large bony hand over the boy's. "It's nothing to feel bad about. You have a sense of knowing when danger is imminent."

Moshe looked confused.

"You know when something bad is about to occur," the rabbi clarified.

"Why does this happen to me?"

"I have been thinking about what happens to you, and I believe I have found an answer in the Talmud," he said, pointing to the large leather-bound volumes resting on the desk in front of him.

"You are a *tzaddik*, Moshe."

"I'm a what?"

"A *tzaddik*, a healer. Not a healer like a doctor, but a healer of souls. A *tzaddik* provides solace to those in despair. Your ability to foresee danger is a clue. The teachings tell us that the *tzaddikim* first begin their journeys as empaths. That's why you feel sick when danger is looming. It's the raw expression of your empathy, Moshe. You have an ability to literally feel the pain of others. The empath is affected by the energy of other people. This is just the seed of your abilities yet to be developed."

He thought about the times when the sickness came. *Are these really signs that foresee danger, as the rabbi says?*

"I am a *tzaddik*," he said. He did like the way the word sounded.

The rabbi smiled. "Yes Moshe, I believe you are."

Moshe took another look at the impressive volumes lying in front of him.

"The books say that there are only thirty-six *tzaddikim* on the earth at any one time. The teachings also say that the journey of the *tzaddikim* offers two paths, one of light and one of darkness," he warned. "The evil ones prey on weak souls, sucking out what they need for their own use until their prey wither and die."

"I want to help people, Rabbi," said Moshe.

"You will, Moshe. But you will need to study with me so I can teach you the ways of the *tzaddik* and start you on your journey." The rabbi rose from his chair and moved to stare out the window.

"Our time is short, Moshe. There are many dangers. Not only is war at our doorstep, but within the year you will be a bar mitzvah. Once you cross the threshold into manhood, you will be a target for recruitment by the dark side." He turned to look at the boy. "This is why you need to be strong and prepared."

....

Lost in thoughts racing through his mind, he didn't notice Max joining him on his walk home.

"I've been calling your name since you left the shul. Are you okay?"

"Sorry, Max, I'm okay," he said unconvincingly.

"You sure, are you sick again? Like the time in the basement?" Max asked.

Moshe did feel sick. He sat on the walkway and leaned against of the wall of the butcher shop. "Something bad is about to happen," Moshe said ominously.

Then it began. Soft low booms sent gentle vibrations that rattled the butcher shop windows. Gradually, the booms became louder, and the rumbles intensified. A faint smell of sulfur drifted past the boys.

Moshe looked at Max with wide eyes. "It's the war. It's begun."

CHAPTER 39

IT'S TOO LATE

Pincus marched down Ludlow and turned onto Grand, heading to the Landsman Society's office in a foul mood. He thought the society's president should not be the one to greet the new families arriving from Krzywcza. Mendel usually handled such interactions, but today he had a meeting with his son's teacher at school that he couldn't miss.

On top of that, the renovations at the shop had now stretched into months instead of weeks. It had all started with that fiasco of the triple homicide. The shop was closed for the police investigation, even before the renovations could begin.

He still didn't believe what Jakob told him about that night. How he had met this Jewish gangster called the Monk. This so called Jewish Monk wanted to meet that Jewish gangster Gorpatsch, who was dating Jakob's girlfriend, Nita. Jakob said that he'd planned to set up this meeting at the shop and inform the police about it, with the intention of getting them both arrested. The end result would be that he'd have Nita all to himself.

But not surprisingly, things didn't go as planned, because Gorpatsch had shot the Monk and the DA, and for some unexplained reason, there had been no arrests. *How could something like this happen in a simple cobbler shop, of all places*, he thought and decided to discuss it further with Jakob.

And what would Clara think? She is expecting me to be creating a good wholesome life for our family. I need to get things under control.

....

The Hertzbergs were already waiting for him at his office. He recognized Chaim and Gussie and their three boys as he walked down the hall. He took a breath as he entered and forced a smile.

"So nice to see you, Chaim," he said, shaking his hand. "Gussie, you look wonderful. How was the journey?" Before anyone could answer, he continued, "Look at your boys, how much they've grown. Please sit and tell me everything."

He had no patience for ceremony. He made it quick, giving them the welcome package that included the list of services the society provided, a directory of housing in the Lower East Side, a sheet listing local employment opportunities, the names and addresses of community synagogues, a brochure about the society's cemetery, and a box from the Landsman's Sisterhood packed with an assortment of useful items such as blankets, a frying pan, and bars of bath soap.

"If you need anything, please don't hesitate to ask," he said, ushering them out the door and on their way to their new life.

Finally, Pincus had time to relax and maybe grab an early lunch. He decided to get a bite to eat at Katz's Deli. On the way, he gave the newsboy a nickel for *The Forward*. As it was late morning, the deli had many open tables, and he found a seat next to the large window facing Delancey Street. He ordered his favorite corned beef sandwich with cabbage on rye bread and a cream soda. Sitting back, he folded his newspaper for easy reading, grabbed half a sour pickle from the jar on the table, took a bite, and nearly choked. The headline emblazoned across the banner of the newspaper read: "War Declared. All of Europe in Turmoil."

CHAPTER 40

AN EYE FOR AN EYE

Jakob looked forward to Gorpatsch's business trips to Berlin and Warsaw, as they gave him and Nita free rein to frolic in the city. Normally they would rendezvous in secret places, which added spice to their budding romance. But with each month that passed, Jakob yearned more and more for the day when they could be together like a normal couple. Whenever he pressed Nita, however, she only smiled, gently touched his cheek, and told him to be patient.

But with the borders closed because of war waging across Europe, all travel plans were cancelled indefinitely. This had several unpleasant consequences. He and Nita would need to find new and innovative ways to spend time together. It seemed that the entire city, from the police to the street sweepers, were the eyes and ears of the city's most powerful gangster. Sneaking around would be futile.

Anyway, there was little time for romance. He worked all day for Pincus, and most evenings for Gorpatsch. After the brutal killing of the Monk, Gorpatsch had taken control of the city's most lucrative rackets. Some nights, Jakob would coordinate liquor deliveries to the brothels. Other times, Gorpatsch sent him to visit those who were in arrears of their high-interest loans.

He had no idea why Gorpatsch had summoned him to his office today. The mustached man had stopped by the shop earlier that day and told him that the motorcar would be waiting for him around the corner at six o'clock.

"I'm leaving now," Jakob said, poking his head into the workroom. Pincus glanced up and gave a brief wave goodbye.

"You okay, Pincus?" Jakob asked.

"I'm fine."

Ever since the shop reopened, Pincus had refocused his efforts on the business.

He imagined that Pincus didn't want to talk about his wife and four children being stuck in a war zone. He should have gone back years earlier. Now it was too late. Hopefully they would survive, and he could get them when the war ended.

....

Jakob kicked off his shoes as usual. The white carpet still looked as perfect and unsoiled as the last time he'd visited.

"Go right in. Mr. Gorpatsch is expecting you," said the assistant, gesturing to the door behind her.

"Jakob, thank you for coming. Please sit," he said, indicating the unoccupied chair in front of the desk.

As he approached, the person sitting in the other chair turned around.

"Hello, Jakob. It's good to see you."

"Captain Becker," Jakob said in surprise.

"I asked the captain to join us," Gorpatsch explained.

Jakob nodded to the captain and sat down next to him.

"As you know, Europe is at war. This has temporarily shut down my business interests in Berlin and Warsaw. When one doors closes, another opens," he said, smiling, leaning back in his chair, and cupping his hands behind his head.

"Germany is at war with Russia, and as you know, there is no love between the Jews and the Russians. It looks like we have an enemy in common with Germany. War always makes for strange bedfellows."

"As Jews, Jakob, it is our duty to assist our friends." He pointed toward Captain Becker. "The German-born captain and I have been talking about how we can help the war effort in defeating the Russians," he said in a serious tone and looking directly at Jakob.

Jakob, who had no idea what Gorpatsch was talking about, sat there dumbstruck.

Gorpatsch deliberately spoke more slowly then so Jakob could understand. "We are going to smuggle guns to the Jews in Galicia, where the fighting is most fierce. I have heard from my connections in Warsaw that the rabbis are encouraging young men to take up arms against the Russians. They have openly declared this as a holy war, classifying the Russians as the most hated enemy since biblical times."

"What does this have to do with me?" Jakob asked.

"Several wealthy and influential Jewish friends have approached me about getting weapons into Galicia." Gorpatsch stood up and walked over to a table where a shotgun lay.

"The captain has procured five hundred Remington pump-action shotguns, a very deadly weapon at close range," he said, lifting the gun and handing it to Jakob.

"We have made arrangements with the Hamburg-Amerika Line to take our shipment to the docks at Hamburg. That's the line you took here, isn't it, Jakob?"

Jakob nodded.

"With immigration grinding to halt because of the war, they are desperately looking for business. Of course, they cannot legally transport arms in a passenger liner, especially in wartime. That's why we have hidden them in crates with shipments of coats and blankets from my factories being donated to the soldiers. If anyone opens the crates, that's what they will find."

Gorpatsch then walked over to the large map of Eastern Europe that hung on the wall and pointed to a series of connected highways marked in red. "The guns will be loaded onto a wagon in Hamburg and will travel this route to Krakow, where we'll make our delivery."

"And you're telling me all this because?" Jakob asked hesitantly.

"The captain and I want you to personally take these guns from here to Krakow."

"Me?" Jakob asked. "This sounds crazy and dangerous."

"I know, and if you refuse, I'll understand, and I won't hold it against you. But you should remember that these Cossacks have subjected our people to countless acts of rape, murder, and unheard-of brutality for way too long. It's time to exact revenge, Jakob. An eye for an eye."

CHAPTER 41

A SECOND CHANCE

Pincus looked around at his tools—the leather press, hammers, punches, and pliers—and thought of his father. *He would be proud of me, proud of the shop I've created here,* Pincus thought. *With just my clothes and these tools in my valise, I've built a successful business.* But then he scowled as his thoughts took a dark turn. *But at what cost? Could the lives of my wife and my four children be the price I have to pay for the choices I've made?*

Hunched over his sewing machine, pumping the pedal, and watching the needle bob up and down, he felt sadness overwhelm him. With all transportation shut down and even the mail delivery canceled because of the war, he had no choice now but to wait for the war to end before he could see his family.

Why did I wait so long? he kept asking himself. *I could have gone back last year. Between the murders in my shop and the start of this war, coming to America could turn out to be the worst decision I've ever made. If something happens to them, I don't know what I'll do.*

The bell jingled, signaling the opening of the front door. Pincus slowly stood up and reluctantly walked to the storefront. "Oh, it's you, Jakob," he said, and turned to walk back behind the curtain blocking the view to his workshop.

"Pincus, I need to speak with you," Jakob called after him. "Come on back, let's talk here."

Pincus sat down on his work stool and watched Jakob as he lifted himself onto the countertop between dozens of pairs of shoes waiting for the cobbler's hands.

"I'm leaving. I need to do something and I won't be back for a while. Maybe a few months," Jakob said.

"Leaving? Leaving for where?"

"I really can't say. But it's something that I need to do."

"Great, that's just great, and what am I supposed to do here without you?"

"Come on, it won't be so hard finding someone to handle the customers. You'll be fine."

"I don't know if I'll ever be fine again," Pincus said with a sigh.

....

Pincus lay awake in his bed. He could hear Jakob snoring a few feet away. "Jakob, are you awake?"

When Jakob continued to snore, Pincus repeated the question loud enough to wake him.

"What is it Pincus? What's wrong?"

"I made a mistake not going back to Krzywcza sooner. Now it's too late. From what I read in the newspaper, my family is living in a war zone. How could I have done such a thing?" he said, struggling to hold back tears. The last thing he wanted to do was to cry in front of Jakob.

Jakob got up, lit a candle, and placed it on the small nightstand next to his bed. "Pincus, I know this is very tough for you. But you must believe that they'll be safe. There's nothing you can do about it now."

"I know that. But I won't be able to live with myself if something *does* happen to them."

Both men sat in silence for a while as the candlelight flickered strange patterns of light on the ceiling. Pincus rubbed away the tears he could no longer hold back.

"Pincus, I need to tell you something." Jakob stood up, walked over to the window, and sat on the sill. He told Pincus about his plan to escort the contraband to the Jewish fighters in Galicia. "I'm to make the delivery to Krakow. That's not too far from Krzywcza is it?"

"A few days' ride by wagon," Pincus said.

"Come with me. You can help me with the shipment, and then I'll go with you to Krzywcza. We'll rescue your family and bring them here."

Pincus, now sitting up in bed, stared at Jakob with his mouth open, the tears no longer running down his face.

"And Pincus, there's one more thing. They are paying me two thousand dollars, a thousand now and another thousand when we make the delivery. I'll split it with you," he said, pulling out a wad of cash from his pocket and showing it to Pincus.

"I don't care about the money," Pincus said, lying back down and staring at the flickers of candlelight on the ceiling. Both men said nothing for a good minute.

Suddenly Pincus jumped to his feet. "I'll do it. I'll go with you. I need to save my family."

"You'd better get dressed first," Jakob said with a smile at Pincus, who was standing there naked except for his briefs.

CHAPTER 42

THE RUSSIAN GUESTS

Clara figured they had enough food at least to get through the winter. If it had not been for Shmuel's warning about the war now raging at their doorstep, they would be starving by now. A large assortment of grains, root vegetables, sugar, goose liver, flour, meat, and beans were stored in the cellar.

Her mother and her daughter Jennie had helped to cook a variety of meals for the family and the usual guests—Shmuel, and Moshe's friend Max, who naturally had open invitations. They ate only once a day, in the early afternoon. Clara looked forward to Shmuel's visits. He came with news about the war that was raging in full force only a few miles away.

What was known was that the Austrian General Conrad had pushed back the unprepared Russian army north and into Ukraine. But the Russians had regrouped and pressed forward, causing the Austrians to fall back, and in desperation they had formed a defensive line along the cities of Lemberg, Prxmysl, and Krakow. She knew these cities well; Krzywcza sat directly between Prxmysl and Krakow.

"Mama, Shmuel is here," Moshe called to his mother as he supervised Anna and Hymie, who were peeling potatoes for the soup.

"Moshe, tell him to take off his boots," ordered Grandmother.

Shmuel kicked off his snow- and mud-covered boots, placed his hat, scarf, and coat on the chair by the door, and gave a Moshe a hug. "Will it ever stop snowing, Moshe?"

"Shmuel, come tell me the news. What have you heard?" asked Clara.

Shmuel greeted the children and their grandmother before walking over to Clara, who sat at the large kitchen table, cutting beets for the horseradish.

"It's not going well for the Austrian army, the rabbi says. The Russians have broken through gaps in the line, and General Conrad had to order the army to retreat into the mountains. All of Galicia is now under Russian control," Shmuel said, grabbing a potato and a knife.

"Oh, this is bad," Clara said. "What about the Germans?"

"From what we hear, the Germans have captured Lodz and are trying to push into Warsaw, but the Russians have held them back."

Moshe and Clara listened intently to every word. "What about the Jews?" Moshe asked. "Last time you told us that we were fighting alongside the Austrians."

"That's still happening, Moshe. Jewish men all across Galicia are being given the rabbinical blessing to fight this holy war against the Russian barbarians."

"Mama, I want to go fight," Moshe said.

Clara dropped the knife, leaned over, and smacked Moshe across the face. "Don't say such a crazy thing. You're twelve years old, and I am not going to lose you."

Moshe touched his stinging cheek. "Okay, Mama."

"I'm sorry, Moshe," she said, hugging him.

....

With everyone asleep, Clara looked out the window onto a moon-lit street covered with a blanket of fresh snow. The winds howled, and occasional bursts of faint flashes of light could be seen over the treetops in the distance, followed by low booms.

She had slept little since the war began. No one, not even her mother, knew that she sat guard every night. Not that she could do much if anyone approached the house. Tonight, under the bright light of the moon, she could see clearly down the street to the marketplace.

Clara couldn't stay awake and fell into a deep sleep. Slumped in the chair, she had a vivid dream of Pincus. In the dream, she opens the front door and Pincus stands there with the same valise he left with. "I'm back, Clara," he says. She slams the door in his face and locks it.

Pincus knocks and knocks and screams, "Clara, please, I'm sorry. Open the door, Clara!"

The rumbling of the floorboards startled Clara awake from the dream. She jumped up from the chair and looked out the window. Marching in formation, moving directly toward her house, was a band of Russian soldiers.

She spun around in a panic. "Children, wake up quickly," she said, not too loudly. "Come, Jennie, wake up," she said, shaking her oldest daughter awake. "Mother, you need to wake up. Everyone into the cellar right now."

With the help of Jennie, the children got to their feet and ran down the stairs into the dark cellar. As soon as her mother's head was clear, Clara closed the cellar door and slid a straw rug on top.

A loud knock rattled the door in its frame. With hands shaking and her heart pounding so hard it hurt, she opened the door. A tall thin man of no more than twenty-five years of age stood there. His faced was smeared with a mixture of dried blood and mud. Light powdered snow had accumulated in the creases of a coat that was clearly too big for his skinny frame.

"What do you want?" She spoke sternly as a way to conceal her fear.

"Madam, please excuse us for the late hour," the man said in broken Polish.

Clara inhaled a breath to calm herself in order to understand the Russian soldier struggling with the language.

"My name is Lieutenant Alexi Ivanov. My men need rest. Would you allow officers to spend night in home? Make us something to eat?" said the young lieutenant.

With her hands shaking uncontrollably, she managed to agree.

The officer turned and waved to two men who stood shivering in the road. The company of enlisted men scattered behind them, seeking refuge in nearby barns and stables.

The officers entered, taking off their coats, hats, gloves, and boots. The snow quickly melted and small puddles of water formed on the wooden floorboards.

They were all around the same age, and none of them looked well fed. Like moths to a flame, they quickly found the stove and huddled around it, relishing its warmth.

"Thank you very much. Allow me to introduce," Alexi said. He put his hand on the shoulder of a much shorter man with a darker complexion. "This is Boris Popov."

Boris gave a slight smile and nodded to Clara.

"And this is my brother Vadim."

"Thank you," said Vadim, who looked identical to his brother Alexi.

"Twins?" Clara asked looking back and forth at the two brothers.

"Yes, I'm older one," said Alexi.

"By two minutes," joked Vadim.

"My name is Clara. Please sit down, let me see what I can find for you to eat. I don't have much, as you can imagine." She placed three bowls on the table and a few pieces of stale bread. Then she ladled warm leftover soup into the bowls.

"Where is family, Clara?" said Vadim.

"I am here alone. My family has emigrated to America." She immediately regretted saying this.

"And you stayed behind?" Alexi asked in surprise.

Thinking fast, she remembered something Pincus had told her. "Oh, I did go with them. But on the voyage to America I became ill, and I didn't pass the medical inspection, so they sent me back. I plan to return as soon as the war is over."

....

The night passed without incident. Clara sat in her chair while the three soldiers slept and snored. In the morning, they thanked her politely and left.

Clara looked out through the window until she felt safe, and then she kicked away the straw mat and opened the cellar door. Grabbing the kerosene lamp, she flew down the steps and saw Moshe lying on the dirt floor looking deathly ill.

"Moshe, are you okay? Are you having an episode?"

Moshe lifted his head and pointed weakly across the cellar into the darkness. Clara moved the lamp and saw her mother lying prone on the ground with her head resting in Jennie's lap.

Jennie looked up with tears streaming down her face. "Grandmother is dead, Mama."

CHAPTER 43

THE PRINCE OF PRUSSIA

I t felt like a lifetime ago that Pincus had first boarded the *SS Amerika*. Back then, he had been poked, stuck, humiliated, sick, and abused. But this time he would spend the extra money he had saved and purchase a first-class cabin. The cost was much less than he expected since traveling in winter to a continent at war was not very popular.

Before the war, Pincus had fantasized this trip as his triumphant arrival home. He would be the returning hero, the man who offered a future in America for the families of Krzywcza. He had relished the idea of being recognized publicly by the rabbi. He'd imagined himself walking with Clara on his arm through the streets of the village, and his name being called out with shouts of gratitude.

Instead his homecoming would be one of shame. How could he have ignored his family for so long? How could he have been so blinded by his own need for success and respect that he would put his family in such danger?

When Pincus put the sign on his shop window announcing its closing, he prayed that Hashem would forgive his disgrace on the day he returned to reopen his shop along with his family safe and sound.

He was taking one last look down Delancey Street before stepping into the wagon that would take him to the pier, when he saw Mendel Beck walking toward him.

"Pincus, I'm happy to catch you before you left," said Mendel, flushed.

"What is it?" Pincus asked.

"Please don't leave Shmuel behind. Somehow bring him back with you. He has been good to your family. Don't leave my boy there," Mendel said in tears.

Pincus put down his valise and put his hands on Mendel's shoulders. "I will bring him home, I promise."

Mendel wrapped his arms around Pincus and hugged him tight. "Thank you. Be safe and come back with your family. The store and the Landsman Society will be waiting for your return."

....

Despite the frigid temperature, Jakob insisted on staying topside until he saw his cargo lifted and safely stored on board the ship.

"There, that's it," he said.

"Can we go inside now?" Pincus asked with chattering teeth as the wintry winds swirled across the harbor. The incessant spray off the whitecaps sculpted immense icicles that rooted themselves into the steel of the *SS Amerika*. Pincus thought the ship looked like it had just arrived from an expedition to Antarctica.

"Let's go get you warm," Jakob said, patting his friend on the back.

....

Later that evening, as the *SS Amerika* set sail out of New York Harbor and into the Atlantic, Pincus watched Jakob button up his jacket.

"That's a nice suit, Jakob," Pincus said, putting away his few pieces of clothing in the elegantly carved wooden bureau.

"Thank you. I bought this for my first date with Nita."

Pincus liked Jakob and, in a way, found his vanity amusing. He wished that he had also bought a new suit. It would have been better than this moth-eaten brown wool jacket that he had worn for the past ten years.

They found their way from their cabin to the carpeted staircase that led to the glass doors opening into the main dining hall. The maître d', clad in a crisp white jacket, greeted them.

"Right this way, gentlemen," he said.

Following the maître d' to their table, Jakob elbowed Pincus and directed him with a nod to the table at the center of the cavernous room. Pincus turned to look at a table for four that indeed deserved his attention. There sat a young man dressed in a military uniform. *How remarkable,* Pincus thought, *he sits as if he were standing at attention. Maybe it's because of all the emblems and metals decorating his blood-red jacket that prevents him from a natural slouch.*

Sitting next to the officer was an even younger woman. She wore a delicate white dress, and a small blue hat was perched on top of her braided bun. Two other men in uniform completed the group.

As they took their seats at their table, Jakob asked the maître d' who they were.

"That is His Royal Highness Price Adalbert. He is the third son of our monarch, Kaiser Wilhelm. The woman next to him is the Princess Adelaide. They are returning from their honeymoon."

Jakob and Pincus sat alone at a table meant for ten. Pincus ran his hand across the spotless white tablecloth. He lifted a knife and admired its polish, then regarded the dinner plate emblazoned with the ship's blue-and-orange insignia. Pincus marveled at the assortment of glassware and how it sparkled from the illumination of the crystal chandeliers slightly swinging overhead.

"Jakob, this is crazy. Here we are traveling like royalty, while my family's lives are in danger," he said as he gestured to the prince and princess.

"Not so crazy," Jakob said quietly. "We need to figure out a way of moving the guns from Hamburg to Kattowitz, and this prince may be the answer."

"Why would he want to do that?" Pincus asked.

Jakob leaned into Pincus and whispered, "We're going to put guns in the hands of soldiers to fight the Russians. We have a common enemy."

"Those men sitting with him. . . ." Pincus glanced over to their table. "They're probably bodyguards. How do you think you'll get close to the prince?"

"I'm going to walk over there right now and ask the prince if he would join me for a cigar and a schnapps after dinner," Jakob said, producing a few cigars from his jacket pocket.

"Where did you get those?" Pincus asked with surprise.

"I bought them from a pushcart on Mulberry," he said, sliding one of the hand-rolled cigars across his upper lip. "Heavenly," he added taking a deep breath. He stood up, buttoned his jacket, and walked across the empty dining hall to the royal table. As he approached, the bodyguards took defensive postures to protect the royal couple. Pincus could see Jakob speaking to the men and then reaching into his pocket to pull out the cigars. The guards looked back at the prince, who nodded and smiled. Next thing Pincus saw was Jakob shaking hands with the prince and princess.

Returning to the table with a big smile, Jakob said, "We are drinking schnapps with the prince tonight in the smoking room."

"Not me Jakob. You're better at this. I'll head back to the cabin and go to sleep. Tell me what happened in the morning."

CHAPTER 44

THE RIGHTEOUS ONE

Moshe sat in the rabbi's study waiting for his daily lesson. Since the war started, the rabbi had insisted that he visit with him every day.

"Moshe, there is much to learn. I must teach you in a short time what has taken me years to understand," said the rabbi.

It had been a few months since that fateful day of the attack by the killers. Mother had had her hands full settling the children after the terrible stabbing. Then she'd had to deal with the humiliating police investigation.

Luckily Captain Berbecki had vacated his post as police captain to become an officer in the Russian army. Any criminal charges against his mother or Shmuel were forgotten about.

With the full outbreak of war and armies from both sides marching across the countryside and through Krzywcza, his mother had new worries. The visit by the three Russian officers to their home had been too much for Grandmother to bear, and her passing had left Mother in a melancholy state.

He wanted to stay with her as much as possible, but she insisted on his daily lessons with the rabbi. "Go. I'll be fine for a few hours."

Moshe still could not comprehend that he had some special powers that he shared with only thirty-five others in the entire world. At first his special ability to help people excited him. But the more he learned, the more he understood the responsibilities his powers entailed. On top of that, some of these other *tzaddikim* had evil intentions, and that put him at risk of falling prey to them.

Since Grandmother had died, he hadn't had any more episodes, even with all the suffering taking place around him. He asked the rabbi in one of his first lessons, "Why don't I feel the suffering from the war?"

"It's not surprising. These premonitions you have occur only when evil is about to affect you or someone close to you," explained the rabbi. "The death and destruction taking place all around us has not found you. At least not yet."

"But how can I live with this reoccurring illness?" asked Moshe.

"Once you learn how to channel your abilities, you'll be able to buffer your physiological episodes. In other words, Moshe, you can numb yourself to a point that you can still feel someone's pain without doing harm to yourself."

....

While he waited for the rabbi, Moshe scanned his eyes across the hundreds of books filling the shelves. *It must have taken a lifetime to accumulate so many books. Has he read all of these?*

"Good morning, Moshe," the rabbi called out, entering the study. "Sorry to keep you waiting. I needed to comfort Mr. and Mrs. Benzur. Their son just joined the army to go fight the Russians."

"I heard that Dovid left yesterday. Maybe I should also go to fight?"

"You cannot go, Moshe. Your work with me is too important to risk your life. Remember what I taught you, that there are only thirty-six *tzaddikim* on earth at any one time. If one should perish leaving less than that number, the world would be in peril. You must continue your studies with me."

"I understand, Rabbi," Moshe said. "Tell me, have you read all these books?"

The rabbi turned to survey the books behind him. "I have, Moshe. It looks like a lot, but you know that I am nearly ninety years old, and that has given me plenty of time to read," he said with a beam of warmth.

"Are you a *tzaddik,* Rabbi?"

"That's a good question, Moshe. I was not born a *tzaddik* like you. But when I have my ninetieth birthday in a few weeks, I will, in a way, become a *tzaddik.* The word *tzaddik* also translates to the number ninety, and if one is so lucky to live to such an old age, our imminent death brings us closer to Hashem." The rabbi paused to allow Moshe to absorb the lesson.

"The basic understanding is that a *tzaddik* is an extension of Hashem placed here in the world to help people, which the *tzaddik* does by tapping into the almighty's powers. A *tzaddik* exists to serve as an offshoot of Hashem. He is the righteous one, the leader and teacher of a generation."

Moshe looked at the rabbi, his mouth open in awe.

"I know Moshe, there's a lot to absorb." The rabbi patted Moshe on his shoulder. "Don't be overwhelmed. I will guide you as long as possible. But I want you to remember one thing right now." He paused and leaned closer. "No one is to know you are a *tzaddik,* ever."

The rabbi's words sent a chill through Moshe. He had known he had a gift that required nurturing, but keeping it a secret added something new and worrisome. Could he muster the strength to live up to his responsibilities?

CHAPTER 45

THE SMOKING ROOM

Jakob sat alone at a table in the smoking room. The prince and his entourage had not yet arrived. A few other passengers were scattered around the other tables. He had never seen such elegance. The walls were finished with dark mahogany wood paneling. Geometrically spaced columns capped with elaborate wood-carved capitals flowed into the decorative plaster ceiling scrolled with symmetrical designs. The ship's blue-and-orange colors were repeated in the pattern of the wall-to-wall carpeting.

While the men at the other tables smoked their cigars, Jakob thought it a good idea to fight the temptation to light up. It would be rude to be smoking when the prince arrived.

As he lounged in the comfortable velvet upholstered chairs, he could easily imagine Gorpatsch socializing in a smoking lounge similar to this one on a business trip to Europe. He also knew that, with him out of the country, Nita would clearly be spending more time alone with Gorpatsch. This sudden image soured his mood. Gorpatsch and Nita were probably hitting the town right now. People would be drooling at the glamorous couple pulling up to his club in his fancy motorcar. What chance did he have, trying to compete with one of the richest men in New York?

Not only was Gorpatsch rich, he was also a criminal master-mind. Jakob had not had a clue that Gorpatsch and the captain had set him up to seek out a meeting with the Monk and then orchestrated the confrontation at the shop. When Gorpatsch had put a bullet between the eyes of the Monk and the district attor-ney, Jakob knew that his life would be linked to Gorpatsch. There would be no easy escape.

But he had to admit to himself that the main reason he'd accepted the offer to run guns was for the money. Two grand was a lifetime worth of earnings. Even splitting the money with Pincus, he would still have far more than he could ever have imagined as a boy growing up poor in Warsaw. He would have enough to marry Nita, buy an uptown apartment, and still have extra to live on without ever working again.

The other reason was to help Pincus rescue his family. How could he not help the only real friend he'd ever had? He smiled remembering their first meeting on the ship and how sick Pincus had been, how Jakob had had to carry him like a child to the deck. It was a strange friendship, but he was grateful for it.

A disturbance in the hallway shook Jakob out of his day-dream. He rushed over to the entrance of the smoking lounge to see what the brouhaha was all about. Just as he approached, he saw Prince Adalbert pull back his arm, a leather glove held in his hand, and attempt to slap it across a man's face. The man, dressed in a fine black floor-length coat, reacted instantly. He caught the prince by the wrist, and twisted his arm, forcing him to the ground on one knee and causing him to release the glove that fell harmlessly to the floor.

Jakob reacted instinctively and shoved the man backwards. He tripped over the prince's knee, stumbled, and fell hard. Jakob pounced, pinning him to the plush carpeting. "Why are you assaulting the prince?" he asked breathlessly, his heart pounding.

"Stop! Get up," the prince called out in a jovial manner.

Jakob turned and looked up, keeping his opponent securely pinned. "Who is this man, Your Majesty?"

"His name is Gerald Richter. He's my friend. We like to play this little game of duel. We've done it since we were children. Now let him go," said the prince, very much amused.

Jakob released his grip and rose to his feet. His face was flushed, his shirt damp with sweat, and he looked befuddled. "I don't understand."

"We were just having some fun. Now help my poor friend Gerald up," pleaded the prince.

Jakob looked down at the man he just assaulted, who lay prone on his back, his black coat draped across the floor, staring back at him. Jakob leaned over, clasped his hand, and helped him back on his feet. "My apologies, Mr. Richter."

"Don't be silly. A perfectly acceptable misunderstanding, Mr. . . um . . . your name is?"

"Jakob Adler, sir. I thought you and the prince. . . ." his voice trailed off.

"Yes, we sometimes get a little carried away with our charades," said Richter, laughing.

"Come now, Mr. Adler, you've earned your drink," said the prince, gesturing toward the smoking lounge.

Jakob followed the prince and Richter quickly through the groupings of tables and chairs to the back of the smoking lounge. There the prince parted a burgundy velour curtain and disappeared into a private room. Richter pulled back the curtain, turned and gestured for Jakob to enter.

It was as if he'd stepped into another world. Not even in the private club that Gorpatsch owned had he ever seen such opulence. The curved walls featured deeply tufted fabric upholstery in the same burgundy velour. Oversized cushions were scattered across a half-round banquette that wrapped around the room and surrounded a round table topped in navy blue felt. The prince slid in with care to avoid hitting his head on the crystal chandelier. Richter and Jakob joined him on either side.

Jakob worried that his opportunity for a private moment with the prince to discuss the guns might have been lost. He needed to learn more about this man before he could risk sharing his plans.

"So, Mr. Adler, let me properly introduce my friend, retired Colonel Gerald Richter," said the prince.

"Retired? You look too young to be retired," said Jakob.

"In my case, early retirement," Richter replied.

"My brave friend here incurred a severe concussion from an explosion on the battlefield in Flanders. As a result, he experiences violent episodes that may endanger his fellow officers and enlisted men under the duress of battle," explained the prince.

"I am sorry to hear that," said Jakob.

"Now he serves the royal court. . . ." He paused, and then continued, "And assists me in my duties."

"I don't think the princess enjoyed having a third wheel on her honeymoon, your highness," Richter added.

"No, she didn't," the prince replied with a chuckle. "Now, tell me about you and your friend. Where is he, and why is he not joining us?"

"That's Pincus. He needed some rest and went back to the cabin. He asked me to send his regrets," said Jakob.

"Why don't you pull out those cigars and let's order drinks," the prince said, summoning over the waiter. "Do you mind if we skip the schnapps?"

Jakob shrugged in indifference.

"Excellent. Have you ever had the pleasure of cognac?" the prince asked.

"I can't say I ever had."

After toasting the meeting of new friends, the prince took a long drag on his cigar, exhaled, looked directly at Jakob, and said, "Tell me why you and your friend Pincus are traveling first-class in the dead of winter to a country at war?"

CHAPTER 46

THE PRINCESS

Pincus awoke early as usual. The first-class accommodation provided the most comfortable bed he had ever slept in. He got to his feet and looked out the porthole. A thick layer of ice covered the glass and blocked his view of the vast ocean. He knew the comfort and warmth of the cabin would be short lived. Soon he and Jakob would try to move five hundred rifles through Germany and then across the battlefield in Galicia.

While he dressed, he could hear Jakob snoring in the other room and wondered how the evening had gone with the prince. Assuming he would sleep a while longer, Pincus quietly left the cabin in search of coffee.

He followed the maître d' to a table near the center of the near-empty dining room. While the waiter poured his coffee, Pincus recognized the princess seated alone a few tables away. He watched the graceful way she scooped the sugar into her teacup with a tiny spoon. But why was she here alone, and where was the prince?

She looked up and caught Pincus staring at her. Unperturbed, she offered a delicate smile and a "good morning."

Pincus felt himself blush. He nodded and looked down at the toast the waiter had just placed before him. He knew he had none of the social graces required to interact with someone like the princess, yet, as he nervously spread strawberry jam across his toast, he could sense her continued stare. He chanced a quick glance and noticed that she had stood up and was walking over to his table.

"Good morning. Would you mind if I joined you?" she asked.

"Please do," Pincus said, clearly flustered.

A waiter standing nearby quickly hurried over and pulled the chair out for the princess. She sat down and smiled. Without the makeup and the elegant dress she had worn the night before, she looked like a teenage girl, perhaps only a few years older than his Jennie. Unlike his daughter, the princess had deep blue eyes and long wavy blonde hair.

"My name is Addie, short for Adelaide," she said, placing the white linen napkin across her lap.

"Pincus," he blurted out. "My name is Pincus."

She laughed. "Why are you nervous, Pincus?"

"I'm not nervous," he said, offering her a forced smile.

"That's good. You shouldn't be. Would you mind if I asked you something?"

Pincus nodded, still having trouble speaking. What if he got caught talking to the princess alone? Even he knew this to be improper and unacceptable behavior for a princess, especially a newly married one. What if the prince walked in, or his bodyguards?

Seemingly unflustered by the prospect of any impropriety, the princess asked, "My husband tells me that you and your friend . . . what's his name?"

"Jakob," Pincus answered.

"Right, Jakob. He's very handsome, by the way."

Pincus looked around the room to see if anyone might be overhearing this scandalous conversation.

"I understand that you and Jakob are planning on rescuing your family from war-torn Galicia. This is very brave," she said.

Pincus nodded. "Yes, my wife and four children are in a small village about two hours east of Krakow."

"That is so romantic. I told my husband that he must help you travel safely through Germany to the border. When you find your family, how do you plan to get them out of the country and to America?"

"I don't know. We still need to figure that out."

She leaned over the table and said in a near whisper, "Go to Arendal. It's a city in Norway. You can take a Norwegian America ship."

Pincus listened with interest.

"This may be the last voyage for these steamships crisscrossing the Atlantic. Such travel is getting too dangerous. But there are other ways."

She took a note pad and a pencil from her small purse and wrote something down. "Take this," she said, sliding the paper across the table.

"I wrote down the name and address of my cousin Carl Mortensen. Tell him we met and show him this note. He can arrange safe passage to America. Carl holds a position with the Norwegian America Line. He can get you and your family safely home. It may be costly. Do you have money?"

Pincus nodded.

"Good. Now I must go. Promise to write and tell me of your adventures once you and your family have arrived in America."

"I will, Your Highness," Pincus said, rising to his feet and this time offering a genuine smile.

She returned the smile, stood up, turned, and walked out of the dining hall.

CHAPTER 47

PETER PAN

Jakob awoke to the sun glistening on the icy portholes. He dressed and made his way down the corridor in search for Pincus and something to eat. When he walked into the dining hall, it was clear he had missed breakfast. The wait staff appeared busy setting up for lunch.

Now where could Pincus be? The frigid weather eliminated any chance of him being topside. He peeked into the library. He had never been in a library before. His remembered his father having a few books and his mother teaching him to read when he was young. But after they were murdered, he had needed to survive in the streets and alleyways of Warsaw. In terms of priorities, browsing through a library came way down on the list.

He stepped into the empty library. A few tables and chairs filled the center space of the room. Books lined the walls. Printed signs divided the sections by language: German, English, French, and Italian. He realized he had never even looked at an English book before. Standing before the wall of titles he found one that interested him greatly, *Peter Pan* by J.M. Barrie. The cover had a picture of a boy swinging a sword with a pirate ship in the background. He sat down in one of the chairs and admired the illustrations, while wishing he could read the words.

After a few minutes, his mind started to wander to the events of the previous night. The prince had not been surprised when Jakob told him about the shipment of guns he had smuggled on board.

"You're not the only smuggler on this ship," the prince had said quietly.

Jakob had told the prince about his plan to transport the guns from the Port of Hamburg to the border town nearest to Krakow. There the guns would be given to Jewish soldiers.

"Why would I want to put guns in the hands of Jews?" the prince had asked.

Jakob had told the prince that the rabbis of Galicia had declared this war against Russia to be a holy war. Jewish men were taking up arms and fighting alongside the Austrian armies in the Caspian Mountains. These guns would help with the fight.

The prince appeared pleased. "These are honorable intentions," he had said.

Jakob still needed to find Pincus. It took a few steps down the hallway to realize that he was still clutching the book in his hand. He looked down to the image of Peter Pan and decided that he would hold on to it for a while, and then he would return it.

CHAPTER 48

THE HEALER

Hours before sunrise, Moshe awoke and quietly washed and dressed while his mother, sisters, and brother slept. Even though the walk to the synagogue took only minutes, Moshe had promised his mother that he would wear his coat, hat, and scarf. With his boots laced up, he opened the front door, kissed two fingers on his right hand, and touched the mezuzah nailed to the doorjamb.

With fighting going on in the surrounding fields as well as in the mountains to the south, the synagogue of Krzywcza had become a first aid station for Jewish soldiers fighting against the Russians. Rabbi Shapira had done his best to organize a makeshift army hospital. However the only doctor was the seventy-year-old Dr. Frenkel. The shtetl's best doctor, Dr. Bachman, had emigrated with his family to America the previous year. Fortunately, a few of the women had trained as nurses and provided most of the urgent care.

Moshe entered the synagogue and walked through the sanctuary to the rabbi's study. Not much had changed since he left the previous night. A dozen or so men still lay on blood-stained blankets on the floor. A few with less severe injuries sat or reclined in the pews. Some slept, but most groaned from the pain of their injuries. It took all his fortitude to fight back tears.

Moshe stopped to greet a few of the wounded who had survived the night. Those who had the strength lifted an arm to grasp his extended hand as he knelt down to comfort them.

After a few minutes, he made his way to the rabbi's study and knocked.

"Come in," the rabbi called out.

"Good morning, Rabbi," Moshe said when he entered. As he removed his coat, he noticed how old the rabbi looked. Maybe it was the dark circles under his eyes. They seemed more pronounced today than he remembered.

"Good morning, Moshe," the rabbi said, rising up from his desk chair and walking around to Moshe. "Some of our boys out there," he said, gesturing to the sanctuary beyond the closed door, "have remarked to me and to the nurses that they feel comforted when you visit with them."

Moshe nodded as the rabbi spoke.

"I want you to understand that your training and education do not only take place in this room, but also out there," he said pointing once again to the door. "As a *tzaddik,* you are not only of the flesh, but also a spiritual being. These men who are on death's doorstep will see you as you are, a connection to Hashem."

The rabbi walked over to his window and looked out at the sun, beginning to illuminate the snow-covered streets. As he turned back around, Moshe saw tears running down his face. Moshe took a step forward and asked, "Rabbi, are you all right?"

"I'm fine, Moshe," he said, smiling and wiping the tears away with the back of his hand. "One of the duties of a rabbi is to encourage those just moments from passing to say the Shema prayer. You know this prayer, Moshe?"

"Of course, Rabbi. Hear, O Israel, the Lord is our God, the Lord is One," he recited.

"Good, Moshe, go now. Tend to the wounded, give them comfort, and let them know that Hashem loves them and is waiting for them."

Moshe could hear the cries of the wounded men in the sanctuary as he left the rabbi's study. His attention was drawn to a young man who lay on the floor, calling out in pain. His head was slightly propped up on a folded blanket. Moshe knelt down and took his hand. The man opened his eyes and fell silent. He squeezed Moshe's hand tightly and offered a slight smile before exhaling his last breath.

Just then a hand reached from behind Moshe and gently closed the soldier's eyelids. Moshe turned to see the rabbi and, unable to contain himself, he laid his head on the rabbi's shoulder and sobbed.

Once he regained his composure, Moshe continued to visit the wounded. He wondered what would happen to the shtetl when the rabbi passed. There were a few young men waiting to take over the spiritual and religious leadership of the shul, but none had the experience or the connection that Rabbi Shapira provided to every member of the community. He would be deeply missed.

Moshe felt that familiar unease sweep through his body. He sat down on an empty space on a pew next to a soldier with a head wound who slid down to give Moshe some space. He put his head between his knees to steady himself. The dizziness passed but not the nausea. Then the sweats came. He felt them rushing down his chest and forehead. He looked up and saw the rabbi looking straight at him with concern.

Suddenly a loud disturbance from the street silenced everyone in the sanctuary. Moshe's friend Max, who helped out occasionally, was perched by the window looking out onto the main street leading to the synagogue's front door. "Russian soldiers," he called out.

A thunderous clash rang as the front doors flew open. In rushed soldiers with rifles drawn who took positions along the walls of the sanctuary's main hall. The nurses screamed in fear. Those soldiers who could stand did so with thoughts of defense but realized their actions were futile.

Moshe was still awash in sickness but struggled to his feet just as Captain Berbecki entered. Leather straps crisscrossed his chest, supporting a wide belt around his waist that carried his holstered handgun. He stomped down the sanctuary's main aisle in his knee-high black boots and climbed the three steps to the raised platform where the rabbi conducted services.

He was not surprised to see the captain as a Russian officer. Moshe had heard his mother speak before the war about the captain's affiliation with the Galician Russophiles, a political organization sympathetic with the monstrous Russians.

Berbecki scanned the room until his eyes fell upon the rabbi. "Rabbi, you are harboring enemies of the state."

The rabbi held out his palms. "These are wounded men, Captain, and need our care."

"They are the enemy and you are under arrest," he said, signaling for his men to seize the rabbi.

"Take your hands off him!" Moshe shouted. The captain's attention and that of everyone else in the room turned to Moshe, who stood on the pew surrounded by armed soldiers with rifles now aimed at him.

"Ah, Moshe Potasznik. It's you again causing trouble," declared the captain.

"The rabbi is not well, please leave him be," said Moshe.

"He looks well enough," the captain replied and signaled for his men to take the rabbi away.

Moshe jumped off the pew and ran up to the steps standing before the captain. "Please do not take the rabbi," he pleaded.

The captain, who was a head taller than Moshe, looked down at him. "Okay, Moshe, I will release the rabbi."

Moshe was relieved. "Thank you, Captain."

"In his place we will take you." He pointed to his men, and they grabbed Moshe, who was too weak to resist, and dragged his limp body toward the sanctuary doors.

The captain scanned the room, sweeping his arm across the space, and shouted, "Take these men outside, drag them if they can't walk, and shoot them."

A gasp of protests and screams was the last thing Moshe heard before he passed out. The lives of the thirty-six soldiers were about to be extinguished.

CHAPTER 49

THE GRAY MAN

Jakob woke to the sounds of the ship's horns announcing its arrival into port. Pincus had already left the cabin, probably hours earlier. Now the next part of their adventure would begin. The prince had offered him a wagon large enough to transport the five hundred guns, two strong horses to maneuver the German countryside, and papers for unimpeded travel from Hamburg to Kattowitz. Once they crossed the border into Galicia, they would no longer be under the royal protection.

He made his way to the dining hall for his last meal before disembarking. To his surprise, he saw Pincus having breakfast with the prince and princess. Jakob couldn't help smiling as he approached their table. "Good morning, Your Highnesses," he said with an instinctual bow of his head. "Good morning, Pincus. Would you mind if I joined you?" he asked.

The prince said, "Please do, Jakob," and indicated the empty chair. "Pincus was just enlightening us on the world of shoemaking. I think between the princess and myself, we must have over five hundred pairs of shoes. We would love to have Pincus live at the royal palace as the king's cobbler," he said with a glance at the princess who nodded in agreement.

"That would be wonderful," Pincus said. "Perhaps in another lifetime."

"Of course, we are just joking," said the prince, who then turned his attention to Jakob. "I'm glad you're here." He looked around to ensure that no one could overhear him, and then added, "Your cargo is being offloaded onto the dock as we speak. When you disembark, go see this man." He handed Jakob a note. "Arrangements have been made."

"Thank you, Your Highness," Jakob said.

"You will also need to stop at the customs office before you disembark. As a foreigner, you will need special permission to travel through the country. I have sent instructions to prepare the documents. But it would be my recommendation that you do whatever it takes not to be stopped and searched. Your cargo will interest many, and these papers may offer no protection after all," he warned.

The moment they stepped off the gangplank and into the Port of Hamburg, their first-class treatment ceased. Unlike the prince and princess, who had a luxurious heated motorcar waiting for them, Jakob and Pincus carried their luggage into the frigid morning. Jakob pulled his coat tighter and said to Pincus, "Let's go find our ride."

After a chilling exploration along the waterfront, Jakob looked down at the note once more. It read:

JÜRGEN HARTMANN
STALL 24 NORTH

"Here we are," he said approaching the frozen gray steel door with STALL 24 NORTH emblazoned above it. He wondered if his knocking would be heard, because as he pounded the door, it felt like he was knocking against a block of solid ice.

The door opened, and an older man looking just as gray as everything around him appeared. "Come in quickly," he urged.

Jakob and Pincus hurried in as the door slammed shut behind them.

"It's not much warmer inside," Jakob whispered to Pincus, who seemed too frozen to speak.

The only source of heat came from several steel barrels with sawed-off tops that served as wood-burning stoves. They huddled, holding their palms toward the flames and trying to absorb some warmth into their bodies.

"My name is Jürgen Hartmann," said the gray man. "I have everything prepared as instructed. Come, let me show you."

Jakob inspected the wagon. It looked sturdy enough to carry the weight of five hundred rifles, and the horses appeared healthy and strong.

"Give the horses plenty of water and rest, and you should be able to make it to Kattowitz in seven days."

Jakob took the reins and summoned the horses forward. They set forth into the gray morning with many unknowns before them.

CHAPTER 50

CLARA'S SACRIFICE

Clara thought she heard her name being called. She placed the pot down on the stove and walked over to open the front door to see if someone was outside. She was greeted by a gust of cold wind, dozens of dead leaves, light powdery snow swirling across the floor, and finally Max.

He looked flustered and frightened.

"Mrs. Potasznik, you must come quickly," he said breathlessly. "They've taken Moshe and shot the wounded soldiers. You need to come now," Max said, his eyes bulging.

"What do you mean they've taken Moshe? Who has?"

"Captain Berbecki. He wanted to take the rabbi, but Moshe begged him not to, so they took Moshe instead," Max tried to explain.

"Jennie." She turned to her daughter. "Take care of the children. I'll be back as soon as I can." She grabbed her coat, hat, and scarf and ran from the house.

As Clara approached the synagogue she saw the horror that Max had hinted at. Motionless bodies of young men lay on the blood-stained, snow-packed earth, a mangled array of twisted legs, arms, and torsos. Rivulets of blood streamed down the wall, which was pockmarked with bullet holes.

Clara screamed. "Who could do such a thing?" she wailed.

"Clara," shouted the rabbi from the entryway. "Come inside quickly."

She entered the sanctuary to the wails and cries of the nurses and midwives who had been attending to the wounded just moments before they were dragged out and murdered.

The rabbi took Clara by the elbow and escorted her to his study. She felt everyone's eyes looking at her.

"Where's Moshe?" she demanded the moment the rabbi closed the door to his study.

"Sit down, Clara, and I will tell you."

The rabbi looked very frail as he related what had just happened. "Your son put his life in danger to save the life of an old man. I pray that Hashem provides a path back for Moshe."

"I am not waiting for Hashem, Rabbi. I am going to find this barbarian and bring my boy home," Clara said.

....

Clara hurried home as fast as she could on the icy street. Not wanting to upset the children, she took a breath before entering. Jennie was waiting for her as she walked in.

"Shmuel and I are going to find Moshe and bring him home," Clara told her. "You will need to take care of Anna and Hymie. I'll be back as soon as I can."

"Mama, it's too dangerous," Jennie cried.

"I'll be fine, Jennie. Now you must be strong and take my place while I'm gone. If you need anything, go see the rebbetzin," she said, giving Jennie a kiss and a hug.

"Children. . . ." She gathered Anna and Hymie to her. "You listen to Jennie. I need to go find your brother," she said, trying to smile. "I'll be home very soon."

A sharp rap at the door interrupted the farewells. "That must be Shmuel," Clara said. "Go let him in, Hymie."

Hymie ran and opened the door. "Hello Hymie," Shmuel greeted him. "Are you ready, Clara?"

"Just about. Did you find out anything?" she asked.

"Most likely he's been brought to the Russian outpost just north of the village. We can get there in about an hour. I have the wagon ready."

....

Clara sat next to Shmuel, who held the reins. The horses trudged through the snow-packed roads, following in the same path the army had marched along just hours before. The night sky had cleared, allowing the full moon to light their way.

She rocked back and forth, pleading, "Hurry, Shmuel."

As they approached the encampment, Clara could make out groups of soldiers huddling around fires. Two on guard duty ordered them to stop.

"Where do you think you two are going?" asked one with a rifle aimed at them.

"Please inform Captain Berbecki that Clara Potasznik is here to see him," she announced.

The soldier stared in disbelief at Clara and Shmuel for a moment and then turned to walk back to the encampment. She looked carefully at the face of the remaining soldier guarding them and wondered if he had taken part in the carnage.

Minutes later, the guard walked back and motioned for them to approach. He ordered them to stop in front of a wooden building surrounded by dozens of snow-covered canvas tents.

Clara climbed down from the wagon onto the frozen mud, feeling stiff from sitting for so long in the cold. Shmuel joined her as they waited for permission to enter. The guard stepped in front of them and opened the heavy wooden door. She grabbed Shmuel's hand for strength and they walked in.

"Mama," Moshe shouted from a chair pushed against the wall.

"Moshe," Clara shouted and ran over to her boy.

The guard held up his arm, preventing her from taking another step forward.

"Mrs. Potasznik, it's nice to see you," said Captain Berbecki as he stood up and walked around from his desk. She couldn't help noticing that his military uniform looked much more impressive than his former simple police captain's uniform. *But if he thinks this gives him the right to hurt Moshe,* she thought, *he is sorely mistaken.*

"Please sit down. We have much to talk about," he said, motioning to the chairs in front of his desk.

"You can see that Moshe is doing very well. No harm will come to him, I promise," he said, standing next to Moshe and giving his shoulder a squeeze.

Clara watched the captain strut around his office. She had never before thought that she was capable of causing another person physical harm, but at that moment she knew she could. She took a breath before she spoke.

"We would like to take Moshe home now, Captain," Clara said, trying to sound pleasant.

"You can take him home, but not yet. You and I still have some unfinished business to attend to," he said with a smirk.

He then turned to his lieutenant. "Take these two outside," he said, pointing to Shmuel and Moshe.

"Mama?" Moshe called. Clara and Shmuel looked over to Moshe, who was now clearly experiencing an episode. His complexion had faded to pure white, sweat poured down his face, and he was slumped over in his chair.

"Moshe!" Clara cried as she jumped up and rushed over to him. "He's sick, Captain. Please let me take him home."

"Nonsense. Now the two of you get up and go with the lieutenant," ordered the captain.

Shmuel went over to Moshe and lifted him to his feet. The lieutenant shoved the two of them through the doorway. The door slammed shut. Clara looked at the captain who stood towering over her like an oak tree.

"You know what you need to do if you want to walk out of here with your boy. The question is, Mrs. Potasznik, are you willing to do what it takes?"

CHAPTER 51

THE GERMAN COUNTRYSIDE

They traveled without incident their first day through the German countryside. Jakob offered his charming smile to the passersby who hurried on, more interested in getting to their destination than standing shivering in the frigid cold chatting to strangers.

As the sun set in the late afternoon, they arrived at the town of Hoort. Jakob suggested they find a place to spend the night. A large sign with a carved image of an eagle, its wings spread wide, advertised the Black Eagle Inn.

"I'll go and inquire," Jakob said.

Pincus looked down the quiet street. A few shopkeepers were closing up for the evening. He knew it was unlikely they'd make the seven-day journey without troubles, but at least the first day had been uneventful.

"We have a room for the night and a barn for the horses," Jakob said. "Why don't you go up to the room, and I'll take care of the horses. I'll be up soon," he added and handed Pincus the room key.

The way to the rooms was through the restaurant and bar. A small gathering of people sat around the tables. A few of them glanced up without interest at the unassuming man walking up the stairs, his key at the ready.

Once inside, Pincus closed and locked the door. The accommodations were certainly a letdown from the first-class cabin and feather bed on the *SS Amerika*, but this wasn't too bad. Sharing a bed with Jakob would probably be something he should expect for a while.

He sat on the edge of the bed next to his open valise, picked up the small, carved shoe his father made for him as a child, and rubbed his fingers across its polished surface. He thought of his father and hoped he would look down upon him and give him strength for his journey to rescue his family. But what if he was too late? The newspapers he'd read on the ship told of fierce fighting taking place from Krakow all the way to Lemberg, and Krzywcza was right in the middle. It was possible that his village could have been wiped out, its civilian population shot dead.

A knock at the door shook him out of his stupor. "Pincus, unlock the door," shouted Jakob over the noise from the crowd below, which had become loud and rowdy.

"Come, let's get something to eat downstairs," Jakob said.

They sat at a table toward the back of the room. A barmaid approached carrying a tray. She placed a tureen of soup on the table, two bowls with spoons already resting inside, and a piece of brown meat simmering on a clay plate with a knife stabbed into it. "I'll be back with your beer," she said.

Pincus looked with disgust at the food and then at Jakob.

"You've been spoiled, Pincus," Jakob said with a laugh. "You'd better get used to this and worse."

As Pincus cautiously scooped out edible pieces of potatoes and vegetables, Jakob carelessly shoveled a spoonful into his mouth.

"You know, Pincus," he said loudly, wiping his mouth with the sleeve of his shirt. "We should keep a watch on the cargo."

"Keep your voice down," Pincus pleaded looking around at the men sitting at the tables surrounding them.

"Since I'm not tired, I'll take the first watch. I'll come and wake you in a few hours," Jakob said, taking a swig of his beer.

"Are you sure? This beer tastes stronger than the beer we're used to," Pincus said pointing to the pint.

"Nonsense, I'm fine. Go on upstairs. I'll grab a blanket and find a spot in the barn. We don't want anyone taking off with our cargo."

....

Pincus opened his eyes to see the sun shining in through the un-shuttered windows. Disoriented, he sat up and could hear a commotion of conversations through the door. *Wasn't Jakob supposed to have woken me hours ago?*

He quickly dressed and ran down the stairs. He looked about the tables, but Jakob was not among the patrons eating breakfast. Forgetting his coat, he ran out into the street, so enraged that the frigid winds had no effect on him. He opened the barn doors and, to his horror, found nothing there. No wagon, no horses, and no Jakob.

CHAPTER 52

MOSHE'S BAR MITZVAH

Clara said little in the days after Captain Berbecki's assault on her and on her village. She talked to no one about it. The rebbetzin cautiously approached, but Clara evaded her. "I just need time," she said, as a way not to offend.

After the dead had been properly buried, life in the village resumed, though under a dark and sinister cloud. People went about their daily lives, but hopelessness spread throughout the village like a contagious virus.

"Mama, please don't be sad," Moshe said, standing next to her as she washed potatoes at the basin.

"Moshe, I am not sad. What matters is that you are okay. My children are the most important thing in my life," she said patting his cheek.

"What about Papa? Is he not important?"

She put down the potato and looked at him. "Your Papa is very important. Wherever he is, we must not forget him and pray for our reunion one day."

"I won't forget him, Mama," Moshe reassured her.

A knock at the door startled Clara, "Who can that be?"

"It's the rabbi," said Jennie as she opened the door.

"Hello, Jennie," he said, giving her a hug and a kiss on her cheek. "You are looking more like your mother every day. So lovely."

"Hello, Clara," he greeted her as he removed his coat. "Come, Hymie and Anna, and give me a hug."

Thanks to Hashem, it's only the rabbi, Clara thought, as she watched her children run over and wrap their arms around his skinny legs.

The rabbi sat down at the table and motioned for Clara and Moshe to join him.

"I've come to discuss the plans for Moshe's bar mitzvah. His thirteenth birthday is only a week away, Clara."

"You must be joking, Rabbi. A bar mitzvah celebration *now*, while we are in the midst of all this madness?"

"A bar mitzvah is no joke," the rabbi said with a smile. "We must acknowledge Moshe's achievements and his rite of passage into manhood."

He placed his hand on Moshe's shoulder and said "I know it's hard to imagine any kind of celebration right now. There is so much pain, especially for you. But it's important that Moshe perform the bar mitzvah ceremony when his thirteenth birthday comes."

....

Bar mitzvahs are typically planned months in advance. So, when the rabbi insisted that it should proceed, she needed to prepare quickly with only days to organize the big event.

When the morning of the bar mitzvah finally arrived, Clara stood before the mirror. Adversity had not been kind to her, she observed, but she would try to look her best. As she fussed over her appearance, she shivered as thoughts of Berbecki flashed through her mind. *I did what any mother would do*, she insisted to herself. But there was nothing that would ever erase the shame of having given herself to that monster.

She imagined the countless women who had no doubt been attacked in the same animalistic manner. The way he had spun her around to face his desk and pushed her down, forcing her to grab the back of a chair; then lifting her skirt and pulling down her undergarments. Seconds later, he had thrust himself into her, sending a screeching pain vibrating throughout her body. The act had taken only seconds, but she knew it would dominate her memories for a lifetime.

"Mother, the children are ready," Jennie called out.

Clara stood up, took a deep breath and walked out into the front room. "Children, let's go to your brother's bar mitzvah," she said with her best forced smile.

....

Every seat at the Krzywcza synagogue was taken. The men who couldn't find a seat stood in the back. Up in the balcony over-looking the sanctuary, the women squeezed in where they could. The entire Jewish population of Krzywcza had come to celebrate Moshe Potasznik's bar mitzvah.

The stories of Moshe's episodes, his healing powers, and his confrontation with the Russian captain had spread like a virus throughout the shtetl. The opportunity of seeing him become a bar mitzvah was the event of the year.

Friends stood up to greet and congratulate Clara as she and her children climbed the stairs to the women's section in the balcony. At the outpouring of love and support, she fought back tears. *Save your crying for the ceremony*, she admonished herself.

The men crowding below on the sanctuary floor all turned and looked up at Clara. They greeted her enthusiastically. She responded by placing her hands crisscrossed over her heart, her head slightly bowed, her eyes briefly closed.

The door to the rabbi's study opened, and out walked the rabbi, wearing his best tallit, followed closely by Moshe. The congregation fell silent at the sight of them.

Clara gasped at her son's appearance. He looked different. A beautiful embroidered white tallit draped around his shoulders. His blue eyes looked up and found her, and he smiled. She couldn't stop the tears any longer as they flooded down her cheeks.

Moshe stood next to the rabbi on the bimah as the ceremony

began. The familiar prayers and songs filled the shul with joy. Clara watched her son, now a man, and felt her heart was bursting with pride.

The religious ceremony ended, and the rabbi stood on the bimah facing the congregation. Moshe sat in a chair next to him.

"Today is a wonderful day. I think it has been a while since I said those words. Let me say them again and cherish each one." The rabbi closed his eyes, spread his arms wide in front of him, and said slowly, briefly pausing between each word, "Today is a wonderful day."

The congregation nodded in approval.

"In all my many years as your rabbi, I have seen many things, both good and bad. I am sure you all can say the same."

Heads nodded in agreement.

"But why do we simplify our memories into these distinct categories of good or bad? How can our complicated lives be boiled down to these two opposites?"

He paused, allowing the question to linger.

"This is how our minds work. Our memories are born of moments that are etched into our consciousness. We store these memories in the rooms in our mind," the rabbi said, pointing his long, crooked finger to his forehead.

"When we are young, these rooms are very large and filled with wonderful, simple memories such as birthday parties. Or maybe something sad like losing a pet," he said for the benefit of a few children poking their young faces through the balcony railing. "As we get older, our experiences, our lives, our moments create new rooms both good and bad. The good moments we store in the rooms that we keep open and easily accessible for times to share with our family and friends. This is healthy and makes us happy."

The rabbi turned briefly to look at Moshe, smiling. "Today will be a happy day that will create a room in your mind, a good memory that you can visit from time to time."

He paused and his expression changed from light and carefree to serious. He clasped his hands together and shook them back and forth.

"We also have bad memories. Dark moments of our lives we don't want to remember. Where do we put these? We tend to lock them up in rooms, wrap them in heavy chains, and hide them in the deepest, darkest corners of our mind."

Clara sat up at this remark. *Is the rabbi speaking directly to me?* She knew any mother would have done the same to save her child, but giving herself to Berbecki was just too hideous a memory, one that she needed to find a deep, dark corner in which to bury.

"This is what our minds like to do. It is our way of coping with tragic events in our lives. It's how we move on." He stopped and glanced up to the balcony where Clara stared back at him.

"While it feels good to bury the bad moments, the bad memories, it is not healthy. We think these rooms are locked up, safe from affecting our well-being. But they are not. These memories have ways of sneaking out through the cracks and poisoning the deepest parts of our minds. What happens next? We start behaving in ways that take us farther and farther away from Hashem."

The rabbi hesitated and looked out over his congregation, now silent and waiting for his next words.

"What is the result as we lose our way? We lock up more bad memories. Our minds become warehouses of dark secrets.

"Each of us must fight the battle every day between good and bad. Between the light and the dark. You may say to me, 'Rabbi I cannot deal with the bad. The darkness haunts my dreams.' I have news for you; the darkness haunts my dreams too."

The congregation gave a collective gasp.

"How do we cope when we have experienced such darkness? Where can we store these memories if we cannot lock them up and throw away the key?"

He paused as if waiting for an answer.

"We accept them, we embrace them. We use them as fuel to move forward. We will not succumb to the darkness. We will move toward the light," he said, raising his arms to the heavens.

"We have, indeed, suffered a great deal. Let us not forget what has happened. Instead let us use this dark moment in our lives to make us stronger, to give us the resolve to move forward as Jews and to follow the teachings of Hashem."

The rabbi summoned Moshe to stand next to him and wrapped his long lanky arm around Moshe's shoulder.

"Today is the day the light takes over the darkness. Today is when we open all the doors in our minds to both the good and the bad. We are no longer afraid. Our village of Krzywcza may be small and inconsequential in this world at war, but we will continue to carry forth the light—a beacon of hope for those who still believe in the power of Hashem."

The congregation waited silently as the rabbi turned Moshe to look at him.

"Today, Moshe Potasznik, you are a man. But you are so much more. You are our beacon of hope. You are our light drowning out the darkness. You inspire us. You inspire me." The rabbi paused to wipe away his tears.

"Not all great men are old men. Some great men are only thirteen years old."

The rabbi hugged Moshe, and then he turned and looked up to Clara in the balcony. He held his clasped hands out to her and said "*Mazel tov*, Clara."

"*Mazel tov*," the congregation replied in unison.

CHAPTER 53

THE ESCAPE

Jakob awoke to find himself bouncing up and down in the back of the wagon next to the wooden crate of guns. He reached for the back of his head and felt his hair stuck together in clumps. Someone must have hit him from behind. The pain he felt and the dried blood on his fingers confirmed that.

He remembered leaving the Black Eagle Inn and walking to the barn. Whoever hit him must have done so then. Did his hijackers know what was hidden in the crate? He parted the canvas flaps and saw they were moving quickly over some unpaved road. The morning light shone through some patches of trees that lined the road.

The wagon slowed and came to a stop. Jakob could now hear two men speaking.

"You go inside and tell Uncle what we have. I'll take care of our passenger and cargo," said the first.

"All right, be careful," replied the other.

"Not to worry. If he gives me any trouble, I'll shoot him," he said with a sharp guffaw.

"Shoot him in the leg. We don't want to kill him. At least not yet," said the second man.

Jakob heard footsteps approaching. The end of a shotgun appeared though the flaps of the canvas panels. Quickly they were pulled aside and Jakob saw the man aiming a shotgun at him.

Jakob noticed the man's dark, deep-set eyes trained on him. His hands seemed steady and sure. He knew that any quick move would result in being shot at close range. He raised his hands slowly.

"Get out," the man ordered.

Jakob got to his feet, walked to the edge of the wagon, and, with survival instincts honed on the rough streets of Warsaw, swiftly kicked the gun aside. The man instinctively fired off a round of shot that splattered across the wooden crate. Jakob leaped off the wagon leading with his fists and pounded the man's face as his landed. The man fell to the ground still clutching the shotgun. With nothing to break his fall, he slammed to the earth hard, knocking the breath out of him.

Jakob swooped down and grabbed the shotgun, cocked it, and pointed it at the man lying motionless at his feet.

"Get up," Jakob ordered.

The man staggered up.

"Walk to the front of the wagon."

Jakob kept the gun pointing at the man's chest as he backed up.

The horses were agitated from the gunshot and commotion.

"Get down on the ground," he ordered.

The man obliged.

Jakob grabbed the horsewhip with his left hand and gave a sharp snap to the rear of one of the horses. The horses budged slightly and moved forward at a snail's pace.

The second man burst out the front door, fired at Jakob but missed him. Jakob fired back, hitting his target. The man fell backwards with such force that he split some of the wallboard covering the outside of the building.

Jakob steadied the horses. Eventually with momentum on their side, their pace quickened. He had escaped alive with the cargo intact. Now he faced two new problems. Where was he, and where was Pincus?

Jakob kept the horses moving steadily for several hours until he came to a village. A young boy walked by, carrying what looked like schoolbooks.

"Can you tell me where we are?" Jakob asked the boy.

"This is Rastow."

"Can you tell me in which direction is Hoort?"

"It's about three miles this way," he said, pointing to a road that veered off to Jakob's left.

"That's great, thank you."

Fortunately, his abductors hadn't taken him too far. With some luck, he could make it back to the Black Eagle Inn, grab Pincus, and be on his way.

....

He arrived at the Black Eagle Inn just in time for lunch. He thought he would walk in and find Pincus sitting at a table, eating and fuming in anger at being abandoned. Jakob tied up the horses and entered the inn. Several tables were occupied by patrons, none of them Pincus.

He asked the innkeeper at the front desk if he knew what had happened to his friend. "He's gone. He thought you left without him," said the man.

"Gone? Gone where?"

"We arranged a ride for him with one of our suppliers. They headed south to Putlitz. It's a day's ride from here. If you hurry, you probably can catch them. He makes a few stops along the way."

"That's good," he said, encouraged. "Tell me, what does this man deliver?"

"He doesn't deliver anything. He picks up."

"Picks up? What does he pick up?"

"Carcasses. Animal carcasses. He sells rotten meat to the pig farmers," the man said.

"Pincus is riding on a wagon with rotting animal carcasses?"

"He wasn't too pleased with that idea either," said the man, laughing.

A few hours later Jakob saw a wagon with its horses tied up in front of a small inn called the Raven. The open wagon had a tarp covering its haul. A man came out carrying a wooden barrel. He flipped back the tarp and dumped some bloody chunks of meat and bones onto the pile. This caused the flies to scatter briefly before they returned to their bounty.

Then he saw Pincus walking out of the Raven Inn and climb up onto the wagon seat.

"Pincus, hey!" Jakob shouted, running toward the wagon.

Pincus turned to see who was calling his name. At the sight of Jakob, he stood up and held his hands out in confusion. He jumped down from the wagon, just as Jakob approached him.

"I'm happy to find you," Jakob said.

Pincus just stood there staring back at him. "What in the world happened to you? You left me back there. I had to ride in this thing."

"I'm sorry, but it wasn't my fault. Let me explain what happened once we are on our way." He took one step and stopped. "Wow, that's some disgusting smell!"

"Not funny," Pincus said, scratching his nose.

CHAPTER 54

BETRAYAL

The journey from the Raven Inn to a mile from the Galician border took an uneventful six days. Even the weather cooperated. The snow melted, and even though the roads became muddy, the horses seemed to have little trouble pulling the heavy load.

They discussed what had happened that first evening in Hoort. Jakob confessed that his behavior in the inn that evening might have prompted the attack. Neither man had any idea who the attackers were.

"I thought you'd left without me," Pincus said.

"Why would I do that?" Jakob asked.

"What was I to think?" Pincus asked.

"I wish I could have seen your face when you saw the wagon gone," Jakob said with a smile.

"I think you would have been more amused with my expression after getting a ride on that wagon with the rotting meat."

Jakob roared with laughter.

"I don't know what was worse, the smell or the flies," Pincus said, shaking his head and laughing along with his friend.

It started small—a military vehicle passed them. Then they saw a few dozen German troops milling about a fire. As they approached the border itself, there was a much more significant military presence.

As far as they could see in either direction, walls made of sandbags formed a boundary. Armed men with long rifles relaxed against the bags as if they were pillows in an Arabian tent. Cannons pointed beyond the border into the Galician territory and seemed poised to fire at a moment's notice.

Jakob directed the horses to the heavily fortified border crossing. German soldiers walked back and forth, apparently with some tasks at hand. As they approached, a German soldier ordered them to stop.

"Where do you two think you are going?" he asked.

"We would like to cross over into Galicia," answered Jakob.

"Why would you want to do that?" the soldier asked.

"That is none of your concern," Jakob said. "We have royal papers giving us permission to pass. Signed by Prince Adalbert himself," he added, offering the envelope of documents to the soldier.

The soldier looked at Jakob and then over at Pincus with an expression of amazement.

"Don't move. I'll be right back," he ordered.

Pincus leaned over to Jakob and whispered in his ear, "I think your tone was a little aggressive."

"Nonsense, that's how to handle these gangsters."

"Gangsters, really?" Pincus shook his head.

"Believe me, I know all about them. They're no different than the scum I dealt with back in Warsaw. Watch now here he comes. We'll be on our way in just a minute," Jakob said.

"Get down and come with me. My lieutenant wishes to speak with you," the soldier said, brandishing his rifle.

The lieutenant was examining their papers as Pincus and Jakob were escorted into his makeshift office. "Where did you get these?" he asked, looking at them over his reading glasses.

"From the hands of Prince Adalbert," Jakob said.

"I see," he paused. "These papers look in order. But I do need to see what it is you have in that crate," the lieutenant said, standing up and summoning a soldier over. "Let's go take a look, shall we?"

Two soldiers quickly pried open the crate. Out tumbled coats and blankets. Jakob reached, in expecting to grab hold of one of the Remington shotguns. But as he dug deeper and deeper into the box, he felt nothing. He looked at the lieutenant and Pincus. "There's nothing here. This is not possible."

"Unless they were stolen on the ship," Pincus said.

"No wonder the prince was helpful," said Jakob.

"Well gentlemen, I don't suppose you still want to cross the border," said the lieutenant.

Pincus gave Jakob a serious look and a nod.

"We still want to cross. I assume the papers allow us to do so?" asked Jakob.

"Sure, by all means. You do know you are crossing into a war zone. Do you have any firearms?" asked the lieutenant.

"We have an old shotgun," Pincus said.

"Well the least I can do is to offer you two rifles and some ammo," said the lieutenant. "I am sure our prince would want no harm to come to either of you," he said.

"Yes, I'm sure our wellbeing is of great concern to the prince," Jakob said sarcastically, raising an eyebrow.

Pincus and Jakob thanked the lieutenant, closed up the empty crate, and slowly crossed the border from Germany to Galicia. Jakob patted Pincus on the back. "Our next stop, Pincus, is Krzywcza."

CHAPTER 55

REUNION

According to the lieutenant, they would have little trouble reaching Krakow. The heavy fighting between the Austro-Hungarian forces and the Russian army was taking place in Limanowa, about twenty-five miles southeast of Krakow.

The journey proved as uneventful as the lieutenant had predicted, except for the cold. Pincus and Jakob wrapped blankets around their shoulders and legs, but they still shivered as their horses moved slowly on the snow-packed road. They arrived late in the afternoon in the city of Krakow.

Jakob asked a man walking alongside the road for a place to spend the evening. He gave directions to a nearby place he knew of.

"It's a small inn called the Anna. They have a barn," he said pointing to the horses.

"That's my daughter's name," Pincus said with a slight smile, and he anticipated his imminent first meeting with his little girl.

A few minutes later, they found the inn. Pincus went inside to pay the manager while Jakob took care of the horses.

After placing their belongings in their room, Pincus warmed himself by the large stone fireplace in the lounge as he waited for

Jakob. A few people sat nearby in comfortable-looking chairs, smoking and drinking and talking about the war. One particular older man had the attention not only of his companion, but of the rest of the room as well.

"The Russians," he said with a hint of disdain, "are being pushed back by General Boroevic. He recaptured the mountain passes and stopped their plans to drive through Krakow."

Pincus observed the elation on the faces of those in the room. This was indeed good news. "What about farther west? We need to travel to Krzywcza," Pincus asked.

"Right now, it looks good," the old man said, taking a drag on his cigarette. "The Habsburgs have recaptured Limanowa and Lapanow. But Prezemysl remains under Russian control."

"Fortunately, we don't need to go that far," Pincus said with relief.

A man leaning against the wall and smoking a cigar asked, "How do you know so much?"

The older man turned his head to see who had questioned his credibility. "My son is an officer serving under the great General Boroevic. I just saw him this morning before he rejoined his platoon," he said with pride.

....

Pincus told Jakob what he had learned when he returned from tending to the horses and wagon.

"That's good news. We should leave first thing tomorrow. Things are changing quickly. Once we get to Krzywcza we can stay just long enough for Clara to gather a few things. Then we will need to travel back the way we came through Germany," Jakob said quietly.

"Hopefully our papers will allow us to cross back over the border. Crossing into a war zone with just the two of us is probably easier than crossing back with a woman and children," Pincus added.

Disjointed thoughts of reuniting with his family kept Pincus awake most of the night. He worried that his children wouldn't remember him. Of course Anna couldn't, as she hadn't even been born when he left. But what about Hymie—what memories would he have? At least Jennie and Moshe were old enough not to have forgotten him.

His most troubling ruminations concerned Clara. Pincus imagined several possible reactions from her upon their reunion, ranging from exclamations of joy to ones of anger at him for having abandoned her and his children.

But then, none of these scenarios would even have a possibility of playing out if he and Jakob were captured by Russian soldiers and shot before they could reach their destination.

When morning finally came, Pincus jumped out of bed to leave those thoughts behind. After a quick breakfast with Jakob, the two men left the Anna.

An hour out on the road, they passed a few dozen Hungarian soldiers. Pincus and Jakob greeted them casually, hoping that they wouldn't be stopped. The weary men, covered in frozen mud and snow, barley acknowledged them.

As they traveled farther from Krakow, Pincus started to recognize the names of the cities and villages and realized they were getting closer to home. After a few days and nights of travel, they approached the city of Rzeszow. Pincus knew the city well. It was where he and his father used to shop for leather hides for the cobbler shop.

The horses moved slowly across the snow-packed road leading into the city. The tall stone buildings he remembered were now mountainous piles of rubble. As they traversed the main road leading into the town center, they could make out a large garrison of the Austro-Hungarian army guarding a fortified crossing. Alongside the road and out into the darkness, Pincus could see dead Russian soldiers lying across the still-smoldering battlefield.

Several soldiers nervously approached the wagon, their rifles aimed at Jakob and Pincus, and ordered them to climb down.

They stood up slowly, holding out their rifles by the stock and placing them on the seat as they stepped off the wagon. The horses, agitated by the soldiers, suddenly jerked forward, causing

Pincus to stumble and fall to the ground, landing hard on his shoulder. He grabbed it in pain.

An officer approached the commotion and asked "What's in the wagon?"

Jakob looked over to Pincus in obvious distress, then back to the officer now waiting impatiently for a reply. "It's an empty crate. That's it."

"An empty crate?" he asked, sounding dubious. "Check it out," he ordered his men. "Bring them to me, when you're done," he added, turning and walking away.

....

After the soldiers confirmed that the crate was indeed empty except for some old blankets, they escorted the men to the captain's quarters. Pincus walked along, clutching his shoulder.

"What did you find?" the captain asked the soldier.

"Nothing except some blankets."

"Do you two have any identification papers?" the captain asked.

Jakob presented the royal documents.

The captain looked up in surprise. "Prince Adalbert gave these to you? Why would the son of the Kaiser give you anything? Can you tell me?"

Jakob told the captain their story, beginning in New York, and prayed that this Austro-Hungarian officer would at least be sympathetic to their intentions.

The captain listened carefully, and when Jakob finished, he said, "Are you telling me the two of you traveled the entire length of Germany before you discovered that the crate that you thought was filled with five hundred Remington shotguns was empty, and that Prince Adalbert, without your knowledge, stole the guns that were meant for Jewish soldiers fighting the Russians?"

"That's exactly what we're telling you," said Jakob.

The captain burst into laughter. "It's been a while since something has been so amusing. This is too outrageous for you to make it up."

Pincus and Jakob looked at each other with relief.

"You must stay the night, and you can go on your way to Krzywcza in the morning," he said and then pointed to Pincus. "Take him to the surgeon and have him take a look at that shoulder."

A few hundred feet from the captain's quarters sat the bombed-out ruins of a church. Pincus followed the soldier, maneuvering around piles of stone that just days earlier had made up the walls of this old church. They entered where the main doors used to be and walked down the center aisle, which had been converted into a field hospital. Injured soldiers were being treated on the wooden pews that acted as hospital beds. Torches lit the cavernous space, creating spaces of light and dark among the caregivers trying to comfort those dying of their wounds.

Pincus had never seen so much suffering before. Many looked too young to fight. Yet here they were, crying out in pain, waiting for death to relieve their misery. He wasn't sure if the throbbing of his injured shoulder was what was causing his nausea, or if it was the bloody sight of the lacerated soldiers.

Clearly annoyed at being interrupted to treat such a minor injury, the surgeon told Pincus that his shoulder was only bruised, not fractured. He wrapped a sling around Pincus's neck, and advised him to wear it for a while in order to immobilize his arm.

....

The next morning, Jakob and Pincus awoke to sunlight shining through the large windows of someone's abandoned apartment. Because of the intense fighting, the city was deserted, many residents having fled into the countryside as the Austro-Hungarian army took back the city from the Russians.

Pincus's shoulder, though sore, felt a little better. They found the captain, thanked him, wished him luck, and drove out of Rzeszow. A half-day's ride and they would arrive in Krzywcza.

CHAPTER 56

PINCUS COMES HOME

Clara's concerns about feeding her family had grown steadily worse. She had carefully rationed her supplies, but as the war dragged on through the winter, the food had dwindled to perhaps a week's worth of meals for her, her children, and the occasional visit by Shmuel.

She felt obliged to take care of Shmuel as one of her own. He had done so much for her and her family, from working the cobbler shop to the crippling injury he had incurred in Lviv trying to protect Moshe.

Clara was staring at the near-empty shelves in the cellar, trying to think of ways to stretch their supplies a few more days, when Jennie came running down the steps.

"Mama, come quickly!" Jennie shouted.

"What is it Jennie? What's wrong?" asked Clara, following her up the narrow wooden staircase.

As she stepped through the cellar door into the living room, still absently clutching a jar of pickles, she froze. The glass jar slipped from her hand and fell to the floor, cracking upon impact. She stared at the open doorway, her mouth agape, a puddle of pickle juice forming around her slippers. There, with his arm in a sling, stood Pincus, smiling.

"Hello, Clara," he said.

"Pincus?"

"Papa!" shouted Moshe, who ran over to his father and wrapped his arms around him.

"Easy, Moshe." Pincus backed off, wincing. "I have a small injury."

"Sorry, Papa," Moshe said as he made room for Jennie and Hymie, who gently hugged their father.

"That's okay, Moshe. I am happy to see all of you. It's been such a long time. And you must be Anna," he said to his youngest daughter, who peeked out from behind her mother's skirt.

"Go on, Anna, say hello to your father," Clara said.

Pincus knelt down and gave his daughter an awkward hug, then stood up again and walked over to Clara, who was still standing in the puddle of pickle juice. He wrapped his good arm around her and kissed her. She looked at her husband and, with tears welling up, reached out and touched his cheek as if she thought she might be dreaming.

"Pincus, it's you. You've come back," she said, burying her head in the crook of his neck and releasing the tears she had held back for so many years, waiting for this moment.

"I've come home to take you and the children to America," he announced.

"Papa who is this man?" Jennie interrupted, pointing to Jakob, who stood in the doorway.

"This is my friend, Jakob," he said, walking over and placing his hand on Jakob's shoulder. "We traveled together from America, and together we will get us all back."

Jakob walked over to Clara. "It is indeed an honor to meet you, Clara. Pincus has told me so much about you."

....

It took some time for Clara to settle down. She asked Jennie to prepare a meal while Moshe ran to tell the rabbi the news. Twenty minutes later he returned, breathless, and said, "The rabbi and Shmuel are coming. They are walking over now."

"Papa, tell us about America," Jennie said, as the children sat around their father.

"I am sure your mother has read to you my letters, but I will tell you again. My life in America has been good."

He began recounting his adventures over the past four years. He told of the success of the Landsman Society, which he said would please the rabbi. He described the cobbler shop, how he and Jakob had built it into a thriving business. Just as he began to describe the journey back home, there came a sharp rap at the door, and in walked the rabbi followed by Shmuel.

"Look at you, Pincus," the rabbi said. He took a step closer and stretched out his arms in preparation for a hug.

"Don't, Rabbi!" Moshe shouted. "Papa is injured. He hurt his shoulder."

"I see," the rabbi said, looking at the sling. He shook hands instead and looked at Pincus for a good while.

He stood aside and asked, "Do you recognize this fine young man?"

"Is this Shmuel?" asked Pincus, unsure of the six-foot, three-inch man standing in front of him.

"It's me, Pincus," said Shmuel, offering his hand.

Pincus looked down at Shmuel's maimed left hand and said, "What happened to your hand?"

"An unfortunate encounter in Lviv," he answered.

"I'll tell you about all that later. It was too complicated to explain in a letter," said Clara. "Please, let's sit down. Jennie has prepared a meal."

The rabbi led a prayer thanking Hashem for delivering Pincus back to them.

"This is our last challah," Clara said, putting the freshly baked twisted loaf in the center of the table.

"Would you please say the blessing, Moshe," asked the rabbi who looked over to Pincus. "He's a bar mitzvah now, Pincus."

After Moshe recited the blessing for the bread, Jennie placed a tureen of soup in the center of the table. Clara carefully ladled out an equal share into each of the nine bowls, leaving the tureen empty.

The blended aromas of the potatoes, onions, carrots, and chicken broth had everyone clutching at their spoons. Clara sat across from Pincus and watched him carefully take a spoonful. He closed his eyes and seemed to drift away for a moment. Placing the spoon back in the bowl, he cupped his hands to his face and started to weep.

Clara rose from her chair and took a step around the table to put her arm around her husband. "Pincus, are you okay?"

Pincus moved his hands away from his face. "I am happy to be home and find everyone safe," he said, looking into the tearful eyes of his children.

With the meal finished and dishes cleaned, the family remained huddled at the table for hours. Clara and the rabbi shared many stories about Moshe and his trials, tribulations, and triumphs. She recounted the support that Shmuel had provided the family and the maiming he had suffered protecting Moshe.

Clara, knowing there would be plenty of time to reminisce, interrupted the storytelling and looked at Pincus and Jakob. "How do you plan on getting us out of here?"

Jakob walked over to the window and looked out to make sure his next words would not be overheard. Standing at the end of the table, he had everyone's attention.

"We are going to travel in the wagon back the way we came. Once we get to Hamburg, we will need to find a boat to take us to the city of Arendal in Norway. When we get there, we have the name of a man who can get us passage on a Norwegian America Line ship," Jakob said.

Clara couldn't believe that outrageous plan. "You want to take the eight of us in that wagon," she said, pointing in the direction of where the horses were tied up, "through the Galician countryside, travel the length of Germany, put us on a boat to traverse the Baltic Sea, find a stranger in a faraway city, and then sail across the Atlantic Ocean to America—all this in the middle of winter and in the midst of a war?"

Jakob looked at Pincus who said, "There's one more thing. We have these." He held out the royal papers. "They provided us clear passage getting here. We are hoping they will do the same getting us back."

Clara looked at the documents and wondered if a piece of paper signed by some prince would be enough to keep her family safe from the ravages of war. But she knew there was no choice but to attempt their departure. The fighting would only worsen, and the stories she had heard about the Russians' wiping out entire villages were becoming ever more frequent.

She looked at the rabbi, who stared back at her, nodding.

"Okay, we will do this on one condition."

"What is that?" asked Pincus.

"That we take Shmuel with us. We owe it to him and to his father to bring him safely to America," she insisted.

"Of course we will take Shmuel. I already promised his father I would."

"Great, it's settled," announced Jakob. "We leave tomorrow morning. Only take the absolute essentials. We can fit two people in the seat up front, and the rest will need to make do in the wooden crate in the wagon."

"We will prepare tonight," Clara said.

CHAPTER 57

AVOIDING KRAKOW

While Hymie and Anna slept, Jakob worked along with Jennie and Shmuel, preparing the wooden crate for the journey. It would be their living space for the next week or two. They laid out the blankets to make it as comfortable as possible. Along with their clothes, they packed a few cooking essentials so they could make do cooking by a fire, when necessary.

Meanwhile Clara, Pincus, and Moshe sat up in the rabbi's study. Dawn was only a few hours away, their departure imminent, but the rabbi had asked them to visit with him before they left for good.

"I know you're anxious to be on your way, Pincus," the rabbi began, "but there is something we need to discuss concerning Moshe."

The rabbi told Pincus and Clara about Moshe's abilities and his belief that the boy carried the blessing and burden of being a *tzaddik*. He told of the several instances of Moshe's episodes, confirmed by Clara. The rabbi spoke of what his teaching from the Talmud taught on the ways of the *tzaddik*. He also warned of the dangers he might face from those wishing to do him harm.

Pincus shared the reading he'd had with Dora Meltzer on the voyage to America four years ago. "She told me that my eldest son had a unique gift."

"Careful, Pincus, she may be a *rasha*. They are the dark counterpart to the *tzaddik*. Moshe must never meet this woman, at least not until he has fully matured and developed his defenses," the rabbi said.

"You say there are only thirty-six *tzaddikim* on the earth at any time, Rabbi. Who are they besides Moshe?" Pincus asked.

"They are unknown, and Moshe must be as well. I shouldn't be sharing what I know, even about your own son. But I believe the circumstances require it."

The rabbi stood up, put on his tallit, and asked Pincus, Clara, and Moshe to stand. He gathered them in close, wrapping his long arms around them and prayed.

O Lord, grant that this night we may sleep in peace.
And that in the morning our awakening may also be in peace.
May our daytime be cloaked in your peace.
Protect us and inspire us to think and act only out of love.
Keep far from us all evil; may our paths be free from all
obstacles from when we go out until we return home.

Pincus stood by the wagon, looking at the home he and his children had all been born in. When everyone had gathered, he announced, "Take your last look, children. Never forget where you come from."

"We won't forget, Papa," Jennie said.

"In America, your lives will be different. They'll be better. But always remember our home, the place of your birth."

"We will, Papa," Jennie said.

"I promise not to forget," added Moshe.

"Me too," Hymie chimed in.

Pincus looked over to Clara expecting her to add a few warm words to comfort the children's farewell. Instead she muttered, while wiping away a tear, "As if things were that simple."

"Don't be sad, Clara," Pincus said, focusing on her tears instead of her remark.

She gave a Pincus a dismissive look and said briskly, "That's enough. We have a long way to travel. Come on, children, let's get going."

Under a cloak of darkness, Clara, Shmuel, and the children settled themselves in the crate. Once inside, with the lid placed on, the crate offered a bit of comfort and warmth, and the spaces between the planks allowed fresh air to circulate.

Jakob grabbed the reins of the rested and fed horses and slowly moved down the street. Jakob turned his head toward Pincus, who was looking around the dark street where he lived his entire life up until four years ago.

"You didn't have a chance to show me around," Jakob whispered.

"There's nothing left to see here. Our lives are in America now."

....

The heavy gray clouds prevented the sun from illuminating the road ahead of them. They decided the first stop would be in the city of Rzeszow. There they could safely stretch their legs, empty their bladders and bowels, and get updates on the fighting.

As they approached the guard posts from the southwest, the same soldiers that had bid them farewell a few days earlier recognized them and allowed them entrance into the fortified city.

Once safely inside, they pulled the wagon over to a field next to a bombed out building. Jakob and Pincus lifted the wooden lid off the crate to see six relieved faces staring back.

"How did you do?" asked Pincus.

"It's fine. Let's get the children out quickly. Hymie is about to burst," Clara said.

"Come, Hymie," Pincus said, reaching in and lifting the boy out. He jumped off the back of the wagon, pulled down his drawers, and peed a long stream.

After a short rest, everyone found his or her place, and they resumed their journey. It took about thirty minutes to make it across the town to the western road leading to Krakow. Hearing reports of their return to the city, Captain Gertz stood waiting for them as the neared the gate.

"Gentlemen, I didn't expect to see you so soon," he said.

"Good day, Captain," said Jakob. "We are heading back to Krakow. Would you know if the road is safe?"

"The road may be safe, but the reports are that Krakow is back under Russian siege. You can't make it safely through the city—especially with your precious cargo." he added quietly. "I'd advise sticking to the back roads south of the city and then making your way north to Kattowitz."

"Thank you, Captain," Jakob said.

"Good luck to you," said the captain, who ordered his men to allow the wagon to leave the city.

· ·

As the sun set before them, and with their rifles by their sides, Jakob and Pincus took a detour off the main road a few miles outside of Krakow.

"How do we know which way to go?" asked Pincus.

"We don't. Let's just hope we find a few friendly faces along the way to guide us."

Sounds of heavy guns and artillery soon broke through the clopping of the horses' hoofs on the packed, snow-covered roads. The smell of gunpowder and sulfur filtered down from the dark gray sky.

"We should stop and make sure everyone is okay," suggested Jakob.

"I don't know, Jakob, the fighting sounds very close to us. Maybe we should try to get some more distance."

The horses followed the narrow path farther and farther away from the blasts and earth-shaking vibrations. Jakob brought them to a complete stop. They sat there for a moment in complete silence. The air, though frigid, smelled clean.

"Let's let them out," Jakob said.

"You must be completely quiet," Pincus instructed as they all climbed out of the crate.

"Where are we?" asked Clara.

"South of Krakow," Jakob whispered. "We will spend the night here. The horses need rest. Pincus and I will take turns on watch. Get the children back inside the crate quickly."

"Do you think it's okay to make a fire?" asked Clara.

"Not here, it's too dangerous," said Jakob.

"Okay, I'll get the children taken care of. Thank you, Jakob."

"You don't need to thank me. We're all in this together."

....

With everyone else asleep in the crate, Jakob sat on the wagon bench with the shotgun lying across his knees. Occasional sounds of artillery drifted over, followed by a slight smell of gunpowder. Clouds backlit by the moon illuminated the small clearing.

Silence eventually took over the night. Nothing could be heard. Not the artillery miles away in Krakow or the small animals in the forest. Sleep had seeped into the world, and Jakob marveled at it. Then he heard it. First the snap of a branch, then the rustle of some dried leaves. He heard footsteps and a moment later ten rifles slid out from the darkness and into the clearing, all pointing at Jakob.

CHAPTER 58

MEANT FOR US

Armed men with rifles took aim at Jakob.

"Pincus, you need to wake up," Jakob said, raising his arms into the air.

"What is it?" he asked, lifting his head out of the crate.

"We have visitors," Jakob answered.

Pincus woke up Clara, Shmuel, and the children, and one by one they climbed out.

Clara pushed Anna and Hymie behind her and grabbed Moshe and Jennie by their coat collars. Pincus took a step in front of Clara. Shmuel stood bravely by, holding on to the knife the rabbi had given him for his trip to Lviv.

Jakob stepped forward and said, "We are trying to escape to the German border. Can you help us?"

A low, raspy voice said, "Why did you come this way?"

"Because of the fighting in Krakow. We detoured to the south, but we lost our way."

The voice continued, "Why would you think it safe to travel through Krakow?"

"We just passed through Krakow five days ago and had no problems," said Jakob.

There was no reply. Clara continued to watch Jakob, wondering what he would say next, but he merely looked at Pincus and shrugged. She could hear quiet, indistinguishable voices all around them.

Then the men in the shadows suddenly withdrew their weapons, as heavy footsteps directed everyone's attention to a large man walking toward them. Stepping from the darkness into the light was a man with the face of a gentle giant.

"My friends, we heard how a certain prince of the Weimar bamboozled you," said the man with a booming laugh, a welcoming smile, and light blue eyes. "We are—or should I say were—your contact for the delivery of the guns."

Jakob smiled and said, "You must be Saul. My contacts in America told me about you."

"Yes, yes I'm Saul. Now let's get you some food and a warm place to rest for the night, and in the morning my men will escort you to the border."

....

Later that night, while everyone else slept, Clara lay awake on a straw mattress on a barn floor with adrenaline still pumping through her. She replayed the moment the guns emerged from trees. How the steel barrels glimmered from the moonlight casting this surreal image of doom. While her first instinct had been to protect the children, Pincus's first instinct had been to protect his whole family, including her.

This act of love was something he had never demonstrated before. Had he changed over the years he'd been away? Before he left for America, Pincus would never have acted so courageously. She recalled back in the shtetl when she had overheard some men walking by the cobbler shop and gossiping about her husband's shameful meekness and desire to avoid confrontation at all costs. The Pincus she was seeing now was not the same man. *I suppose that happens to people under great stress*, she mused. *I hope this change proves to be permanent.*

Then she thought of Moshe and the events of that prior evening. Why hadn't he had an episode moments before they emerged out of the crate? He always senses danger to himself or to his family. It then occurred to her that there had been no danger after all. She remembered looking at Moshe in the heat of the moment, with the guns trained on them, and he had returned her look of panic with a calm gaze. He had known everything would be okay.

Moshe's ability to foreshadow events didn't relieve Clara's terrible burden, the secret that continued to haunt her dreams. She shuddered, thinking of Berbecki's violation of her body. Could she ever overcome the heartache she felt that her once-fond memories of Krzywcza, the birthplace of her children, would forever be tarnished? On top of all of that, this was something that she would never share with anyone, especially not with Pincus. No one could ever know the sacrifice she had made to protect her oldest son.

CHAPTER 59

A GOOD JEW

Their host Saul ended up being a warm and generous man. He told of their militia of Jewish fighters throughout Galicia and their holy war against the Russians.

"Those guns would have been a great help against the barbarians," Saul lamented.

They certainly would have, Jakob agreed silently. *If only I could get my hands on that crooked prince.* But he kept his vengeful thoughts to himself and said, "We are sorry, Saul, for having allowed the prince to con us. It is very embarrassing."

"That's all right. Your intentions were noble. I am sure that our rich Jewish friends in America have heard about the mishap and are right now scheming to replace the lost guns with a new shipment.

"At least you got yourself the royal travel documents. That should get you through Germany without any interference from the military. Bandits, on the other hand, won't care about the prince's papers," Saul warned.

....

The next morning, they offered thanks and goodbyes to Saul and his men. Saul provided a map and directions to Berlin.

"My men will escort you to the border. Once in Germany, stay on the main roads all the way to Berlin. When you get there, go to this address." He wrote the name and address on the map. "He is a good friend, a Jew. Tell him I sent you for his assistance. He will help get you to Hamburg and on a boat to Arendal."

"All I know is your first name. What do I tell your friend?" Jakob asked.

"Just say 'Saul from Krakow'—that's enough."

Saul and his men provided a generous amount of food, water, and extra blankets to make the dark journey in the large wooden crate more manageable. Fortified with rest and these new supplies, Clara, Shmuel, and the children climbed back into the crate, and Jakob and Pincus drew the lid over them.

CHAPTER 60

BERLIN

Pincus opened the map and consulted it. "It's here—number eighteen Schiffbauerdamm. It faces the Spree River."

"We can't pull up to the front of an apartment building in the middle of Berlin pulling this," Jakob said, pointing to the wagon behind him. "Let's find a safe place for the wagon and the horses. Is there a park nearby?"

"Here," Pincus said, "it's close by." He leaned over indicating a place on the map.

The cold January early morning had few people roaming the Berlin streets. The horses made their way slowly, attracting little attention. As they waited for some military vehicles to pass, Pincus grabbed a day-old newspaper out of a trashcan. The front page told of tremendous food shortages and indicated that Berlin would be the first city in Germany to ration bread.

"It says that residents should expect long lines for the basics like bread, meat, potatoes, and milk," he told Jakob.

The park proved to be a good place to wait. The whirling, bitter winds kept the usual morning walkers home, and piles of snow provided decent cover. They removed the lid to the crate.

Clara, Shmuel, and the children took the opportunity to relieve themselves in the nearby thick brush.

"I'll go find this man," Jakob said. "Shmuel, you come with me. Pincus will stay here."

They walked along the river, now choked by large glacial blocks of ice. The buildings along the Schiffbauerdamm looked dark and dreary. Minutes later they found 18 Schiffbauerdamm and entered the protected vestibule area. Jakob scanned the names of its residents posted on the wall.

"Here he is," Jakob said, pressing the bell next to the name of Isaac Kerr.

"Do you think he'll let us up?" asked Shmuel.

"We'll see."

Ten minutes passed and nothing.

"Ring it again," said Shmuel.

Just as Jakob reached to press the bell, a man appeared in the lobby looking out at them through the glass door.

"What do you want?" the man demanded.

"Are you Isaac Kerr?" asked Jakob.

"Who wants to know?"

"We've been sent by Saul from Krakow," replied Jakob.

The door opened and the man said, "Follow me quickly, don't speak."

....

A few hours later, as they prepared to get on their way, Jakob told Clara and Pincus about the conversation he and Shmuel had had with the writer Isaac Kerr.

"He's an interesting man," he told them. "He writes books and articles on Jewish oppression in Europe. He says that we are very smart to be going to America. Life for Jews will be getting much worse."

"That's interesting," Pincus interrupted. "But what about getting us out of the country?"

"He gave me the name of a ship's captain in Hamburg from whom we can buy passage to Arendal. It's going to cost us plenty.

He told me that the Hamburg Shipyard has become a port for the German Navy and their new U-boat submarines, a very effective weapon. They've been destroying British Navy ships in the North Sea. Even if we can get passage on a steamship with a Danish flag, we won't know for sure that we'll be safe, even though Denmark is a neutral country. The U-boats have been attacking, regardless of the ship's flag, and many ships have been flying false flags."

"That's it then," Pincus said. "And let's pray to Hashem that this will be my last time in Hamburg."

CHAPTER 61

HAMBURG SHIPYARDS

As their horses and wagon approached the shipyards, Pincus barely recognized the place where he had stood over four years ago before his voyage to America. The government had transformed the home of the Hamburg-Amerika Line and other transatlantic shipping companies into the base of the German Naval Fleet. Hundreds of men worked on large steel frames, pulling on giant chains, elevating elongated oval metallic gray shapes of new U-boats being prepared to launch into battle. Naval officers in white uniforms directed the men about the shipyard.

Pincus did remember the boat slip that had been home to the *SS Amerika*. In its place now stood the new *SMS Kronprinz*, its tremendous array of guns reaching out twenty feet beyond its stern.

Saul had told them to move quickly through the Hamburg Shipyards and find Captain Walter Schwieger.

"He is a former captain on the *SMS Oldenburg*. His ship was decommissioned before the war, and they forced him into retirement. His life's ambition was to lead a battleship into war, and now he's being sidelined during one of history's greatest conflicts. He transports passengers illegally as a way to thumb his nose at the German government. You fit his passenger profile perfectly. He'll be happy to take you to Arendal if you pay him what he asks."

"This is it," Pincus said as they stopped in front of a dilapidated, weather-beaten, wood-clad building.

The sign out front simply read

CAPTAIN WALTER SCHWIEGER

I guess his name is all you need to know, Pincus thought.

Jakob said, "I'll go buy our passage. Why don't you check on everyone?"

Pincus opened the lid.

"We have to get out of here *now*, Pincus. I can't stand another minute in this box," Clara insisted.

"Okay, Clara, we're here. Jakob is inside arranging our passage right now." Without waiting for Jakob, Clara, Shmuel, and the children climbed out of the cramped and smelly wooden crate they had lived in for the past ten days.

Moshe pointed to the *SMS Kronprinz* and asked, "Are we going on that?"

"No, my boat is a little smaller."

Moshe and everyone else turned toward the man with the gruff and gravelly voice.

"My boat is over there, the *Oldenburg II*," he said, pointing to a section of the shipyard with small boats bobbing in individual slips.

"This is Captain Schwieger," said Jakob. "He has agreed to take us to the Norwegian America Line in Arendal. We need to gather our things quickly and follow him. We are leaving now."

"Now?" asked Clara. "Can we get a few minutes for the children to relieve themselves?"

The captain turned around, showing his deep wrinkled, weathered face with faded translucent eyes. He sneered at Clara and said, "We leave now or never."

"They are closing down all nonmilitary activity at midnight. The captain is right. We must leave right now, or we'll be stuck here," Jakob said, gesturing to the scene around him.

....

The ship moved swiftly through the Elbe River and then into the choppy waters of the North Sea. The captain permitted Jakob and Moshe to join him on the bridge. The grumpy captain took a liking to Moshe's curiosity and allowed him to take the wheel.

"Hold tight, Moshe, these waters are unforgiving. That's it," he encouraged. "You'd make an excellent seaman," the captain bellowed.

He asked Moshe, "Do you know why I named my boat the *Oldenburg II*?"

Moshe shook his head, impatient for an answer.

"I named her after my last assignment as the captain on the *Oldenburg*, the Germans' greatest battleship," he said with pride. "Before some dummkopf decided to decommission her and retire me after thirty years of devoted service to the Prussian Empire."

Nearly ten hours later, they entered the channel leading to the shipyards at Arendal. With the arc of the sun scarcely traversing the horizon at this time of year, night barely turned to day. But there was enough light reflecting off the steel facades of the ships bouncing in the choppy waters to make out the harbor as they approached.

The captain pulled into a slip not too far from the Norwegian America Line and asked Moshe to assist with the docking. As they disembarked, the captain walked over to Pincus and asked, "Moshe is your son?"

"He is, Captain," Pincus said.

"I never had any children. You know, the life at sea leaves no time for a family. But your boy Moshe is special. I don't know what it is, but he has a very calming effect on me, and I am not a calm person. It reminds me of a time when I was a child. It's hard to describe."

The captain crouched down to shake Moshe's hand. He took off his hat and placed it on Moshe's head. Moshe touched it and asked, "Is this for me?"

"It is indeed. You are now Captain Moshe."

Moshe thanked the captain, who embraced him warmly. He ran to his parents, clutching the hat.

"Look, Papa, what the captain gave me. He says it was his hat from the real *SMS Oldenburg*."

"That's quite a gift, Moshe," Pincus said, looking at Clara.

CHAPTER 62

THE *BERGENSFJORD*

Jakob found the Norwegian America Line ticket office hidden behind large crates waiting to be loaded onto a cargo ship. "It's here," he yelled over the noise and activity of the busy shipyard.

Pincus responded with a wave and led Clara, Shmuel, and the children over to him. Each one carrying a small valise, they hardly looked like passengers about to purchase two first-class cabins for passage to America.

The ticket agent looked at Pincus, Jakob, and their entourage standing behind them, and shrugged. Jakob paid him $200 in US currency, and they had their passage to America.

As they gathered their meager belongings, Pincus said to the children, "I'll tell you about my first voyage to America and how Jakob and I met after we get ourselves settled."

As they walked from the ticket office to the first-class boarding area, Pincus watched the steerage passengers standing in long lines, huddled in groups in order to stay warm. The ramp for first-class offered a covered gangplank that quickly ushered the passengers on board and into their cabins.

Jakob presented their tickets to the officer who scornfully looked them over. Their clothing and luggage suggested steerage, not first class. Jakob smiled at the officer who returned the greeting with a smirk and instructed a young crewman to take their luggage.

"Is this all you have?" asked the crewman.

"We travel light," replied Jakob as they handed over their luggage that consisted of several old valises, some of them tied up with twine to keep them from popping open.

The valises were loaded on a dolly and pushed up the ramp as the Potaszniks, Jakob, and Shmuel followed closely behind.

The two cabins were situated directly across from each other with the center hallway running in between. They gathered around as Clara announced that Jennie, Anna, Hymie, and Moshe would stay with her in one cabin and Pincus, Jakob and Shmuel in the other.

"Please, Mama, may I stay with Papa in his cabin?" Moshe pleaded.

"If it is all right with your father," said Clara.

"Of course. He is a man now," Pincus said, pulling Moshe close.

....

They unpacked their few belongings into the elaborate wood-carved drawers and cabinets, taking up only a fraction of the space allotted for first-class passengers. Pincus watched Jakob slip on his dinner jacket and realized that Clara would not have anything appropriate for the first-class dining hall.

"Do you suppose the ship has a clothing store on board?" Pincus asked Jakob.

"I believe they do, and I know what you're thinking."

....

As Clara held on to his arm, Pincus led them into the dining hall.

He leaned over and whispered, "You look beautiful."

She thanked him, and he looked past her at their children. Each wore new clothes that Pincus had purchased at the ship's store. Jennie looked like a grown woman, in a beautiful blue dress.

Anna looked adorable in a plaid one-piece that was probably meant for a boy. But she didn't seem to notice or care. Hymie wore something similar in a solid green fabric. The men, including Moshe, all looked handsome in dinner jackets, white shirts, and pressed pants.

When Pincus had come to Clara's cabin to present her with her dress, she had gasped. "I've never owned a formal gown like this before, except for one my mother made me when I was a little girl."

As she stood in front of the full-length mirror in her cabin, Pincus by her side, he admired how beautiful it looked on her. A soft flowing fabric casually sculpted her curves. The light salmon color went well with her complexion and her auburn hair, which she had pinned up into a bun. A short lace jacket in a similar color layered over her shoulders, covered her neck, and ended just below her elbow, leaving her forearms bare. To top it off, a celadon-green ribbon was wrapped around her waist, tied off with a bow along her hip, and draped down to a few inches from the floor.

"I don't even want to know the cost of this extravagance," she said.

"Good, because I wouldn't tell you anyway. You've been through too many years of suffering not to enjoy this moment," he said as he kissed her.

CHAPTER 63

JAKOB MEETS THEODOR

The voyage to America took ten days. While Pincus spent time with Clara and the children, Jakob had time to get to know Shmuel. He told Shmuel how he had met Shmuel's father and brothers in New York and how Mendel was really the man responsible for the success of the Landsman Society.

"Pincus likes you to think otherwise," he told Shmuel privately. "He may be the president and likes to take all the credit, but your father is the one running the organization."

He told Shmuel how he and Pincus had built up the cobbler shop into a thriving business, leaving out the illegal activities he'd used the shop for that had brought in the bulk of their profit.

"I wish I could work there," he said sadly. "But a one-armed cobbler isn't much good."

"Don't worry. I'm sure we'll find you work that will suit you," said Jakob.

....

Leaving Pincus, Clara, and the children in their cabins, Jakob and Shmuel spent their evenings in the men's smoking lounge. Jakob easily conversed with many of his fellow passengers. He learned that most were traveling on the *Bergensfjord* as a last chance to cross the Atlantic. The German U-boats were becoming too much of a threat, even for neutral countries like Norway. There were stories of enemy ships falsely flying colors of other nations, and the German Navy had become suspicious of any ship traveling through the North and Baltic Seas.

On one evening, Shmuel excused himself early.

"I'm tired tonight. Would you mind if I go back to the cabin?"

"That's fine. I probably won't stay much longer. I'll see you in the morning."

With Shmuel gone, Jakob wandered over to where several men hovered, curiously watching a poker game. He approached the table, which was cloaked in cigar smoke, stood next to one of the men, and took a moment to admire his perfectly tailored jacket that ended at his knees. The jacket opened like drapes to reveal a black vest with pinstripes in a matching charcoal shade. The gray trousers featured a dark black pinstripe. Even his stylish gray-black mustache and dark eyes coordinated well with his outfit.

The man looked over at Jakob, slipped his left hand into his vest pocket, and offered his right. "Good evening, sir. My name is Theodor Bergman," the gentleman said.

Jakob straightened his spine and returned the handshake. "Good evening, Mr. Bergman. I am Jakob Adler."

"Won't you join me for a cognac? I'm getting bored watching other men play cards."

"I would be honored, sir," Jakob replied.

Several hours and quite a few cognacs later, Jakob and Theodor were trading stories, each of them trying to outdo the another with more and more amazing tales.

Jakob learned that Theodor Bergman was a German businessman with factories that produced various types of firearms.

"The war has been good to me," he boasted and whispered that he wished it would continue.

Jakob told Theodor about his attempt to smuggle five hundred guns from America to the Jewish fighters in Krakow.

"That sounds exactly like the prince," Theodor laughed.

"You know the prince?"

"Of course, I know him. We do business together. Who do you think buys my guns?"

A brief interruption paused the conversation as Theodor greeted a few friends who approached the table. Jakob was introduced to other wealthy industrialists in such booming businesses as railroads, steel, and shipbuilding.

Soon they were alone again. Theodor gave Jakob a pensive look and said, "Tell me, who sent you to Galicia with these American guns?"

Jakob hesitated at first, but then realized Bergman would make a good ally and might help him with Gorpatsch, who certainly wouldn't be pleased that they'd been conned and lost his rifles.

"Do you know Leo Gorpatsch?" Jakob began carefully.

"You're involved with that thief?"

"Involved? I wouldn't say that, exactly. Let me just say our paths have crossed a few times," he said. "Anyway, how do *you* know Mr. Gorpatsch?"

"We've done business together over the years. He used to spend time in Berlin before the war. I sold him guns." He paused and then went on, "He's a thug. So, I shouldn't have been surprised when he hijacked one of my shipments and stole ten thousand dollars worth of goods."

Jakob listened without interrupting.

"I've been looking for a way to take my revenge on Leo. Perhaps now I've found it." He leaned back, took a long drag on his cigar, tilted back his head, and exhaled a stream of smoke that exploded into patterns as it hit the wood-paneled ceiling.

CHAPTER 64

BACK IN THE LOWER EAST SIDE

P incus wrapped his arm around Clara as they stood side by side grasping the railing of the first-class promenade. No amount of driving snow blowing across New York Harbor could have dampened their spirits. The children stood next to them, transfixed by the giant metal statue rising out of the swirling waters.

Pincus turned to his children and said, "She is called the Statue of Liberty, and she is saying, 'Welcome to America.'"

As a first-class passenger, Pincus had savored each remaining moment on this ship, knowing that once they disembarked, his elevated status would cease to exist. However, there was still a last indignity that his family's first-class tickets would spare them: the demeaning health inspections and humiliating questions required to pass through customs and immigration at Ellis Island. The privileged class were simply given a cursory exam aboard the ship and quickly admitted into the country.

The porter followed Pincus and his family onto the waiting ferry for lower Manhattan, where they handed off their luggage and ended their first-class life. But Pincus didn't care. He had rescued his wife and children and brought them to a new and safer life in America. Still, there would be a few manageable challenges, such as finding a larger apartment, reopening the cobbler shop, and getting the children into school. But this was nothing like the life they had left in Krzywcza.

To the children's delight, as well as Clara and Shmuel's, they took a taxi from the Battery Park docks to the Ludlow Street apartment.

As they pulled up to the building, Pincus turned to Clara. "This is it," he said, pointing to the sign swinging back and forth in the wind. "Our shop is here and up the stairs is the apartment. We will be cramped until we find a larger place. Tomorrow we will make some inquiries."

No one seemed to care. Moshe dashed up the stairs, followed by Hymie, who was trying to keep up.

"Slow down, boys, you don't know where you're going," shouted Pincus. He held Clara's hand as he led her up to their floor.

As Clara examined the decrepit conditions with a look of horror on her face, Pincus assured her, "It's only temporary. I waited for you to come so we could choose a larger and nicer place together."

Despite the inconvenience of eight people living in a one-room apartment, they all slept well that night.

Pincus woke at four o'clock and hurried to the shop. It was just as he had left it. A large pile of mail lay on the floor by the front door mail slot. He would have Jakob sort through it.

A few hours later, Jakob came in and said, "I'll go speak with Manny this morning. I'm sure he can find you a larger place. Shmuel can stay with me unless he wants to go and live with his father. He's already gone out looking for him."

Later that morning, Clara and the children came down to the shop.

"This is your shop, Papa?" Moshe asked.

"This is it. What do you think?" he asked proudly.

"It's great, Papa," Moshe said.

"Pincus," Clara interrupted, "we need to go to market. Can you take us?"

"Yes, of course, Clara. Just wait until you see the pushcarts on Delancey. All the choices will make you dizzy. Let me lock up and we'll go."

....

Pincus treated them to a tour of Delancey Street.

"Look at all these fruits and vegetables! They have everything here—breads and meats, knishes, pickles—" Clara said. "I've never seen so many things. It's almost too many choices."

As they finished their shopping for the day and began to walk toward their lodgings, Clara turned and smiled at Pincus, then looked behind her to make sure all her children were still following. Suddenly startled she asked, "Where's Moshe?"

Pincus turned and scanned the busy street. "He's over there, sitting on that stoop."

They ran over and found Moshe's head tilted forward resting in his palms.

"Moshe, are you sick?" Clara asked in a panic.

He lifted his head and she saw he was exhibiting the same symptoms as his previous episodes.

Pincus picked him up, and Moshe wrapped his arms around his neck and legs around his hips. "Hold on to me tight and I'll carry you."

With bags full of groceries and Moshe in the arms of his father, they rushed home. As they turned the corner onto Ludlow, they saw several police cars parked out front.

"What is going on, Pincus?" Clara asked.

"I have no idea."

They walked up to the storefront, and Hymie said, "Why is Jakob in that police car, Papa?"

Pincus looked over and saw Jakob staring back through the window of one of the patrol cars parked askew.

A policeman walked up to Pincus and asked, "Are you Pincus Potasznik?"

"Yes."

"My name is Captain Becker. Please put the child down.

You will need to come with me to the station. You are under arrest," he said and directed one of the officers to handcuff him.

"What is going on?" Pincus yelled. "Arrested for what?"

"Money laundering among other crimes. But you will learn more at the arraignment," said the captain.

Pincus lowered Moshe to the sidewalk. The officer grabbed his wrists and snapped on the handcuffs. With his arms stretched behind him, they pushed him into the backseat next to Jakob.

"Papa, where are they taking you?" asked Jennie.

"It will be all right. Go upstairs, I'll be home soon," said Pincus.

Clara stood there with grocery bags clutched in both hands, Moshe sitting ill on the frozen sidewalk, and Jennie staring at the police cars as they pulled away.

As Pincus turned to watch them through the back window, he gave a feeble smile, trying to let them know that everything would be all right.

CHAPTER 65

LUDLOW JAIL

Pincus and Jakob were locked in a small cell inside the Seventh Precinct station on Pitt Street.

"Jakob, can you tell me what is going on?"

"We've been arrested, Pincus," Jakob said.

Pincus rolled his eyes. "Enough with the sarcasm. Is there something *else* you need to tell me?"

"Don't act so surprised Pincus. You knew what was going on at the shop. You just chose to turn a blind eye to it."

"What are we being accused of? The cop said money laundering. What would that be?" asked Pincus.

Jakob put a finger to his mouth and said in a near whisper, "It's not just money laundering. I was collecting loan payments for Manny. We used the shop as a place for borrowers to drop off cash. I took a five percent cut and handed the rest to Manny."

"I did have an idea you were involved with some bad guys, but not to this extent. You put my entire family at risk, Jakob."

"You know that wasn't my intention. Please forgive me."

"How did they find out about it?" Pincus asked, with a sigh of resignation.

"I think Gorpatsch is behind this. Captain Becker is on his payroll and set us up. I'm sure he's not happy we lost his guns to the prince."

"How would he know about this already?"

"Gorpatsch has eyes and ears everywhere. I wouldn't be surprised if the prince sent word. The two of them probably set us up from the very beginning," Jakob said.

"Maybe they didn't think we would make it back?"

"Probably not. But I met someone on the ship. If I can get word to him, I think he can help us."

....

Later that day, Jakob and Pincus were brought before a magistrate for their arraignment. They were charged with usury and money laundering, crimes that, if convicted, meant many years in prison. Bail was refused because they were considered a flight risk due to their recent trip to Germany.

They were transferred to the prison on Ludlow Street, only a few blocks away from the apartment and the shop.

"I didn't even know there was a jail on our street," said Jakob who stretched out on one of the two benches lining the cell walls, while Pincus paced back and forth, rubbing his hands together.

"I can't believe you're so relaxed right now, Jakob. We're in prison! How will Clara know where to find us?" Pincus asked.

"She can go to the police station and ask," said Jakob.

"Hopefully Shmuel located Mendel. He will know how to find us."

"That's right, and then I can get word to Mr. Bergman. He's our ticket out of here."

CHAPTER 66

CLARA MEETS LEO

Clara did her best preparing breakfast. Unlike her kitchen back home, she had little to work with. None of that mattered now. Pincus had done it again, abandoned her and the children. How could she have been so wrong about him? He had just demonstrated tremendous courage and fortitude in rescuing them from war-torn Galicia. How could it unravel so quickly?

However, she knew she needed to be strong, as she had been in the past. *I have done it before*, she reminded herself: *managing the cobbler shop back home, taking care of four children and my mother, and surviving a year of war. There is just one thing I will never do again*, she vowed.

A sharp rap at the door startled her. The children all looked at the door and then back at her.

"Stay put, I'll get the door," said Clara.

She opened the door an inch and peeked out.

"Shmuel, thank heaven it's you," she said and opened the door to Shmuel and his father, Mendel.

"Clara, my dear, it is good to see you," exclaimed Mendel. "Look at your children, how they have grown."

"It's good to see you too, Mendel. It's been a while."

"Where's Pincus?" he asked.

Clara told Mendel and Shmuel the story of Jakob and Pincus's arrest.

"I have no idea where they took them," Clara said. "Can you help me find them?"

"Let's go to the station on Pitt Street and find out. Shmuel, stay here with the children until we get back."

After pleading for several minutes, they finally learned where Pincus and Jakob were being held.

"Let me see," said the desk sergeant looking a clipboard, "Pincus Potasznik and Jakob Adler. Here they are. They have been interned at the Ludlow Street Jail."

They hurried out and back the ten blocks toward Ludlow. Breathlessly Mendel and Clara entered the prison and asked to see the men. A clerk told them to wait and disappeared behind a wooden door. A few minutes later he returned and told them that they would need to come back later during visitor hours between three and five in the afternoon. As it was still early morning and the prison only a few blocks from the apartment, they decided to wait at home.

They returned a few minutes before three. After filling out a form, they were escorted into a small room with a table and four chairs, two on each side. On the wall facing them was another door, where they assumed Pincus and Jakob would soon appear.

Clara stared at the door handle and as soon as she saw it move she grabbed Mendel's hand. "Here they come," she said.

Instead of her husband and Jakob, a well-dressed man with a short-cropped red beard entered.

"Good afternoon, Mrs. Potasznik," he said, removing his hat and offering a handshake.

Clara, not knowing this man but not wishing to offend, took his hand.

"And you must be Mendel Beck," the man added.

"I am. Who are you and when will we get to see Pincus and Jakob?" Mendel asked as they shook hands.

"My name in Leo Gorpatsch. I am a business acquaintance of Jakob Adler and, in a way, of Pincus Potasznik as well."

"When can I see my husband?" Clara interrupted.

"That's why I'm here. I'm afraid that you won't see him for a while. Your husband, along with his buddy Jakob, seems to have lost some property of mine, and unless there is compensation for my loss, I can't imagine Pincus or Jakob will ever be walking the Lower East Side streets again as free men."

Mr. Gorpatsch stood up, replaced the hat on his head, adjusted it, said, "Good day Mrs. Potasznik . . . Mr. Beck," and left the room.

Clara turned to gape at Mendel. She felt her mouth trying to move, but no words would come out.

CHAPTER 67

THE PLAN

Back home, Clara paced the few steps it took to walk from wall to wall in the tiny tenement room. Mendel and Shmuel sat in the only two chairs, and the children huddled on the worn wooden floor.

"Who is this Leo Gorpatsch?" asked Clara. "Mendel, do you know this man?"

"I think I have an idea of who he is," said Mendel. "Pincus told me that Jakob got himself mixed up with a couple of rival gangsters. A meeting was arranged between them at the shop one evening. Unbeknownst to Jakob, the police had the place staked out. Shots were fired, and one of the gangsters was killed along with the district attorney."

Clara gasped. "Right downstairs in Pincus's shop?"

"Right there—although I realize it's hard to imagine," Mendel agreed.

"Afterward, no one heard about any charges or arrests made. Some people are saying that the surviving gangster was Leo Gorpatsch, the man we met. Rumor has it Police Captain Becker is on his payroll."

Clara shook her head in disbelief. "How can this be happening?" she asked in despair.

Shmuel stood up and walked over to Clara. "We've been through tough times before, Clara. I'll do whatever it takes to get Pincus and Jakob released."

She patted Shmuel affectionately on the cheek. "Thank you, but I can't ask you to risk your life again for my family. You have gone through so much," she said, gently touching his maimed hand.

"I'll go see this Captain Becker alone. I've had experience with men like him before," she said with a glance over at Moshe. "I won't leave without arranging a meeting with Gorpatsch."

"What will you say when you see Gorpatsch?" asked Mendel.

"I don't know, Mendel. I'll think of something."

CHAPTER 68

CLARA MAKES A DEAL

Clara had to wait hours before Captain Becker would agree to see her. During this time, she couldn't help recalling her early interactions with Captain Berbecki, and the collision course they had sent her on. This time, she would do everything in her power to handle this captain in a businesslike manner.

"Mrs. Potasznik, the captain can see you now," said the desk sergeant, who fortunately spoke Yiddish.

Clara stood, smoothed out her dress, and thanked the sergeant with a nod. As she entered the captain's office, she led with an outstretched arm poised for a firm handshake. But no one was there to return it. She looked around the room. There was no place to hide. She poked her head back in the waiting area. The sergeant was also gone. Confused, she turned back into the office and saw Leo Gorpatsch sitting in the chair behind the desk.

"Mrs. Potasznik, please come in. I'm so sorry I startled you," he said.

"I thought I was seeing Captain Becker," she fumbled.

"The captain is unavailable, but you can speak with me. Please sit down and tell me how I can be of service."

"Fine. I wish for Pincus and Jakob to be released."

"That's not likely, Mrs. Potasznik. I do apologize, but you must understand that I cannot allow my employees to cause me significant monetary losses without serious consequences."

"Please amuse me, Mr. Gorpatsch, and tell me what these losses are?" Clara said.

"And if I tell you, what do you plan to do about it?" Gorpatsch was clearly amused.

"I will attempt to make right whatever harm Jakob or my husband have caused you."

"Well, I am impressed, Mrs. Potasznik. You certainly carry yourself quite well. I appreciate such a quality in a woman."

"Thank you, sir," she replied.

"I offered Jakob two thousand dollars to deliver much-needed guns to Jewish fighters in Krakow," he began.

"A noble cause," Clara added.

"Indeed, Mrs. Potasznik."

"Please call me Clara," she remarked.

"Very well, Clara. Please call me Leo," he volleyed back.

Clara smiled.

"So, as I was saying. I offered him two thousand dollars. I paid Jakob a thousand up front. He would have received another thousand if he'd delivered the guns successfully. Unfortunately, a young and sly prince of Prussia snookered your husband and Jakob. The loss of the guns, including the lost profit, comes to another thousand. If you want to settle the score, you would need to come up with two thousand dollars plus interest."

"Let me see what I can do, Leo." Clara paused to allow the idea to sink in. "I would need to speak with my husband first. He will direct me how to accumulate the money you require."

"This is intriguing. I will allow it. Please let me know when I can expect the money, Clara."

"Give me a week, Leo," Clara said.

"Agreed," he said, slamming his fist on the table. "I like you, Clara!"

CHAPTER 69

VISITORS' DAY

Living in a prison cell for two days had Pincus continuously scratching at phantom itches. He watched Jakob sleep the entire night as if he were still in his first-class bed on the *Bergensfjord*. Being locked away without any outside contact was unbearable. What would Clara be thinking? *She must be disgusted with me again. This is the second time I abandoned her and the children. I wouldn't blame her if she never spoke to me again. Would she leave me and take the children away? I suppose I deserve it.*

Pincus heard footsteps approach from down the hallway. He shook Jakob who had nodded off, and said, "Wake up. Someone is coming."

"Adler, Potasznik let's go. You have a visitor," the guard announced.

Pincus exchanged a quick glance with Jakob, who was already on his feet. The guard opened the door and gestured for them to walk on ahead to the door down the hall. They were led into a small, windowless room with a table and four chairs, and a door faced them on the opposite wall.

"Sit and wait here," the guard ordered and stood alongside the table.

A minute later the other door opened and in walked Clara. "Clara!" Pincus exclaimed and stood up.

Two strong hands forced him back down. "Don't stand until I tell you to stand and don't touch the visitor," the guard instructed.

"It's okay, she's my wife."

"I don't care if she's your mother. Sit and don't touch, or this visitation is over."

"All right, I will. Clara, are you okay? How are the children? We need to get out of here. Did you speak with Mendel? He can get us a lawyer through the society."

"Slow down, Pincus. Everything is okay. The children are fine. I've spoken with Mendel, and we're working on a few things," Clara said in a slow deliberate manner.

"Clara," Jakob interrupted. "I met a man on the *Bergensfjord*. His name is Theodor Bergman. He has an office in the Germania Bank Building on the Bowery. Tell him what's happened. I think he can help."

....

The Germania Bank Building was only eight blocks from the Ludlow Street Prison. In fifteen minutes, Clara stood in front of the ornate granite facade of the six-story building that wrapped itself around the corner of Bowery and Spring Streets. She stepped into the vestibule and located BERGMAN ARMS, SIXTH FLOOR on the highly-polished, brass-framed directory on the wall.

She hurried through the lobby of the Germania Bank to the elevator. She took a breath and offered a courteous smile to the operator as she entered the car. Nervously she watched the hand sweep across an arc that indicted the floors they passed. The car jolted to a stop at six. The uniformed operator pulled the doors open and looked at Clara.

"First time in an elevator?" he asked.

She smiled and nodded. "Yes, thank you," she said and hurried off.

A few plaques on the wall with arrows pointing left or right indicated the names and direction of the offices on the sixth floor. Right at the top she saw it, Bergman Arms with an arrow to the right.

Clara removed her coat, neatly folded it, and draped it across her arm. She smoothed out any creases in her dress and finger-combed her hair. This Theodor Bergman must be a very important man if he manufactures guns, especially during wartime. Jakob said he'd met this man on the *Bergensfjord*. It must have been in the men's smoking lounge.

All these thoughts buzzed through Clara's mind as she opened the impressive set of mahogany doors into his office. She had no idea what to expect, but she never thought she would see a large open office with huge windows flanking both sides. The room was flooded with sunlight that streamed in from the south. In the middle of the room sat the largest desk Clara had ever seen. It looked like a Roman temple with carved columns at the corners and capitals at its top supporting a four-inch-thick mahogany desktop. The man sitting behind the desk looked up at the intruder.

"May I help you, madam?" he asked with a heavy German accent.

"I am so sorry to just walk in. I thought I would find a secretary or an assistant," Clara said awkwardly in a mix of Yiddish and German.

The man stood up. The large desk seemed suited to his stature. He walked around the desk and extended his hand. "My name is Theodor Bergman. Please have a seat and tell me who you are."

Clara firmly shook his hand. "My name is Clara Potasznik."

"That's an impressive handshake from a woman, Mrs. Potasznik."

"Thank you, sir."

"Well, it's nice to meet you. Please tell me how I may be of assistance."

Clara related the entire story, beginning with Jakob's deal with Leo Gorpatsch and ending with Jakob and Pincus locked up in the Ludlow Street Prison.

"That is an amazing story, and yes, of course, I do remember speaking with Jakob on the *Bergensfjord*. We discussed Leo Gorpatsch. He's been my nemesis for too long. Perhaps the time has come to exact my revenge and at the same time help your husband and Jakob."

CHAPTER 70

RELEASED

Early the next morning, Pincus and Jakob walked out onto Ludlow Street and saw Clara and Shmuel waiting for them. "How in the world did you get us out, Clara?" Pincus asked.

"Jakob's friend proved to be very influential. He knows a federal judge, a fellow German, who allowed bail to be set, which Mr. Bergman paid. So, you're free, for now . . . until the trial," Clara said.

As they walked the few blocks back home, Clara added, "We need to go see him after dinner tonight at his office. Mr. Bergman has a few ideas on how to deal with Leo Gorpatsch and get you two out of trouble."

Once at home in their cramped one-room apartment, Pincus assured the children that everything would be fine and they were not to worry.

"Papa, why were you arrested?" asked Moshe.

"It seems that the man who asked us to bring guns to the Jewish fighters in Krakow didn't like the fact that we lost them to the Prussian prince. But it looks like we have a very important man who wants to help," Pincus explained to Moshe and the other children.

At lunchtime, Mendel came for a visit. As they sat at the kitchen table, Mendel said, "I've been hearing grumbling from some board members. They are not happy that the president of the Landsman Society has been arrested. It doesn't look good. Some are asking for your immediate resignation."

"Schmucks, all of them. I haven't been charged with a crime. The arrest was bogus. It's Leo Gorpatsch who's behind this. He has the police and the politicians in his pocket. It's about getting his money back for the guns we lost. I doubt it's even about that."

Pincus leaned over the table to whisper so the children wouldn't hear. "What I believe is that Gorpatsch wants Jakob to disappear. They are both dating the actress Nita Naldi, and Gorpatsch is jealous. He wants her all to himself."

"Really, Pincus? You think all this mess is because of a love triangle?"

"I do, Mendel. Anyway, it doesn't matter. We're working on a way to clear this all up. Tell those schmucks that I won't resign. They'll have to wait until my term is up and vote me off."

CHAPTER 71

JAKOB AND NITA

Jakob found Nita in her dressing room getting ready for the evening performance of *Forbidden Fruit*.

"Jakob, I heard you were arrested. What happened?" Nita asked, looking at Jakob's reflection in the mirror as she applied her makeup.

"It's your friend Leo again. He set us up and got us arrested. Remember the story I told you about the guns and the Prussian prince?"

"I do, Jakob. That was funny."

"Funny? Well, not really—considering it was Leo who set us up in Germany and who's turned out to be the one who masterminded our arrests. Luckily, Pincus and I were able to find a way out. At least for now."

"I'm sorry, Jakob. That's awful. I didn't mean to make light of it. Maybe one day we can laugh about it. But, as you see, I need to get ready for the matinee. The show starts in a few hours. Can we discuss this another time?"

"Of course, Nita. I just came by to ask you if you want to make a life with me. Just me. Not this three-way craziness."

"Jakob, you know that's impossible. How can we make a life together? You know nothing about me."

"I know the only thing that's important, and that is that I love you," he said, giving her his most charming smile.

"That's very nice, Jakob. But I have a history that may change your mind about me."

"Nita, do you think you are the only one with secrets, the only one with a questionable history? Think again. There's nothing you can say that could ever change my mind about you."

Nita spun around in her chair from the mirror to look directly at Jakob. "I appreciate that, Jakob, but I would feel better if I could tell you my story first, before you make such a claim."

Jakob removed a hat—one that Nita would be wearing in her scandalous and popular new show—from the nearest chair and sat down. "I'm all ears," he said.

"My real name is not Nita Naldi," she began. "My parents, Joseph and Bridget Dooley, emigrated from Ireland before I was born, and like many fellow Irishmen, they had little money. They found a cheap tenement on Orchard Street. This is where I was born.

"Father got involved with a gang called the Hudson Dusters, and like all gangs, they demanded goods from local merchants in exchange for protection."

Jakob nodded, acknowledging his familiarity with this type of nefarious business.

"One day they ran into a saloonkeeper who refused to deliver six barrels of beer for a gang party the Hudson Dusters were planning. My father, along with several of his fellow cronies, broke into the saloon to take what they considered to be rightfully theirs. To their chagrin, the police were there waiting for them. Father never came home that night. My mother identified the bullet-ridden body at the city morgue the next morning.

"After Father's death, Mother needed to find work. She ended up doing the only thing she had any skill for, and that was sewing in a sweatshop located in a room in a tenement building on Grand Street. She found a job paying ten dollars a week.

"When I turned twelve years old, she took me along with her. 'You need to work too if you want to eat,' she told me.

"Two years later, she became ill from cholera and died."

"I'm sorry, Nita."

"Thank you," Nita replied, nodding her head. "Anyhow, once she was gone, I continued to work, sewing clothes from six in the morning to six in the evening, seven days a week. I forced myself to go out on Saturday evenings, which meant just an innocent walk along Delancey Street.

"On one such walk on a summer evening, I heard singing coming from an Irish pub. The joyful sounds lured me to the place. I covered my head with a scarf so I wouldn't attract attention. Then I walked down four brick steps to the front door and slipped inside unnoticed. I found a place against a wall that gave me a partial view of a woman on stage singing joyously and a man hunched over a keyboard accompanying her. The audience seemed transfixed by the beautiful, slender woman with curly blonde hair.

"After the applause died down, the singer announced, 'I am going to sing a song I think many of you know. Please feel free to sing along with me.'

"The piano player began the introduction, and immediately the audience knew the song and cheered. They sang out the words and filled the room with sweetness."

"What was the song?" Jakob asked.

Nita leaned over from her chair, reached for Jakob's hands, and sang:

Let me call you sweetheart
I'm in love with you.
Let me hear you whisper
That you love me too.
Keep the love light glowing
In your eyes so true.
Let me call you sweetheart,
I'm in love with you.

Jakob felt himself blushing at Nita's lovely voice.

"Everyone sang and swayed from side to side in perfect unison. I felt joyful and knew at that moment what I wanted to do with my life. Whoever this beautiful singer was on stage, that would be me. That was the day Mary Dooley died and Nita Naldi was born."

Before he spoke, Jakob leaned in and kissed Nita tenderly. Then he said, "Now, why in the world would that story change the way I feel about you? I think I love you even more, knowing this about you."

"You're sweet, Jakob. But please be realistic. Even if you don't judge me, you know Leo would never allow me to marry you. He is a very powerful man, and I'm afraid that he would hurt me if I ever broke up with him."

Jakob jumped to his feet, knocking over his chair. "Damn it, Nita! We can't live our lives this way. I love you, and I want to marry you."

"Jakob, I love you too. But I don't see how we could ever be free of Leo."

"You leave that to me," he said.

He stormed out of her dressing room as Nita called out after him, "Don't do anything you'll regret."

CHAPTER 72

LEO'S PLAN

L eo sat in his office on the top floor of the Flatiron building overlooking the late-night traffic along Broadway. He had recently learned that Jakob and Pincus were out of jail. Some German judge had reversed the magistrate's decision and allowed bail to be set, and a $1,000 bond had posted. It wasn't hard to figure out who would have that kind of money and influence with a federal judge of German descent. *It must be my old friend Theodor Bergman*, Leo thought. *But why would Theo be interested in Jakob and Pincus? He's probably looking for a way to get back at me for the Berlin heist*, he reasoned.

....

Later that afternoon, the mustached man escorted Jakob into Gorpatsch's office.

"Hello Jakob. I see you managed to find your way out of Ludlow Prison," Gorpatsch said, offering Jakob a seat in front of his desk.

"No thanks to you," Jakob replied.

"If I had my way, you would still be rotting there."

"Based on what charges? This is a country of laws. Not even you are above them."

"True, Jakob, but let's not argue. You should have been more careful and not boasted to the prince what you were up to. But what's done is done. Keeping you locked away won't do anything for me."

Jakob nodded.

"I've come up with a plan for making you square with me," Gorpatsch said, standing up and leaning against the windowsill behind his desk.

"It's not hard to figure out that Theodor Bergman is the one who pulled the strings to get you out on bail." He looked at Jakob, waiting for some reaction. When none came, he continued. "I assume you know that Theodor Bergman is the owner of Bergman Arms. One of the largest arms dealers in Europe. He's making a fortune from the war."

"I've heard something about that," Jakob said casually. "What's your plan?"

"You go and speak with Bergman. Tell him I want to settle our differences. It makes no sense for us to be at odds. I'll make good on what I cost him in Berlin in exchange for an alliance."

"You want me to set up a meeting between you and Theodor Bergman?" Jakob said.

"That's right. You can act as the neutral third party. I'll let you select the location. Choose a spot that makes you feel safe."

"I did that once before at the cobbler shop and it didn't turn out well," Jakob reminded him.

"I thought you might mention that." Stroking his beard, he went on, "I needed to get rid of the Monk. He was bad for business. This is different. I carry no such ill will toward Bergman. In fact, he is very useful to my future plans, as are you, Jakob," he said, resuming his seat behind his desk.

"You set up this meeting, and afterwards we'll talk about bringing you into my organization full time. No more collections at the cobbler shop. You'll have people working under you. A position with responsibilities and a future."

Jakob looked at Gorpatsch for a moment before answering. "Okay, Mr. Gorpatsch, I'll set up this meeting under one condition."

"What would that be?" he asked.

"That you have the charges dropped against me and Pincus today. Not after the meeting, today. I need to assure Pincus and Clara that this is resolved so they can get on with their lives."

"Consider it done."

CHAPTER 73

THE DONNYBROOK

Jakob found an Irish pub on Clinton Street called the Donnybrook, which seemed like a good compromise meeting place for a German and a Jew. The Donnybrook was laid out like most Irish pubs in the city with a long wooden bar hugging its length and tall, backless, cushioned bar stools. Glass shelves with a mirror backdrop featured its many whiskeys. A dozen rectangular tables with four chairs occupied the remaining space.

In the back sat a round table. Jakob made arrangements with the owner of the pub to reserve this particular table since it was secluded in the rear. This would be advantageous for a getaway, since the back door was just a few steps away through the kitchen and out into the alleyway.

Both men agreed to an afternoon meeting when the place would be quiet. Acting as a mediator, Jakob set the ground rules. The meeting would be just the three of them. Each man would come alone with no bodyguards or backup. There would be no weapons allowed into the pub. Jakob had arranged for Luke, one of the Donnybrook's larger bouncers, to do the pat-downs.

Jakob arrived early to make sure the table remained unoccupied. As three o'clock approached, the two men arrived within a minute of each other. Luke conducted thorough pat-downs, and all three men took their seats at the back table.

"It's good to see you, Theodor. You're looking well," said Gorpatsch.

Bergman sighed, shook his hand, and replied, "Leo, you thief. Did you think you'd be able to hide from me forever?"

"Now, Theodor, this is no way to start our reconciliation."

"Is that what this meeting is about?" asked Bergman.

"Didn't Jakob tell you? I want to make things right between us. Why can't we settle our differences and move on? I'm prepared to compensate you for my poor decision in Berlin. I'm here to apologize, Theo."

"Only a fool would trust you, Leo," Bergman said.

"You are indeed the wise one," Gorpatsch said, as he quickly rose from his chair, a miniature pistol suddenly appearing in the palm of his hand.

CHAPTER 74

TWO SHOTS

Leo fired twice, one shot for Bergman and one for Jakob. Both hit the target right in the middle of the man's forehead. They fell over in their chairs nearly simultaneously. Their heads smashed against the travertine floor, and blood quickly pooled beneath them.

Gorpatsch calmly picked up his coat and hat and walked toward the front door. Blocking his exit stood Luke, the six-foot six, 350-pound bouncer.

"You just shot those two men," Luke said.

"Very observant," Gorpatsch said sarcastically. "And if you don't want to be the third, I suggest you get out of my way."

Luke's gaze shifted from Gorpatsch to something over his shoulder.

Gorpatsch spun around to see what had distracted Luke from the intense encounter, and he couldn't believe his eyes. Walking toward him, carrying a shotgun aimed right at him, was Pincus. Gorpatsch tried to comprehend the sight of this slight man with round, wire-rimmed glasses, wearing a round felt hat and a long black coat, and walking toward him with purposeful determination.

"Pincus, what are you doing?"

Those were the last words ever spoken by Leo Gorpatsch.

CHAPTER 75

PINCUS'S REVENGE

As Pincus pulled the trigger, the shotgun seemed to explode. Gorpatsch was blasted off his feet and crashed through the plate glass window and onto the sidewalk. His torso was ripped apart from the shotgun and the rest of his body sliced up by shards of glass.

Pincus looked out through the large hole that was once the Donnybrook's window and saw Gorpatsch lying dead in a pile of packed snow that was turning red as he bled out. He turned around and handed the shotgun to Luke, who accepted it numbly, in shock at what just transpired.

Pincus walked over to Jakob. He got down on his knees and looked at him. Jakob stared blindly into nothingness. Pincus gently closed his eyelids. With tears rolling down his cheeks, he leaned closer and whispered, "Goodbye, my friend. I will never forget you."

Pincus stood up and walked out the way he had come in, through the back door.

CHAPTER 76

MAN OF THE YEAR

"We're going to need a larger apartment, Pincus," Mendel said, adjusting his tie as Pincus watched from a wobbly chair in the tiny kitchen.

"I'm sure, with three teenage boys," agreed Pincus as he looked around at the cramped and cluttered apartment.

"But I would live anywhere as long as I have my Shmuel."

"He's a special boy. Clara and I are eternally grateful to him. Does he have plans?"

"Rabbi Shapira was a great inspiration to Shmuel. He learned so much working as his scribe that he's decided to continue his studies and become a rabbi. Last week he registered at the Rabbi Isaac Elchanan Theological Seminary on Henry Street."

"That's wonderful news," Pincus said.

"It is. I'm very pleased. But now," Mendel said, looking at his watch, "we should probably head over to the reception hall."

Tonight would be a big night for the Landsman Society and especially for Pincus. He was to be named the society's Man of the Year, in honor of his heroic rescue of his family and Shmuel from the battlefields of Galicia, as well as for having gunned down Leo Gorpatsch, the most notorious gangster on the Lower East Side.

Pincus Potasznik and his exploits had made front-page news in all the city papers. They had proclaimed him a local hero.

Tonight over a hundred families from Krzywcza would be honoring the man who not only was a local celebrity but who had helped them find housing, employment, health care, and more in America, as well as providing them with the inspiration to keep fighting against all odds.

"I'm proud of you, Pincus. You've come a long way since your days as a cobbler in the shtetl," Mendel said.

"Thank you. When I think back over these past years, it's hard to imagine it's my own life," said Pincus, as the men stepped out onto the busy street on their way to the reception hall.

A few months earlier, Pincus had resigned as the society's president and Mendel had replaced him with a unanimous vote. As the new president, Mendel would be presiding over tonight's program. *He deserved a chance to lead*, Pincus thought, *because he was the real driving force of the Landsman Society from day one.*

Like a returning hero, Pincus caused a stir as he entered the hall. Most of the thirty large round tables were already full. Children ran about looking for friends, while the women chatted among themselves, and the men blew cigar smoke up into the large brass-and-crystal lighting fixtures that hung throughout the ballroom.

Pincus spotted Clara and the children at the table of honor right up front, only a few feet from the dais. He gave Clara a gentle kiss on her cheek and smiled at his children as he took his seat. Mendel walked to the podium and banged a gavel to bring the meeting to order. After a few moments, the audience fell silent and the proceedings began.

"My friends," Mendel began, "we have all traveled a long distance to be here today. While we have unique stories to tell about our journeys, there is one common thread we share, and that is our faith. But what is faith? As our great Rabbi Shapira taught us, faith is a belief in something that is not based in fact.

So why do we choose to believe in something when we have no proof of its existence? Why do we leave our birthplace, our homes to travel to a faraway land? Do we base our decision on hope? Hope is only a wish for something better. Faith, on the other hand, is a belief in the strength of one's community. It is the knowledge that together we can overcome obstacles. Individually, we have only hope, but together, we can bravely face the unknown with our faith.

"Ladies and gentlemen, children, today we are here to honor a man who has epitomized such a belief in faith. He is a man who has ventured into the cauldron and returned. He is a remarkable person, father, husband, and friend. But before we bring him up here to say a few words, there is someone else who deserves to share equally in this honor, and that, my friends, is Clara Potasznik."

At the mention of her name, the audience rose to its feet and burst into applause. Clara sat stunned, seemingly transfixed, while her eyes darted around the table at her children, who gazed back lovingly. She turned to Pincus, who took her arm and encouraged her to stand. The thunderous applause continued. She blushed and acknowledged the appreciation with a gentle wave.

....

Later that night, after the guests had filed out of the ballroom, Mendel sat at the head table with Pincus and Clara. Pincus reached out and took Mendel's folded hands, which rested on the wine-stained tablecloth.

"Mendel, you have been a true and loyal friend for many years. I want you to know how much I appreciate you and all you have done," he said.

"Thank you for saying that. We've been through a lot together."

"Clara and I will never forget you and Shmuel. You've been a big part of our lives."

"Why would you say that, Pincus? Are you planning to go somewhere?" Mendel asked.

"Clara and I have found an apartment in the Bronx. It's in a nice neighborhood with good schools. We need to get out of the Lower East Side. It's not a good place to raise children."

"This is a surprise. What about the cobbler shop?"

"We'll open a new one on the Grand Concourse. I've already found a location. Moshe wants to learn the business, so I'll take him in."

"That sounds wonderful. Perhaps you'll invite me and the boys to visit once you get settled," said Mendel.

"Absolutely, Mendel. You can count on it."

CHAPTER 77

THE CEMETERY

Pincus walked the pathway in the Beth David Cemetery, where the Landsman's Society of Krzywcza's section had two grand brick columns holding large wrought-iron gates at its entrance. The columns displayed in a series of brass plaques the names of the founding members, and Pincus's name sat at the very top. *This will be my life's legacy*, he thought.

Just beyond the entrance sat his family plot, currently with only one tombstone. He rolled the stone he'd picked up the other day around in his fingers. Before he placed it on top of the granite marker, he stopped to look. The tombstone read:

JOSEF HOROWITZ
A.K.A. JAKOB ADLER
BORN DECEMBER 11, 1885
DIED JANUARY 16, 1915

"It's a beautiful spring day, Jakob," Pincus said aloud, looking up at the blue sky. "I wish you were here to enjoy it."

He stepped forward and placed down the stone among the others. As he did, he noticed a woman walking toward him carrying a small bouquet of flowers. He turned to address her.

"Hello, Nita, it's nice to see you again."

She brushed aside a lock of her red hair and said, "You must be Pincus."

"I am," he said, sticking out his hand.

Shaking his hand, she looked down at the grave and said, "I remember meeting you at the Yoselle Rosenblatt concert at the Grand."

Pincus nodded and said, "Yes, a wonderful performance."

"Do you miss him?" she asked.

"Terribly. He was like my brother. We went through so much together."

"Did you know that he told me he loved me and wanted to marry me? And I said no because of Leo." She bowed her head in shame, then looked up to Pincus. Tears welled up in her blue eyes. "Jakob set up the meeting to kill Leo so he could be with me. That's why he's dead. It's my fault."

"That's not true, Nita. It was Jakob and I who conspired with Theodor Bergman to snag Gorpatsch in an ambush. Actually the plan had nothing to do with you. I was to hide out in the backroom with the shotgun cocked and ready. When Jakob thought the timing was right, he was to signal me, and I would step out and shoot Gorpatsch. Things fell apart when Gorpatsch turned the tables and surprised us with his hidden pistol. If our plan had worked, Jakob would still be alive. It's not your fault."

"Thank you for saying that," she said, looking again at the gravestone. "I never knew he'd changed his name from Josef Horowitz," she chuckled.

"It had something to do with an accident in Warsaw before he immigrated to America," Pincus said.

"Well, my name isn't Nita Naldi either. I guess we all have our secrets. I shared my story with Jakob right before he was killed. I never got a chance to hear his story."

They stood silently for a moment before she said, "I wish you and your family all the best." Then she kissed Pincus on the cheek, turned, and walked away.

....

As Pincus left the cemetery, he wondered if Nita would recover from her loss. Having two lovers murdered is unimaginable. But for some reason, he suspected she would overcome it. She seemed the type.

Pincus hurried from the cemetery, hoping to catch the 2:48 train to Manhattan where he would get a connection to the Bronx and the new home he and his family had just moved into.

Clara seemed pleased as well. It had taken a while for them to get to know each other again. When they had resumed sleeping in the same bed, Clara had lain on her side with her back to Pincus, at first. One night, he had tried resting a hand on her hip, and when no protest had come, he had gradually moved his body closer to her. Within a few weeks, as the tension had melted away, Clara had allowed Pincus to embrace her each night.

He worked with Moshe every day at their cobbler shop on the Grand Concourse, passing down knowledge from master to apprentice. *A third-generation business would certainly beat the odds for any commercial enterprise*, Pincus thought proudly. But then, everything he had accomplished over the past five years had involved beating the odds. *But if the rest of my life is peaceful, even dull and boring, I will die a happy man*, Pincus thought, smiling to himself.

CHAPTER 78

DORA RETURNS

It took Moshe only a few months to learn the trade. Eventually Pincus would leave him alone to manage the shop and tend to the repairs and polishing. Moshe enjoyed the work, and the customers loved Moshe. Once they met Moshe, their mood seemed to change. If they walked into the shop grumpy, after a few minutes with the young cobbler, they left feeling more cheerful.

Soon his regular customers were telling their friends about the cobbler shop on the Grand Concourse. They said things like, "When you go, make sure you only deal with Moshe, not the father. He's not so nice, but Moshe on the other hand, such a doll." And "I don't know what it is, but when I leave I feel so good. He has an amazing effect upon me."

....

As summer approached, Pincus told Moshe that he was going to spend a week at Orchard Beach with Clara, Jennie, Anna and Hymie. If he wanted to come, they would close the shop.

Moshe thought about it and decided he would stay home. He didn't want to disappoint his customers by not being there.

Clara cooked extra meals for Moshe and left explicit instructions on how to warm up each one. He thanked her and promised he would eat everything she made.

"Nothing will be thrown away," he said.

They promised to buy him a souvenir as they said their goodbyes.

Moshe enjoyed the peace and quiet of the apartment. He slept soundly every night without his brother, Hymie, constantly asking him to do things in the middle of the night, like taking him to pee or getting him a glass of water.

Business in the store was good. Moshe had to stay late many evenings to catch up on his work. He seemed to be spending way too much time chitchatting with his customers.

One evening, shortly after had he had turned the sign around to say CLOSED, a woman knocked at the door. Moshe called out from the back of the shop that he was closed. But the knocking continued. He put down the new leather sole he was preparing to nail onto a waiting shoe and walked to the front.

A woman's face peered through the glass front door.

"Would you mind please letting me in? I promise not to take long," she pleaded.

Moshe looked closer at her face. She looked pretty with bright blue eyes and blond hair in tight curls falling upon her shoulders. He opened the door.

"Thank you very much," she said breathlessly, as she entered the shop.

Moshe looked at her and asked, "How may I be of service?"

She pulled a pair of tall boots out of a cloth bag and handed them to Moshe.

"I would like to have the soles replaced. These are very old boots. I had them made for me in Berlin and they cost me a fortune. Aren't they lovely, Moshe?"

Moshe didn't think twice about the fact that she knew his name. Most likely a referral, someone had told her to ask for him. He was used to it.

He examined the boots. They were indeed beautiful, tall and

slender and crafted with two types of leather. The base of the boot was sculpted in black with a pointed toe and a three-inch heel. The upper was made of gray leather and highlighted with twelve rows of grommet holes for the laces, which would finish just below the calf. His father would have loved to see shoes of this quality. Moshe hoped she wouldn't need them before Pincus returned so he could see them.

"These are indeed very handsome, miss." He paused and looked at her, waiting for her name.

"Dora Meltzer."

Moshe wrote her name and address on the work ticket.

"I can replace the soles for two dollars. When do you need them?"

"Oh, there's no rush," she said.

"Would it be okay to wait a few days? I would love for my father to see these boots. It's not often we get a quality footwear to work on."

"Of course, that would be fine," she said with a charming smile that caused Moshe's pulse to quicken.

"And now, Moshe, let's put aside this pretending and talk about why I am really here."

"I don't understand."

"Let me tell you about myself. I practice the art called the wisdom of the hand. It is a Hebrew palm-reading technique that goes back to the 1500s. People come to see me for advice on business, family issues, sickness, and most often, advice on love," she said, looking directly at Moshe.

At that, Moshe felt a touch of nausea wash over him, but it was not overwhelming, not like it had been for him before, and it soon passed.

"Five years ago, I met your father, Pincus, on the *SS Amerika*. He and his friend Jakob came to see me in my cabin for a reading. I read your father's palm and I saw you. I told him his eldest son had a special power that very few people have."

She reached out and grabbed his right wrist. She turned his hand over and gently ran a caressing finger across his palm. Moshe froze at her sensual touch.

"Moshe, let me look at you," she said.

She held his wrist and traced the lines of his palm with the soft touch of her right hand, decorated with deep blue nail polish.

"There it is, the simian crease. It is true, Moshe. You are one," she said, looking into his eyes as she held on to his wrist.

"I don't know what you're talking about," Moshe replied and tugged his hand back.

She tightened her grip and resumed her reading. "You have the power of the empath. I see it clearly. Oh, you are special, Moshe. You are a *tzaddik*."

He forcibly pulled his wrist out of her grasp and said, "Please, Miss Meltzer, I would like you to leave."

"Moshe, don't you understand? You have abilities that are unique and could be very powerful. I understand that you want to help people. You cannot do this here, in a cobbler's shop. You need to be on a bigger stage. I can help you, teach you."

She took a step back toward the door.

"Come with me now. My car is right outside. You can live with me in my beautiful home."

Moshe looked at the elegant woman standing before him. She stirred unfamiliar erotic feelings deep inside him. He wanted to go with her. But he remembered the rabbi's warning and pushed away the urges.

"You must go now, Miss Meltzer. I am not interested in your offer," Moshe said. The nausea returned, forcing him to sit down and place his head on his knees.

"Moshe, my dear boy, are you all right?" Dora asked.

"You must leave now, please," Moshe begged.

"Nonsense. You need me to take care of you," she said. She walked over to the door and tapped on the glass. A man who was waiting outside entered. He needed to duck his head as he walked in.

"This is Mr. Marcus. He will help you, Moshe."

Moshe looked up at the man who stood over him. His angular face and bony limbs gave him the appearance of a giant insect transformed into a man. Mr. Marcus stooped down, scooped

Moshe up in his arms, and carried him like a small child to the front door and out into the awaiting car parked in the street.

Moshe glanced over and saw Dora pick up her boots, place them into her bag, follow them out of the shop, and shut the front door. Mr. Marcus started the engine and pulled out into the traffic on the Grand Concourse. Dora leaned up against Moshe and forced his mouth open. "Drink this, Moshe, it will make you feel better."

Moshe tried to resist, but he was too sick and allowed the fluid to enter his mouth. Moments later he was asleep.

CHAPTER 79

WHERE'S MOSHE?

The subway ride home from Orchard Beach gave Pincus time to reflect. They'd had a wonderful relaxing vacation on the beach—a full week of sunshine and warm temperatures. His three youngest children had swum in the ocean and run carefree along the sand.

At last, his life had settled down. His relationship with Clara had improved, and the children were healthy and happy. Now with Moshe running the shop and the society's purpose winding down with most of the Jewish population of Krzywcza emigrated, he looked forward to his free time.

When the train pulled into the Fordham Road station, Pincus said, "Let's surprise Moshe and stop in. He'll still be there."

Pincus, Clara, and the children, each carrying a valise, stepped out of the subway stairwell and into the bustle at the intersection of Fordham and the Grand Concourse. The shop was a few blocks down.

As they approached the store Clara noticed the sign first. "Why is the CLOSED sign on the door?"

"Maybe Moshe forgot to turn it around," Pincus said.

Pincus turned the unlocked doorknob and entered. The lights were on, and it looked as if Moshe might have stepped out for a moment and forgot to lock the door.

"He probably went somewhere and will return any minute," Pincus said. "Why don't you take the children home? I'll wait for Moshe."

Clara agreed and left.

....

Pincus figured that he might as well reopen the shop, so he flipped the sign back around. Moments later, customers came in to either drop off or pick up. A few customers asked about Moshe. He told them that Moshe had stepped out for an errand and would return momentarily. But after an hour had passed and there was no sign of Moshe, Pincus started to worry.

What could have happened to him? He took a step out onto the sidewalk and looked up and down the busy concourse of pushcarts and pedestrians. He walked back in and that was when he spotted a work ticket lying on the pavement. He picked it up and looked at it. It said:

DORA MELTZER
97 ORCHARD STREET
BLUE SHOES
REPLACE SOLES—$2

"Dora Meltzer," he said aloud. Sounds familiar, he thought. How do I know this name? He stared at the paper for another minute and then it occurred to him.

"The palm reader from the *SS Amerika*!" he blurted out. *The rabbi warned me that she might be a* rasha *and would come for Moshe.* He turned the sign back around to CLOSED, locked the door, and ran home to tell Clara that he needed to go rescue their son.

CHAPTER 80

DORA'S MENTOR

By the time the motorcar pulled up to the entrance to 97 Orchard Street, Moshe was drugged and sleeping heavily. Dora had rested his head on a pillow so he wouldn't bang it against the car window. He had responded very quickly to the elixir she'd prepared. Maybe she had made it too potent, and it might take a while for it to wear off. But there was no rush. Moshe would be staying with her for quite a while.

Mr. Marcus lifted Moshe in his arms and carried him to a bedroom at the top floor of her townhouse. Dora had become very wealthy since arriving in America five years ago. Her reputation as a palm reader brought her many clients, including former presidents, actors, and wealthy businessmen.

She explained to her clients that there was an art as well as a science in being able to see into someone's soul through the lines and bumps of a palm. The great rabbis of the past have said that, in order to read palms, one must have knowledge of the mystical origins of people's souls.

Dora Meltzer had such knowledge, but had squandered it doing silly and boring readings. She did them to pay the bills.

Her true desire was to go beyond her current level and have the power to manipulate the weak-minded to her wishes and desires. She could create great wealth and influence world events. This would certainly be more exciting then telling a forlorn wife that her husband was cheating on her again.

To do this, she would need to enhance her knowledge with that of the *tzaddik*. She had learned the dark arts of chiromancy, or palmistry as it is called in America, from a rabbi in Berlin when she was a teenage girl. She thought back to the day she had met him.

As she stood in line at the bakery waiting her turn, an old man had walked up to her. He stood as tall as she and stared at her a few inches from his face. Her initial reaction was to jerk back, but she didn't move. She knew this was a clear invasion of her personal space, but she didn't feel invaded. She felt curious.

"Your name is Dora?" he asked.

"How do you know my name?"

"I've been looking for you." he said, without further explanation. "Would you come to my home tomorrow?" He handed her a piece of paper with his name and address:

RABBI HERZFELD
AM KROGEL 35
APARTMENT 6

"Come tomorrow morning at nine," he said and turned and walked out of the bakery.

The next morning Dora found the address and knocked on the apartment door. The old rabbi answered.

"Come in, Dora. I am happy you came."

The apartment smelled of mildew and other vaguely unpleasant odors. Probably the cats, she thought, when she saw a few dart across the floor as she entered. The rabbi sat down in an old, worn-out chair and asked Dora to take the chair across from him.

"Have you ever heard of chiromancy?" he asked.

"I have not," Dora answered.

"Which hand do you write with?"

"I write with my right hand," she said, holding it up.

The rabbi reached out quickly, grabbed her outstretched hand, and turned it with her palm facing up.

"Let me look at you," he said.

He traced his finger along the lines of her palm.

"This line here that curves around the meat of your thumb is your life line. This one that crosses straight through is called the head line. This is the heart line and here is what is called the girdle of Venus. This is the sun line, the Mercury line, and the fate line."

She followed along, fascinated.

"Each of these lines has a meaning. But in addition, we look at the shape of your hand. There are shapes that represent earth, air, water and fire. Let me look at yours," he said, examining her hand by turning it over to study it from various angles.

"Your hand is of fire."

"Fire?" She asked, holding it up to see if it was about to spontaneously burst in flames.

"The fire sign tells me that you are a person with unlimited energy and ambition. Perhaps a little short-tempered but highly imaginative," the rabbi said, looking at her for acknowledgement.

"Yes Rabbi, this is all true."

....

Dora spent the next three years studying the dark arts of chiromancy. She became the rabbi's best student, learning all he could teach her, and soon it came time for her to move on.

"I have no more to offer you, Dora. You have mastered all my skills and more. The next step is for you to go beyond being just a reader of souls and becoming a master of them. If you can learn the ways of the empath, the *tzaddik,* you will find no greater power."

The rabbi told Dora about the *tzaddikim* and their powers.

"People are drawn to them. They have an ability to offer comfort to even the most disturbed. You can only look into a man's soul, Dora. But the *tzaddikim* can actually touch it. They are the direct hands of Hashem."

"How do I recognize one?"

"You can tell one by reading his palm. The sign that you have found one is what is called the simian crease. This is the fusing of the heart and head line, a very unusual occurrence."

He traced it out on her palm.

"This combining of these two lines represents a spiritual connection to the almighty. You will see this not only in the *tzaddik*, but in the parents as well."

The rabbi stood up and walked over to a pile of books on his desk.

"Dora, if you ever find a *tzaddik,* you must be very cautious. The *tzaddikim* have the ability to destroy us. We are considered their mortal enemy. They call us the *rasha*, the dark side. It's nature's balance of light and dark."

Dora listened intently. She never could have envisioned herself being associated with the dark side—until the allure of chiromancy had seduced her.

"Here it is," he said, opening the ancient volume to a particular page.

"These are the prayers you say if you ever have a *tzaddik* in your web. Memorize them; you cannot take this book with you. Chant these prayers and you will gain control over your *tzaddik,* and his powers will become yours."

He handed her the book.

"But do not keep the *tzaddik* long, or you will become a target for retribution from the other thirty-five. They do not like one of their own being mistreated," he warned.

CHAPTER 81

PINCUS TO THE RESCUE

The D train from Tremont Avenue to the Grand Street station involved two transfers and took 59 minutes. The three blocks from the station to 97 Orchard Street took Pincus fifty-nine seconds.

He ran up the steps to the front door and rang the bell. When no answer came immediately, he banged on the door with both fists.

The door opened and Mr. Marcus greeted him.

"Good day, Mr. Potasznik. It is nice to see you once again."

"You have my son. Step aside and let me enter," Pincus demanded.

"I'm afraid that is not possible. Your son Moshe came of his own free will and wishes to remain here until he decides otherwise. Good day, Mr. Potasznik," Mr. Marcus said, closing the door.

Pincus stood there staring at the large wooden door and brass knocker. He would apparently need help. He could go to the police, but Captain Becker would probably not be inclined to help, considering Pincus had killed his major source of income,

Leo Gorpatsch. The only other option would be to go see Mendel. Perhaps he could think of something.

The last time he had seen Mendel had been the day they had moved to the Bronx, nearly two years earlier. Mendel wrote occasionally and had told him that since the Landsman Society had officially closed, he would take a position as manager in the housewares department at Macy's on Herald Square.

Pincus found Mendel demonstrating the newest vacuum cleaner from Hoover for a young couple.

"Its all about the revolving brushes. They vibrate the carpet fibers that loosen up the trodden-in grit and dirt," he said with a forced smile. "It beats as it sweeps as it cleans."

Finally he finished, and Pincus approached him. "Mendel, can I talk to you?"

"What are you doing here?" Mendel asked.

"Moshe has been taken by some crazy palm reader named Dora Meltzer. She has him locked up in her townhouse on Orchard. I went over there demanding his release and the door was slammed in my face."

"That's a lot to absorb, Pincus. Let's go find a place to talk privately."

CHAPTER 82

MOSHE'S MORNING

Moshe awoke the next morning still under the effects of the drug. His eyelids felt like heavy curtains. His blurred vision couldn't make out any details. He propped himself up on his elbows, but that caused his head to spin. Collapsing back onto the soft mattress, he dozed off again.

"Master Moshe, please wake up," came a voice that penetrated Moshe's sleep. He heard it again, and a hand shook his shoulder. Slowly he awoke and opened his eyes. Staring at him stood the tall Mr. Marcus.

"Where am I?" Moshe asked.

"You are a guest in the home of Miss Meltzer. She would like you to wake and join her for breakfast."

The last thing he remembered was being forced to drink something. Moshe rubbed his eyes and swung his feet off the bed and sat up. He saw his clothes folded neatly on an ottoman in front of a large upholstered wing chair on the other side of the room. He looked up at Mr. Marcus, whose nod indicated he had removed Moshe's clothing the previous night and put him to bed.

Slowly the events of the previous night returned.

"You drugged me," he said.

"It was required," answered Mr. Marcus.

"Why am I here?"

"Miss Meltzer will explain. Now do I need to help you get dressed?"

"No, I'm getting up," Moshe said.

....

As he washed up in a private bathroom and dressed, Moshe worried about the cobbler shop and his parents. *What will they think? How will they find me, when they have no idea where I am? Why do I always wind up in these troubling situations?*

Moshe found the carpeted circular staircase leading downstairs and followed the voices coming from somewhere toward the back of the first floor. At the foot of the stairs, he stepped onto a black-and-white checkerboard pattern of large ceramic tiles. The tiles met a twelve-inch-high, black-painted, wooden baseboard that wrapped around the entire lobby. Two twelve-foot-high doors were also black and had polished chrome hinges and hardware. He took a step toward them when Mr. Marcus appeared.

"Right this way, Master Moshe. Miss Meltzer is waiting for you in the conservatory."

Moshe followed him through the tallest room he had ever seen. The ceiling soared nearly twenty feet. Even Mr. Marcus seemed dwarfed. A pair of windows nearly as tall flanked a fireplace that featured a white marble mantelpiece and hearth. A glass-topped cocktail table with polished chrome trim and legs stood on a black, gray, and white geometric rug between two white sofas upholstered in wool chenille .

The conservatory was another treat for the eyes. This room was constructed of white wrought-iron framing and crystal-clear glass. The eight walls formed an octagon, and each wall, except for the one attached to the living area, was glass. The geometry continued to the ceiling, which consisted of an array of glass triangles meeting at a peak, where a chain hung down supporting a delicate crystal chandelier.

As Moshe entered, he could see the back of Dora Meltzer as she sat in a white iron chair whose back resembled a seashell. Mr. Marcus announced Moshe's arrival. Dora quickly stood up and rushed over to Moshe.

"I hoped you slept well, Moshe," she said. "Please come join me."

"Why am I being held here against my will? I demand to be let go."

"Nonsense. Mr. Marcus, please offer Moshe coffee and orange juice."

Moshe sat down without taking his eyes off Dora. Her blond hair and delicate blond curls framed her white smooth skin, round wide-set blue eyes, and pink full lips. She wore an ivory lace throw over a blue silky housecoat that crisscrossed across her breasts, exposing cleavage that Moshe tried not to stare at.

"I'm not thirsty," Moshe said, placing a hand over the empty coffee cup as Mr. Marcus attempted to fill it.

"Nonsense," Dora insisted. "I'm not going to drug you again. I did it last night for your own good," she said with a warm smile.

"Why did you force me to come here?" Moshe asked.

"Do you not like my home, Moshe?"

"Your home is beautiful, but why am I here?"

"You are here because I want you to teach me the ways of the *tzaddik*."

"I don't know what you are talking about," Moshe snapped back.

"Please don't pretend," she said reaching out and touching his hand. "You will remain with me as long as it takes for me to master the knowledge of a *tzaddik*, and then you can go home to your hovel in the Bronx."

"That's it—you're a *rasha*," said Moshe, remembering the rabbi's warning.

"Let's not resort to name-calling," she said with a charming smile.

"What makes you think you can keep me here?" Moshe demanded.

"Like you, I have developed some abilities. As a palmist, I can see people's past and future, and just like you, I know when danger is approaching. So, we are well protected in my little castle," she said waving her arms to dramatize.

"What could I possibly teach someone like you?"

Dora leaned in and said, with widening eyes, "You will show me how you touch people's souls. How you connect with them. I want to learn how to go deeper."

"I don't know how I do that. It just happens. It's not me; people feel a certain way when I am with them. It's not something I can teach."

"Well, we will see about that. Now why don't we get to know each other a little better?" she asked, biting into a succulent red strawberry.

CHAPTER 83

THE SEMINARY

Pincus sat with Mendel and Shmuel waiting for Rabbi Kagen to enter his office. He smiled as he looked around; the space reminded him of Rabbi's Shapira's office back home, its cluttered collection of books and papers filling every nook and cranny.

After Pincus had shared with both Mendel and Shmuel what Rabbi Shapira had told him about Moshe, Shmuel had suggested they speak with Rabbi Kagen, as he was the seminary's best mind on mystical Judaism. Shmuel advised Pincus to speak slowly and loudly to the rabbi. "He is very old and hard of hearing. He also doesn't see well," he advised.

The door opened, and in walked the rabbi, escorted by his assistant Sara.

"Here Rabbi, you're at your chair. Sit down."

The rabbi slowly lowered himself into the desk chair and looked toward the visitors sitting across from him.

"Hello Rabbi. It's me, Shmuel Beck. I am here with my father, Mendel, and our friend Pincus Potasznik," Shmuel said loud enough for the old rabbi to hear.

"Ah Shmuel, it's good to see you," the rabbi said, taking off his hat and placing his hand on his yarmulke, making sure it was still in place.

"Thank you, Rabbi," said Shmuel.

"You have a wonderful boy, Mendel. Having him here at the seminary is a joy," the rabbi said.

"Thank you, Rabbi," Mendel said.

The rabbi then looked over to Pincus and asked, "Did Shmuel say your name is Pincus Potasznik?"

"Yes Rabbi," Pincus said.

"Well what an honor having the famous Pincus Potasznik sitting in my office."

"I wouldn't say I'm famous, Rabbi," Pincus said.

"You're famous at the seminary. You have been the topic of conversation for months with the students."

"Thank you, Rabbi," Pincus said shyly.

"So tell me, why are you here? What can an old rabbi do for the great Pincus Potasznik?"

Pincus explained of how he learned from Rabbi Shapira that his son was one of only thirty-six *tzaddikim* on the earth. He explained about the episodes and Moshe's abilities to provide comfort to the distressed.

"Your rabbi sounds correct. He may just be a *tzaddik*. I would like to meet your son," the rabbi said.

"That's the problem, Rabbi. Moshe has been abducted by the palmist Dora Meltzer," Pincus said.

The rabbi's pensive mood became disturbed, and he said, "Ah, Dora Meltzer. That name has been whispered around the seminary. Some say that she is evil. Your son could be in danger."

Pincus went on to tell him how he had met Dora Meltzer on the *SS Amerika* and how she had seen Moshe in his reading.

"Oh, my. You must get Moshe out of her clutches. Did your rabbi tell you about the *rasha*?" he asked.

"He told me that the *rasha* is wicked. The opposite of the *tzaddik* and its mortal enemy."

"This is all true. If Dora Meltzer is indeed a *rasha,* and your son may soon be under her spell," the rabbi warned, "you must rescue him and bring him back to the seminary where we will perform an exorcism to drive out the evil spirits."

"Thank you, Rabbi," said Shmuel, rising from his chair.

"There's no time to waste, Pincus. You must go now, all of you, and rescue Moshe before it's too late," said the rabbi.

CHAPTER 84

THE SEDUCTION

It had been many years since Dora had learned the dark arts of chiromancy. She had done very well for herself. But she was hungry for more, and the only way to advance her powers would be through a *tzaddik*. Now she had one in her web.

Dora knew that it was preferable for the *tzaddik* to submit to the *rasha's* advances willingly and without resistance. But if that were not possible, there were other methods of persuasion.

She watched Moshe through her bedroom window wandering the walled garden below like a caged animal. She would attempt seduction first. He did seem to be old enough to be lured by her erotic charms.

Mr. Marcus led Moshe out of the garden, up the staircase, and down the hallway, where he knocked at a pair of doors.

"Send him in," Dora called out.

The doors opened and a frightened Moshe entered.

"How old are you, Moshe?"

"I'm fifteen," he answered.

"That's a good age. Come and sit. I want to talk with you."

Moshe found a chair as far away from her as possible.

"Moshe, you are shy," she said standing up from her vanity table and walking over to him. She had applied her most alluring makeup, which highlighted her eyes and lips. She wore the same blue silky housecoat but without the lace throw.

She saw Moshe clutch the arms of the chair as if he were about to be forcibly removed. He stared up at her as she approached.

"Moshe, you have never been with a woman before, have you?"

He sat there, unable to speak.

She gently ran her fingers through his curly brown hair.

"You are very handsome, Moshe. Would you like to touch me?"

Moshe nodded.

She took his hand and led him to her bed. He sat on the edge of the large soft mattress, covered with an oversized bedspread and dozens of decorated pillows. She stood before him and untied her belt, revealing her naked body underneath. Her firm breasts remained partially covered, while her soft flat belly, as well as everything below it, was now exposed.

She took Moshe's hands and placed them on her hips. Dora gently pushed him back on the bed and climbed on top. The housecoat slipped off her shoulders, and she gazed down at the mesmerized eyes that scanned her naked body.

"Would you like me to undress you, Moshe?"

He nodded.

CHAPTER 85

THE RESCUE PLAN

Pincus, Mendel, and Shmuel found a quiet table toward the back of Katz's Deli to discuss their plan.

"Let's recruit some men from your shul, Mendel, and knock down her door," said Pincus.

"We might get ourselves arrested if we do that. After all, there's no proof that Moshe was taken unwillingly," Mendel advised.

"There has to be a way for her to give up Moshe without resistance," Pincus said.

"Or to lure them out of the house with a ruse and grab Moshe," said Shmuel.

"What are you suggesting, Shmuel?" Asked Mendel.

"As far as we know, Dora has no special powers or abilities. Even if she knows the prayers, she can't succeed with them alone. She will need to consult with a rabbi versed in the dark arts of Kabbalah. A professor I know at the seminary is an expert on Kabbalah and is against these evil practices. Maybe if I told him the details, he would help us."

"Help us, how?" asked Pincus.

"He can approach her and offer his expertise in harnessing the powers of the *tzaddik*. Dora would not find it unusual if such a person were to contact her. She would probably expect it."

"Okay, then what?" asked Mendel.

"Then he would explain that in order to perform the ceremony, she would need to bring Moshe to his hidden sanctuary. I know the perfect place. It's on Willet Street just off Grand. It was built in 1826 as a Methodist church and served as a stop on the Underground Railroad. Ten years ago, a congregation of Jews from Bialystok converted it into a synagogue. They painted the sanctuary ceiling with zodiac symbols to correspond with the Hebrew calendar. A friend of mine at the seminary is a member. If I tell him what we are planning, I'm sure we can get access to it for a night."

The men nodded their approval.

"That's where we hide out and grab Moshe," said Pincus.

....

Shmuel found Professor Rabbi Frenkel in his office and explained the plan. At first he thought it ludicrous. But when Shmuel offered more background to the story, the rabbi became convinced that this would be indeed be a mitzvah.

Shmuel told his dad and Pincus that all was in place. The Willet Street Synagogue was theirs for the evening. Rabbi Frenkel would knock on Dora Meltzer's door that afternoon to introduce himself and offer to perform the ceremony.

CHAPTER 86

THE RUSE

Dora watched Mr. Marcus lift up Moshe and carry him out of her bedroom. She had put a few drops of barbital, a sleeping potion, in his tea after their lovemaking. The time had come to take him to the Willet Street Synagogue for their appointment with Rabbi Frenkel. Perhaps this would unlock the key to the *tzaddik's* energy.

Her seduction had clearly had no effect on Moshe except to satisfy his lustful desires. Perhaps he was too young and too innocent to understand what a powerful woman like Dora could provide for him. She would need outside assistance, and just as she'd wished for it, it had come. Earlier that day, Rabbi Frenkel had appeared at her home with knowledge about her captured *tzaddik*.

"I can help you break though to his soul. Your witchcraft and palm-reading and even your womanly charms stand no chance against the powerful forces of the *tzaddik*," said the mysterious Rabbi Frenkel.

"How did you know he was here?" she asked.

"The *tzaddik* are indeed hidden to most except those who have mastered the dark arts of Kabbalah," he told her. "They leave bread crumbs—you just have to follow the trail."

His instructions were to bring Moshe to the Willet Street Synagogue at midnight.

....

With Moshe drugged and propped up in the back seat of the motorcar, Dora got in, and Mr. Marcus drove five minutes to the synagogue.

They had been told to park in the alley and enter through the back door. Mr. Marcus found it easily and saw the rabbi standing in the open doorway as they drove in.

"Quickly now. Bring him inside," he instructed.

Mr. Marcus lifted Moshe from the back seat and carried him up the metal steps into the rear of the synagogue. Dora followed closely behind them.

As she entered the sanctuary, Dora felt her eyes widen. A soft glow filled the sanctuary space, which was illuminated by hundreds of tall candles burning in decorative golden candelabras. The carpeting, drapes at the bimah, and cushions on the pews were in a deep red fabric. A tall, delicate series of stained glass windows rose around the sanctuary's perimeter.

What convinced Dora that this would indeed be the perfect place for the ceremony were the zodiac signs painted on the ceiling. She knew of no synagogue—at least in New York—that honored the astrological symbols. Only a rabbi versed in the Kabbalah would know how to draw on the powers from the heavens.

"Lay him down on the bimah," said the rabbi.

Mr. Marcus gently put Moshe down on the large wooden table normally used for Torah readings during services.

"Please have Mr. Marcus leave us," said the rabbi.

"I will stay," insisted Mr. Marcus.

"He cannot stay, Dora. He is not of our faith."

Dora nodded and Mr. Marcus left the synagogue to go wait in the car.

As soon as the back door slammed shut, Pincus, Mendel, and Shmuel jumped out from behind a pew a few rows back, and the rabbi stepped between Dora and Moshe.

"Have you set me up, Rabbi?" Dora growled.

Pincus walked down the center aisle. "It's over, Dora. I'm taking my son home."

Dora turned around to look at Pincus, Mendel, and Shmuel walking toward her.

"I don't think so," Dora said, reaching into her pocket and pulled out a pistol.

She pointed it at Moshe. "Either Moshe leaves with me alive or he leaves with you dead. It's your decision, gentlemen."

Pincus looked at Dora with his arms outstretched. "No one needs to get hurt. Put down the gun and we all can leave peacefully. Just give me back my son."

"I guess you underestimated me," she said with a smile. "Rabbi, would you be so kind as to ask Mr. Marcus to come back in please."

"You won't get away with this," Pincus said.

"If you look at this from my point of view, it appears I will."

A voice appeared from up in the women's section in the mezzanine overlooking the sanctuary floor. "Put the gun down, Dora."

All eyes turned upward to the balcony and there stood Clara with a rifle trained on Dora's heart.

"It is indeed over. Put down your gun—the police are on their way."

....

After the police came and took Dora and Mr. Marcus away, Pincus, Mendel, and Shmuel all looked at Clara.

"How in the world did you know about this?" asked Pincus. "And where did you get that rifle?"

"Your friend and accomplice Rabbi Frenkel is married to Etta Frenkel, an old friend from Sanok. We found each other a few months ago at the butcher shop and have renewed our friendship. So when the rabbi came home and told Etta of your clandestine plans to rescue Moshe, she thought it would be a good idea to tell me. Which she did, thank goodness."

The men all looked at the rabbi.

"Normally she can keep a secret," he said defensively.

Everyone broke out into laughter.

"But what about the rifle, Clara. Where did you get that?" asked Shmuel.

"Oh, that's not real. I picked that up at a toy store on Grand. Good thing Dora didn't look too closely," she said, precipitating another round of laughter.

"Mama, is that you?" Moshe asked, propping himself up on his elbows, rubbing his sleepy eyes, and pushing a few of his brown curls away from his face.

"It's me, Moshe. Papa is here too. We've come to take you home."

CHAPTER 87

THE EULOGY

After twenty years of living in America, Clara had made many dear friends who were distraught to hear of her passing. Moshe, along with his brother and sisters, greeted and thanked them for coming. They offered the same answers over and over to each mourner. "Yes, she had been ill for some time . . . it was the pneumonia . . . she was too young, only fifty-five years old."

Clara had passed the previous day, on a Friday afternoon. The funeral would be delayed until Sunday, because of the Sabbath. She had been ill for some time, but that didn't prepare Pincus for the shock of losing his beloved wife.

"Papa, please calm down," Moshe begged his father, as he sobbed in his bed.

"I can't live without her," Pincus choked out.

"Yes, you can, we'll help you," Moshe said, gently lifting his father's head and placing another pillow to prop him up.

"She can't be gone," Pincus moaned.

Moshe clutched his father's cold hand between his own. "Mother has passed on. It was her time."

As Pincus drifted off, Moshe told him he would handle the burial arrangements at the Landsman Society's gravesite in the Beth David Cemetery. Then he went downstairs to say goodbye to Mendel and Shmuel, who had driven up to the Bronx from their apartment in Greenwich Village.

"Your mother meant a lot to me, Moshe," said Shmuel.

"She was indeed special," added Mendel.

Moshe turned back to look at the living room Jennie prepared for the shiva. The larger pieces of furniture had been moved into another room and replaced with a series of small wooden chairs that lined the long wall facing the fireplace. The mirror hanging over the stone fireplace had been covered with a sheet. Against the wall with the windows looking out onto Pondfield Road sat a large table with food and beverages. His parents had made a good life in their beautiful home in Bronxville.

Jennie walked in from the kitchen and looked around.

"Where is Papa?" she asked.

"He wasn't feeling well, so he went upstairs to lie down," said Moshe.

"I'll go check on him," Jennie said.

"Good, because I'm all of a sudden not feeling very well either. I think I need to lie down," Moshe said.

Jennie looked at her brother as he turned pale and began to break out in a cold sweat.

"Oh, no, Moshe!" she yelled and ran upstairs.

....

The next morning, Moshe called the Beth David Cemetery to inform them that two plots would be needed that day, not just one for Clara. Pincus Potasznik had passed the day before of heart failure.

Moshe and his siblings sat together giving each other comfort as the coffins were removed from the home and put into the two waiting hearses.

"Moshe, are you feeling okay?" asked Jennie.

"I'm fine. It's just hard accepting that they're both gone. At least with Mother, we had time to say what needed to be said. I should have known this could happen," Moshe lamented.

"Don't be hard on yourself. Who can predict such a thing?"

Mendel and Shmuel, who had returned early the next day upon hearing about Pincus's death, helped the family to the waiting cars.

"I can't believe Pincus passed so quickly after Clara," Mendel consoled Moshe.

"I can. They loved each other that much," added Shmuel.

"I agree. He died of a broken heart," Moshe said, clutching Mendel's arm.

....

The synagogue had the largest congregation in Bronxville. Its newly built sanctuary held over 400 people. When Moshe entered, he saw that every seat had been filled, and a few people stood along the sidewalls and the back wall. He greeted many of them as he walked down the center aisle to the first row reserved for his wife Leah and their children Barbara and Elaine, as well as Jennie, Hymie and Anna's growing families.

Moshe heard the words of the rabbi's prayers, but they seemed distant. He thought of the things he wished he had thanked his father for.

Thank you, Father, for saving us from the ravages of war.
Thank you, Father, for building a life for our family in America.
Thank you, Father, for teaching me the cobbler trade.
Thank you, Father, for loving our dear mother.

He felt a tug on his arm and a squeeze on his shoulder. Moshe turned to look at Leah, who was trying to bring him back from his wandering thoughts.

"It's your turn, Moshe," she said.

Moshe looked up to the bimah and saw the rabbi looking back at him and gesturing for him to come up and deliver his eulogy to the congregation. He felt for the folded papers tucked into his jacket pocket.

Moshe rose and walked over to the two closed caskets. He kissed the edge of his tallit draped over his shoulders and transferred the kiss by touching each casket. He climbed the three steps up to the platform and turned to face the congregation. Moshe looked out among the many faces of friends and family members.

He slowly removed the papers and placed them on the empty bimah. He reached into his pocket for his reading glasses and found it empty. Quickly he patted his other pockets and realized he had left them at home.

He folded the papers and replaced them in his jacket pocket. The congregation murmured. Moshe looked up and smiled.

"It seems I forgot my glasses. But not to worry, the words do not come from here," he said, patting the pocket where he just slipped in his written speech. "They come from here," he added, placing his palm over his heart.

Sounds of approval rippled through the riveted assembly.

"We have come a long way," he began, catching the warm faces of Mendel and Shmuel sitting a few rows back.

"We have been blessed to have known two remarkable people in Pincus and Clara Potasznik, Mom and Dad. I'm sure many of you have heard about some of their exciting adventures. But there is one story I want to share with you today, and that is the only story that matters in the end—the story of their love.

"Of all the many things our parents taught me and my brother and sisters, the most important is that love is the light that triumphs over darkness. Their amazing lives have provided us with numerous examples of overcoming hardships and great loss with the power of love. Even with their last actions, they show us once again what love means." Moshe paused to look over to the caskets sitting side by side.

"It should not surprise anyone who knew my parents that one could not remain without the other. The power of their love would not permit the separation of their souls."

Moshe looked out again and saw many tears flowing. He closed his eyes and opened his palms out to the congregation.

"I feel you, they feel you. Your blessings comfort them as the pass on."

....

Later that day, with the burials completed and the mourners gone, Moshe stood with Shmuel at the two mounds of fresh earth forming the graves.

"So Jakob finally has company," said Shmuel.

"He's been alone for over twenty years." Moshe sighed, looking at the small pile of rocks on top of Jakob's tombstone and the fresh flowers placed on the grass before it.

"I guess she still visits him," Shmuel said.

"Nita comes every Sunday. We probably just missed her."

CHAPTER 88

THE ADVENTURES OF
PINCUS AND CLARA

Moshe's six grandchildren gathered around him, waiting to hear once more about the exciting adventures of Pincus and Clara.

He began the story by telling of Rabbi Shapira asking Pincus to travel to America.

"The great wise rabbi with a long white beard told Pincus to start the Landsman Society of Krzywcza. He told Pincus to help bring the Jews from our little shtetl to the New World," Moshe said proudly.

He described the day that Pincus said goodbye to Clara, who was pregnant with Anna, and how he traveled alone on a grand steamship called the *SS Amerika*.

"The North Sea is very rough and windy. The ship bounced around like a leaf on the sea. Pincus got seasick and was rescued by a man named Jakob Adler, who became his best friend and business partner."

The children sat mesmerized, even though they had heard the same story told exactly the same way many times before.

He described where his parents had lived on the Lower East Side. The streets were made of cobblestones. People bought fruits, vegetables, and breads from pushcarts. Children ran through the streets only speaking Yiddish.

"Pincus and Jakob had the finest cobbler shop on Delancey Street. They made a lot of money, and when they had enough they bought tickets on a steamship to come back home to Poland and rescue us from the war."

The children loved the part about the Prince of Prussia who helped Pincus and Jakob travel through the battlefields.

"Once we got lost in a forest. A band of Jewish soldiers found us and gave us food and water and led us back to the German border," he told the children.

They couldn't wait to hear about the steamship *Bergensfjord*.

"Because your great-grandfather Pincus was a wealthy man, we traveled in a first-class cabin, very fancy. When we reached America, we gathered on the top deck of the ship and stood at the railing. All of us standing side by side, and what did we see?" He asked the children.

In unison the children replied loudly, "The Statue of Liberty."

....

With Leah in the kitchen preparing lunch for the grandchildren, Moshe thought he would add something new to the story.

"You know, children, there is a part of the adventures of Pincus and Clara I never told you about."

They quickly sat back down, curious what their grandfather would say.

"Have you ever heard the term *soul mate*?"

The children shook their heads in unison, which made Moshe smile.

"You remember that I told you Clara died from pneumonia on a Friday and the very next day Pincus died of a broken heart. That was because they were soul mates, and Pincus could not allow their souls to be separated. It is said that when two souls find each other, they are bound together for eternity. This is what a soul mate is. One day each of you will find a soul mate of your own. Someone to love and have a family with."

The children sat in silence.

He continued, "Did I ever tell you what my grandfather, Scheindl the cobbler, used to say?"

Again, the children shook their heads.

"He said that the best way to understand the soul of a man. . . ." He paused to place his hand over his heart, ". . . is by examining his sole," he said, pointing to his shoe.

ACKNOWLEDGMENTS

The inspiration for *A Cobbler's Tale* was drawn from the true story of my great-grandparents, Pincus and Clara Rubenfeld, and their son Moshe, my grandfather. Even though their actual story is not as dramatic as this fiction, Clara and the children did survive the bloody battles of World War I before Pincus came back for them in 1920.

While Moshe Rubenfeld was not a *tzaddik*, he did have a unique ability to bring joy to his children, grandchildren, friends, and the many people he interacted with in his fruit and vegetable store on Manhattan's Upper West Side.

ABOUT THE AUTHOR

Neil Perry Gordon grew up in the village of Monsey, a suburb of New York City, and still lives today not far from his childhood home. His joy of art and fiction writing was kindled during his education at the Green Meadow Waldorf School.

He has written two trade books, *The Designer's Coach* and *An Architect's Guide to Engineered Shading Solutions.* Both books, as well as many trade articles, have been well received and have affirmed Neil's expertise in the window covering industry.

A Cobbler's Tale is Neil's first novel and is based loosely on the story of his great-grandparents' immigration to the Lower East Side.

Made in the USA
Monee, IL
21 December 2020